SHIFT

a Fletcher Wise novel

by
Patrik Martinet

ACKNOWLEDGMENTS

Thank you, Elayne Morgan, for your amazing editing skills.

Thank you, Jake, of J Caleb Design, for your incredible cover.

And a special thanks to everyone who read early drafts of *Shift* and encouraged me to publish it

SHIFT

CHAPTER 1

October 19th, 2015

I want a divorce, Fletch."

The words echoed in Fletcher's head as he stared at the clock on his desk. He tried to concentrate on the missing persons case sitting idle on his computer, but all he could think about was what Kate had said last night. She'd blindsided him with the declaration, refused to discuss it with him, then barricaded herself in their bedroom. He'd slept on the couch and when he woke up in the morning, she was gone.

Despite what she'd said, they needed to discuss this. There was no way he was going to let this happen without at least talking about it. He decided to text her.

"What time will you be home?"

While he waited for her to reply, he looked at her picture on his desk and wondered how things had ended up where they were. They'd had their fair share of problems, even been through counseling a time or two, but divorce?

After several minutes he got his reply.

"Probably not til late if at all."

"What do you mean?"

"I might stay with my sister."

Fletcher clenched his jaw and put his phone down. He wasn't going to argue with her via text message. He did his best to turn his attention back to the case, but it was proving nearly impossible to concentrate. The details of the case were already more than familiar, but he was trying to find a new lead.

Tyrell Gibson's parents first reported him missing the afternoon of September 26th, which was nearly a month ago. He hadn't found anything new since the initial investigation, and at this point the chances of finding Tyrell alive were next to nothing. He hated the idea of giving up, though. It wasn't in his nature. He glanced over at Kate again and shook his head.

According to Tyrell's parents, Tyrell hadn't come home from his night shift at the Burger Mania on the corner of Watson and Willow. They didn't think much of it initially because he often spent the night at a friend's house. Fletcher thought it was odd that they allowed that on school nights, but they said they didn't have a problem with it as long as he kept his grades up in school. When asked about whether he had called or texted to say he wouldn't be home, they said no, but they hadn't worried because he was bad at keeping his phone charged. Fletcher found that hard to believe—what teenager was ever without a cellphone these days? But there wasn't a reason to think they weren't telling the truth.

Fletcher looked at the clock again. It was twenty to five. Knowing he wasn't going to accomplish anything else for the rest of the day, he logged off the computer.

"Bugging out early?" Eric Harris said from across their two desks.

Fletcher looked past the two monitors at Eric. He'd worked with Eric on street patrol for several years, but Eric was a new detective and he'd been assigned to train him. "Yeah, I figured I'd head over to Ponderosa's a few minutes early."

Fletcher stood and pushed his chair in.

"Roger that, IO," Eric said. "I'm right behind you anyways."

"IO?" Fletcher said with a raised eyebrow.

"Intellectual One. It's a mouthful, I know, so I figured I'd abbreviate it."

"Wouldn't want a nickname to be annoying, now would we." Fletcher grabbed his phone off his desk and said, "See ya in a bit."

He was out the back door of the station fifteen minutes early. He dug his keys out of his pocket, unlocked the door of his '89 Chevy S-10, and plopped down into the worn seat. Glad the day was finally over, he let out a deep sigh of relief. He rested his head on the headrest and wearily closed his eyes. His thoughts swirled around work and his failing marriage. Mentally he went round and round before he reminded himself of why he'd left work early. He opened his eyes, but his phone started buzzing before he could fasten his seatbelt. He pulled it out of his pocket and looked at the name on the screen: Sergeant Frey.

"Dammit," he said. The phone continued buzzing while he considered letting it go to voicemail. There were plenty of other detectives who weren't just getting off work and could handle whatever it was Frey was calling for. After a few more buzzes he sighed—in an altogether different way than the previous one; this sigh was one of resignation—and answered the call. "What's up?" he said with as much enthusiasm he could muster, which wasn't much.

"Detective?"

"Yeah?" He didn't want to sound disrespectful, but knowing Frey, he would take it that way. He was going to get a tongue-lashing about this, he just knew.

"I need you to come down to 1542 Lakeview Drive."

"Why?" Yep, he was definitely going to get a tongue-lashing.

"We've got a possible homicide."

"Homicide?" He clenched his eyes shut and pinched the bridge of his nose. "All right, be there in a few."

Fletcher begrudgingly got out of his truck, shoved the manual lock down, and walked toward his unmarked cruiser. His hope of having an early beer was gone. In fact, he knew he had better odds of winning the lottery tonight than of having a beer at Ponderosa's.

Eric emerged from the station as he approached the cruiser. He joined Fletcher at the car and said, "So much for bugging out early, eh?"

Fletcher sighed again. What was this one—despondency?

"Mind if I ride with you?" Eric said.

"Would it matter if I said I *did* mind?"

"No, not really. I'd probably wonder why you were being a dick, though."

Fletcher had a mind to keep the passenger door locked and make Eric drive his own cruiser. He certainly wasn't in the mood to listen to Eric's mind-numbing chatter as they drove across town. But instead, he said, "Get in."

Fletcher started the engine, fired up the mounted laptop, then glanced at the clock on the dash: 4:49. *I should be on the way to the pub. No, I should be in the pub. And instead of drinking away my sorrows I should be drinking...* Fletcher stopped himself short, refusing to finish his train of thought. Nothing good would come of continuing. He picked up the hand-held microphone and said, "Detectives Wise and Harris available, en route to the scene."

"Roger," a familiar female voice answered.

"God," Eric said, "what I wouldn't give for the opportunity to investigate her."

Fletcher pinched the bridge of his nose again and closed his eyes. Tina was a dispatcher who had been with the department for nearly as long as he had. They'd become friends over the years and their paths occasionally crossed outside of work— such as the department Fourth of July party, or when he was at Ponderosa's. He would be lying if he said she wasn't attractive, because she was—very—but he tried not to think about her like that anymore. Despite his best efforts, though, when he heard her voice over the radio he sometimes relapsed and thought about her the way he knew Eric did. Eric was a man with a one-track mind, and his reputation in the department had preceded him. But Eric was single. He could think and do whatever he wanted. Fletcher was married. Happily. Or at least until last night he'd thought he was. His marriage wasn't perfect, but whose was?

The address of the scene of the crime popped up on the laptop's map display with a *ding*, and Fletcher redirected his attention to the situation at hand. He acknowledged receipt, then pulled out of the parking lot. He turned right onto Gurley and merged with the traffic trying to get out of town for the day. That was one of several reasons he enjoyed going to Ponderosa's after work—he could avoid most of the rush-hour traffic, such as it was in a modest city like Prescott, Arizona. Kate was never home for dinner anyway, so he was rarely in a rush to get home.

Eric messed around on his phone as Fletcher drove. It looked like he was sending text messages left and right. Fletcher reckoned Eric could fire off texts faster than he could rounds in his gun. He often wondered who Eric was always texting but had quit asking long ago because Eric always replied, "No one in particular." But he didn't complain. He was glad for the relative silence, broken only by the incessant click-clacking of Eric's phone.

More often than not, if Eric wasn't on his phone he was a nonstop chatterbox. However, after a few minutes he set his phone on his lap and said, "So, how are things with Kate?"

All good things come to an end, Fletcher thought. And he wasn't talking about his marriage. He looked over at Eric out of the corner of his eye.

"What?" Eric said.

"I don't really want to talk about it, presently."

"Talk about what?"

"You know, for a detective, you can be really obtuse sometimes."

"Obtuse?" Eric said, trying the word out as though he'd never heard it before. "Here you go, getting all Mr. Smarty Pants on me again."

Fletcher glared at Eric. He hated that Eric so willingly participated in the name game. He knew the other detectives had put him up to it when he'd switched from the beat to their department. "She told me she wanted a divorce, Eric."

"Oh... Shit. I'm sorry, man. I didn't mean to—"

"It's all right," Fletcher said with a wave of the hand.

"Knowing you, I figured you guys would patch things up."

"What's that supposed to... never mind." Fletcher did *not* want to discuss his marital problems with Eric, a man who changed sexual partners more often than he changed his underwear.

Fletcher navigated the rush hour traffic and finally turned into a subdivision off Watson Lake—the same area in which Tyrell had gone missing, he thought idly. He made an immediate right onto a side street and stopped in front of a squad car blocking the road, its lights flashing. An officer standing by the trunk waved Fletcher by, and he drove around the vehicle and up to where several more squad cars gathered.

He parked the car and said, "Grab the kit, would ya?"

Fletcher radioed that they were on scene, but remained seated as Eric climbed out. He stared blankly down the road at the flashing lights, Kate's words still echoing in his head. He pulled his phone out of his pocket and texted her to let her know he was going to be late. He hoped she decided to come home so they could talk.

Fletcher looked up at Eric, who was standing by the hood gesturing at him, and sighed. He slid his phone back into his pocket and got out of the cruiser. They walked the rest of the way down Lakeview Drive toward 1542, passing a few groups of curious neighbors gathered on driveways. They were talking amongst themselves, every one of them gawking as if they'd never seen such a commotion before. Given Prescott's sleepy nature, he imagined they hadn't—at least not in this particular neighborhood. The most excitement they probably got out here were the semi-regular first responders attending to one of their elderly neighbors.

The house in question, which was on the left just before the road ended in a cul-de-sac, had its perimeter roped off with police tape. An ambulance was parked on the curb just past the driveway with EMTs gathered at the back door. There was a yellow VW bug parked in the driveway, as well as another group of neighbors gathered in the middle of the cul-de-sac. Officer Spencer Barr leaned on the trunk of his cruiser, which was parked in front of the house. "How goes it, Wise Guy?"

"Well, I'm not drinking beer," Fletcher said. "You?"

"Oh, you know…"

He did not, in fact, know.

Seeing someone in the back of Barr's cruiser, he peered in and saw a woman sitting there, looking straight ahead, her hands behind her back. Her hair was neatly done and she was wearing a yellow dress-miniskirt thing. He ignored her for the moment and walked toward the driveway. He was met at the tape by Officer Peter Copeland.

"Detectives," Copeland said. "What's up?"

"I'm not drinking beer," Fletcher repeated. Copeland handed him a clipboard, which he signed.

"I had big plans tonight," Eric said.

"Oh yeah?" Copeland said. "Which were what?"

"Do you really need to ask?" Fletcher said, slapping Eric in the chest with the flat side of the clipboard.

"You're probably right," Copeland said with a shudder.

"You're just jealous," Eric said.

"Just sign," Fletcher said.

"Can you imagine what it's like working with someone as wound-up as this guy?" Eric curled his fist into a ball and gestured at Fletcher with a thumb. "He's like a—"

"A what?" Fletcher interjected. Eric didn't answer, so Fletcher ignored him and ducked under the tape. Fortunately, Eric had sense enough to follow. Given Fletcher's clout in the department, it wouldn't take much complaint on his part to get Eric's training transferred to someone else. He made his way over to Sergeant Frey and said, "What do we got?"

"Marlon Williams, early twenties, shot twice—chest and abdomen," Frey said. "Barr and Thorton cleared the house and reported the victim deceased. Neighbors reported hearing a couple gunshots, then, a minute or so later, a woman screaming. They say a woman exited the house by the front door and sat in the middle of the driveway. Stayed there until Barr and Thorton arrived."

"They find anybody else?"

"Not yet. She's in the back of Barr's car." Fletcher looked over his shoulder at the squad car behind him, remembering the woman sitting in the back. "She's been pretty talkative and spins quite the tale. His words, not mine."

"He interrogated her?"

"Nope. She started talking the moment they arrived."

"What kind of tale?"

"Ask him."

"All right." Fletcher ducked back under the tape and walked back to Barr's car, Eric tagging along behind him. "Got a talker, eh?"

"Sure do," Barr said. "Started yapping the moment I walked up to her and wouldn't stop until I put her in the car."

Fletcher looked in at her again. She was still staring straight forward and rocked slightly back and forth. "What's her name?"

"Renee Denovan."

Fletcher looked up at Barr. "And she's the shooter?"

"Not according to her."

That didn't surprise him. Even in the face of mountains of evidence, criminals often denied their involvement in a crime.

"So what'd she say?"

"When Thorton and I arrived, she was sitting in the middle of the driveway with her legs crossed." *Odd,* Fletcher thought. *Why wouldn't she have fled the scene?* Sticking around wouldn't help with whatever alibi she'd concocted. "He went inside, and I guarded her. She didn't need guarding, though, because she wasn't going anywhere. She just sat there and rocked back and forth." Fletcher peered back inside the car, where Renee was still rocking slightly. "When Thorton came back out he reported that a man had been shot twice and confirmed he was dead. After that, she wouldn't stop talking. It was like I accidentally chopped the head off a sprinkler with my mower and couldn't get the water to stop flowing."

Fletcher looked at Barr again, this time with disbelief.

"What?" Barr said.

"You mow your lawn at the same time you're watering it?"

"No."

"Then how'd you chop the head off? Don't they pop up or something when they turn on?"

"I don't know. Why you gotta analyze everything?"

"He's in a mood," Eric said.

Fletcher pinched the bridge of his nose.

"All I know is somehow I musta chopped one while I was mowing, 'cause the next time they came on it was like Old Faithful. Anyway, she was like that: started talking and wouldn't stop till she was sitting in the car."

"Okay, get back to the part where she supposedly started yapping."

"As I was saying, she spun quite the tale. Talking all crazy and shit."

"What do you mean?"

"After Thorton reported that the victim was deceased she started saying, 'I didn't do it, I didn't do it,' over and over. She mumbled something about being in a coffee shop then a dark room."

"Darkroom?" Fletcher said. "Like for developing film?"

"Dunno. But then she claims that somehow she was magically here."

"What do you mean, *magically*?"

"Says she doesn't know how she got here."

"That her car? The V-dub?"

"It's registered to her," Barr said.

Well, how she got here is pretty obvious then, isn't it?

"But she claims she didn't drive it here."

"So she had an accomplice," Fletcher thought aloud.

"Well, as of yet we got no one."

"One'll turn up, I'm sure. She couldn't have teleported here."

"But that's exactly what she's claiming."

"Wait… what?"

"Said one second she was in the coffee shop, then magically in a dark room, then from there to here."

"She actually said she *teleported* here?" Fletcher said with exasperation.

"She didn't use that word exactly, but yeah."

"Well, that's a new one," Fletcher said. He looked over at Eric, who shrugged his shoulders.

"What are you looking at me for?"

"Here's the kicker," Barr said.

"There's a kicker? How can you possibly trump teleportation?"

"She sat there rocking back and forth babbling nonsense for a spell and then—you're never gonna believe this—she claimed she was a man."

CHAPTER 2

S he claimed *what?*" Fletcher said.

"That while she was in that dark room, she was a man," Barr said.

Fletcher looked in at Renee, dumbfounded. He had been a detective for a long time, and in that time, he thought he'd heard it all. But this was new. No one had ever claimed to teleport to a crime scene, let alone become the opposite sex in the process. "Anything else?"

"Nope. After that she went radio silent."

All he could say to Barr was, "Thanks."

"No prob, Wise Guy."

Fletcher ignored the comment and started back toward the house.

"Sounds crazy, if you ask me," Eric said.

"You don't think she actually believes that, do you?"

"Then she must think we're crazy if she thinks we'll fall for a story like that. She was a man... give me a break."

"Well, the interrogation should be interesting, if nothing else." Fletcher checked his phone as they made their way toward the house.

"Quite the story, eh, Smarts?" Sergeant Frey said when they

arrived back at the house.

"You could say that," Fletcher said, putting his phone back in his pocket. "Witnesses saw her coming out of the house?"

"Four of them."

Fletcher looked over at Officer Thorton. "And no one else was in there?"

"Besides the victim, no one," Thorton said.

"The victim was dead when you arrived?"

"He wasn't breathing and had no pulse."

Fletcher noticed a woman standing by the garage with a couple of officers. She had one arm wrapped across her stomach and was dabbing at the corners of her eyes with a wadded-up tissue. "Who's that?"

"Jennifer Williams, the victim's wife," Frey said. "Johnson and Everett are just finishing up getting her statement."

"Thanks," Fletcher said. He gestured to Eric with his head and together they walked to the front door. Eric handed him a pair of booties from their kit. Once he had them on, he stepped inside. A faint smell of gunpowder greeted him. He immediately saw the gun on the ground to his right, about five feet away. The corpse was farther into the living room, about ten feet from the gun.

Three other detectives—Hampton, Reynolds, and Peterson—were already combing the room. *See*, Fletcher thought, *there's absolutely no reason for me to be here.* He was literally minutes away from Ponderosa's. He should be finishing his second beer by now. He wanted to go home so he could talk with Kate—assuming she decided to come home tonight.

He walked over to the corpse and surveyed it. The man's shirt appeared blood-soaked in two separate locations: his chest just to the left of his sternum, and his stomach. "What do you think?" he asked Eric.

"Well, from the blood stains—"

"You mean red liquid substance?"

"Right. The *red liquid substance* staining his shirt here and here would indicate that he was shot twice."

"That appears to be what happened," Fletcher said. He stood back up and looked over at the gun on the other side of the room. "What are the odds it was suicide?"

"Little to none."

"Why?"

"Cause the gun's too far away."

Fletcher nodded. "But...?"

"We'll have to wait for the autopsy to know for sure."

"Right."

Fletcher left the other detectives to continue their inspection of the house and walked back toward the front door. He removed the booties and stepped onto the concrete front step.

"Take her to the station and do your thing, Smarts," Frey said.

Fletcher considered objecting. The other detectives were perfectly capable of doing their own thing. An interrogation was an interrogation and they were, after all, perfectly qualified detectives. He'd always thought the entire team was very capable. Well, with the exception of Eric. But he was still learning—at least, that's what Fletcher kept telling himself. "All right," he resigned.

He looked around for Eric and rolled his eyes when he saw Eric was on his way toward the ambulance where, he surmised, Eric was going to hit on the EMT, who just happened to be a rather attractive woman.

"Hey!" Fletcher called.

Eric veered right and met Fletcher at the perimeter tape. "What?"

"This isn't 'hit on the hot EMT' hour." He started back toward Barr's cruiser.

"It's always that time."

"Well then, by all means," Fletcher said with a gesture behind them.

"Serious?"

"Do you *think* I'm serious?"

"Man, you know, sometimes you can be a real buzzkill."

"And most of the time, you're a real pain in my ass." When they got to Barr's cruiser Fletcher said, "Any chance Eric can ride with you?"

"Hey!" Eric exclaimed.

"Why, so he can hit on the suspect?" Barr said.

"*Hey!*"

"No, you're right," Fletcher agreed. "See ya at the station." Barr nodded.

"You know, you're being a real dick," Eric said as they made their way to Fletcher's car.

"You always say that."

"But you've ratcheted it up like three notches tonight."

"I wish I could say I'm sorry but I can't."

"See, that's exactly what I mean."

"Just get in the car. And try to keep the chatter to a minimum."

Fletcher checked his phone again before he got in the car. Still no texts from Kate.

On their way back to the station, Fletcher looked left when he drove past the split in the highway that led to Prescott Valley, the neighboring town where he and Kate lived.

I want a divorce, Fletch.

Just like that. There'd been no big discussion, hours and hours of going round and round about how horrible their marriage was. Nothing. She just blurted it out, so cavalier. It was like she was simply announcing she wanted to go out for Chinese food.

"Want something from the wheel of death?" Eric said when they got back to the station.

"No thanks," Fletcher said. He hadn't had much of an appetite all day.

"Well, I'm starving."

Fletcher followed Eric to the break room and got a cup of

coffee. He leaned against the counter and watched Eric hold the button down on the vending machine, making it spin in a circle. "Were you hoping the options would change the second time around?"

"There's never anything good in here."

Which was exactly why Fletcher never ate from it—even when he did have an appetite. "Come on, we gotta go."

"Just a sec." Eric put some money in the machine and pulled out a sandwich.

As they made their way through the station, Eric grumbled through bready mouthfuls about how disgusting the sandwich was. By the time they got to the interrogation room, Officer Barr was standing at the door.

"You Mirandize her?" Fletcher asked.

"Not yet," Barr said.

"No worries." Fletcher looked through the one-way glass and saw Renee sitting at a table. His immediate thought was that she didn't strike him as someone who had just murdered someone. She looked more like someone who was about to go to CJ's or on a date or something. Her dress was body-conforming enough to be suggestive and her hair was neatly done. It wasn't even slightly disheveled, which would have suggested some sort of physical confrontation. No sign of bruising. Besides her smeared mascara, nothing seemed out of the ordinary. Well, except that she wasn't wearing shoes. *Not typical killing attire*, Fletcher thought. She was fidgeting with a paper cup.

"You wanna talk to her?" he asked Eric.

"*Me?*" Eric's voice was slightly elevated in pitch.

"Who else would I be talking to? You gotta do it sometime if you want to be a detective. And now's as good a time as any." Besides, his mind wasn't really in it. He should have told Sarge to shove it.

"I... I'm not ready for this, Sensei."

"Sensei? Really?"

"Good one," Barr said. "Haven't heard that one yet."

"Yeah," Eric said, looking from Barr to Fletcher. "You're my teacher, right?"

"Now's not the time," Fletcher said. He wasn't interested in Eric's games right now. Although, now that he thought about it, was he ever? "I'm not feeling it. We just gotta get her to admit what really happened—not that 'I was a man' crap—before she figures out she oughtta lawyer up."

"Nah, man. Maybe I could handle a drug or theft charge, but not homicide. I'm not ready for this."

Fletcher shook his head. "Suit yourself, but you're coming in with me. And you're reading her her rights." He opened the door before Eric could protest and walked into the interrogation room. "Good evening, Ms. Denovan," he said. Renee looked up at him briefly, then quickly looked back down, placing both her hands in her lap. Her eyes were red and her cheeks moist. "My name is Detective Wise." He gestured to Eric and said, "And this is Detective Harris. We'd like to talk to you a bit about what happened today."

Renee nodded without looking up.

"But first—" Fletcher gestured to Eric.

"You have the right to remain silent," Eric read from his notebook. "Anything you say can and will be used against you in a court of law. You have the right to an attorney. If you cannot afford an attorney, one will be provided for you."

"Am I under arrest?" Renee said. She looked rather taken aback.

"No, not yet," Fletcher said. Thankfully she hadn't requested a lawyer—that would have really drawn things out. "But we do want to ask you some questions."

Fletcher sat in a chair opposite Renee and placed his coffee cup on the table. He pulled his notebook out of his jacket pocket as Eric sat beside him. He looked at the empty cup in front of Renee and said, "Can we get you anything before we get started?"

Renee shook her head.

"All right, then." He took a sip of his coffee. "If you could, for the record, please state your name?"

"Renee D-Denovan."

"And how old are you?"

"Twenty-two."

"Address?"

"241 East Pine Street. Apartment 412 B."

"That in Prescott?" Fletcher asked, already knowing it was. It was the address of an apartment complex south of downtown. He'd visited a time or three back when he was on street patrol.

Renee nodded.

"Could you answer yes or no, please?"

"Y-yes," Renee said. "Sorry," she added.

"It's okay. Can you tell me the nature of your relationship with Marlon Williams?"

"I... I don't know who he is."

"You don't know Mr. Williams?"

"No, sir. I've never seen him before."

"Do you know Marlon's wife?"

Renee shook her head.

"Yes or no, Ms. Denovan," Fletcher said.

"No."

"If you don't know either of them, what were you doing at their house?"

"I... I don't know."

"You don't know?"

Renee shook her head.

"Ms. Denovan, I'm going to need verbal answers, please."

"I don't know," Renee said. She reached up and wiped tears from her eyes, further smearing her mascara.

"All right, then," Fletcher said. "Why don't we start off by you telling us about your day." Fletcher took a sip of his coffee. "How you found yourself at the Williams' residence."

"I don't know how I got there. One minute I was at Connie's

Coffee Shop, then somehow, I was in a dark room. I was trapped there for... I don't know... then I was just there."

"So you just appeared at the Williams' home?"

"Yes."

Fletcher resisted the urge to shake his head. Nobody in their right mind would believe such a thing. People don't just appear in different places. "Okay. Before we get into that, let's go back to the coffee shop. Try to tell me exactly what happened today, in as much detail as you possibly can."

Renee nodded. She sat quietly for a moment, fidgeting with the cup, then said, "I went to Connie's for a date—I mean, it wasn't really a date, not really." She hesitated again, but then continued. "My roommate Liz thought I was crazy for meeting someone I'd met on the internet. I kept telling her that he wasn't a stranger—well, not a total stranger; we'd been chatting online for a couple weeks—and that I didn't see how meeting someone online was any different than her meeting someone at CJ's."

Fletcher looked over at Eric, who shrugged his shoulders. CJ's was a local bar on historic Whiskey Row downtown. Eric had dragged him there far too many times, and he knew for a fact that Eric often went home with women he'd met there. Apparently, Eric agreed with Renee.

"For some reason," Renee continued, "she thinks meeting guys at bars is different. I told her everyone starts out as strangers, no matter where you meet, but that didn't stop her from insisting that there was no way I could know whether he was a serial killer or not." Fletcher jotted down a note reminding him to ask her about this. "I told her we were just meeting for coffee, and she relented when I promised I wouldn't go back to his place. I don't know who she thinks I am. I'm not like her; I don't sleep with guys on the first date."

Fletcher looked over at Eric again, and Eric silently mouthed, "What?"

"I followed the YIM safety guidelines," Renee continued, "and arranged to keep the meeting short and in a public place."

Fletcher made another note. "Liz wanted to know how long I was going to be there so she could keep tabs on me. I told her maybe an hour or so—I was supposed to go to work later, anyway. She made me promise *again* that I wouldn't go back to his place, and then I left.

"I drove to Connie's Coffee Shop and ordered a coffee. Only the guy I was meeting never showed. I just kept sitting there waiting. I eventually texted Liz, and just as I was thinking about leaving, something... something really weird happened."

Here we go, Fletcher thought when Renee paused. *Let the yarn spinning begin.*

"My heart started racing—you know, kinda like when something scares you—and my vision went blurry like I couldn't focus. Then my skin started tingling all over and everything went black. My heartbeat slowed and the tingling stopped, but I couldn't see anything. I could tell I wasn't sitting on a chair anymore. I was on concrete or something, with my back against a wall. I felt weird and smelled fresh paint. I knew something was wrong when I tried to get up. My stomach"—Renee's hands went out in front of her abdomen like a pregnant woman cradling her unborn baby—"I couldn't bend forward." Fletcher narrowed his eyes. Renee looked to be quite fit. "I couldn't lean forward enough to get on my hands and knees. I had to roll to the side and use the wall to help me do it. My arms felt heavy, and my back hurt.

"Somehow, I... I don't know how, but I was in some sort of a room."

Fletcher mentally rolled his eyes, and stared straight at Renee to prevent himself from physically rolling them. No one—especially no jury, if it came to that—would believe she had teleported.

"I know you probably think that sounds crazy, and I don't know how to explain it." Renee looked up, hopeful. But seeing Fletcher staring at her, she looked back down. "One second I was sitting in the coffee shop and the next I was in a dark room.

I felt my way around and found a door, but it was locked. The lights didn't work, either. I called out for help, but... I know you're not going to believe me, but... I wasn't myself." Renee visibly shuddered. "When I called out for help my voice... it wasn't mine. It was... deeper. Manly. And it wasn't just my voice—my body... I was... fat."

She must think we're stupid, Fletcher thought. It was one thing to hear Barr talk about it, but hearing it straight from her was really too much.

Renee looked at him and must have sensed his disbelief. "I know you think I'm crazy—"

"I don't think you're crazy," Fletcher said truthfully. At this point he didn't necessarily think she was, but he *did* think she was lying.

"—but you have to believe me. I swear, I don't know how, but I wasn't myself. Somehow, I was... I think I was a man." Renee immediately averted her eyes as if she was embarrassed to admit such a thing.

Fletcher looked over at Eric who tried to inconspicuously circle his finger around his ear on the side of his head not facing Renee. Fletcher looked back at Renee and studied her for moment.

She was right; he didn't believe her. Her story was a load of crap that no judge, let alone a jury, would ever buy. So why would she tell it? Couldn't she come up with something a little more believable? Renee had quit talking, so he prompted, "What happened next?"

Renee looked at Fletcher as if she had been lost in thought. "I, uh..." She drifted off again.

Fletcher resisted the urge to say something sarcastic about how she was a man. Sarcasm was one of his many faults. Being sarcastic wasn't a fault in and of itself, but as Kate liked to remind him, sometimes he didn't know when to turn it off. At least at work he had some modicum of control. Instead, he waited patiently, knowing Renee was trying to gather her thoughts.

Eventually she continued. "It seemed like I was in there forever. Then my heart started racing again and the tingling returned. And then it was so bright I couldn't see anything and my ears were ringing. And I smelled... I didn't know what it was... fireworks? My eyes adjusted to the light and I realized I was standing in another room—a living room. Then I saw him..." Renee paused again. "He was lying on the ground." She looked up and directly into Fletcher's eyes. "I was so scared."

"Who did you see?" Fletcher said.

Renee sat in silence. She reached up with one hand, touched the rim of her cup with a finger, then put her hand back in her lap.

"Ms. Denovan?"

"I didn't shoot him, I swear!"

"Shoot who?" Renee didn't answer. "Mr. Williams?"

Renee nodded.

"Can you answer yes or no, please."

"Y-yes. I swear," she repeated, "I didn't kill him. It wasn't me."

They sat in silence. It appeared to Fletcher that Renee was finished with her tale. And what a tale it was—one that would surely go down as *the* craziest the department would ever hear. She hadn't confessed to the murder—they rarely did—so now it was his turn to ask her questions. But just to make sure she was finished, he asked, "Anything else you'd like to add?"

Renee shook her head and said, "No."

"All right, then. I'm going to ask you some questions now, if that's all right with you." Renee nodded. "You said that, on this date of yours, you were following the guidelines of YIM. What's that?"

"Your Ideal Mate," Renee said.

"Which is what?"

"An online dating site."

"Okay," Fletcher said, making some notes. "What sort of

guidelines were you following?"

"They recommend that on your first date you meet in a public place, keep the initial meeting short—an hour or so—and to let someone else know where you'll be."

"Sounds like good advice," Fletcher said. "And what did you mean when you said your date wasn't a serial killer?"

"For some reason Liz stubbornly clings to this outmoded stigma about online dating that you can never know whether the person is a serial killer or not. It's ridiculous, if you ask me."

"What's Liz's full name?"

"Elizabeth Warner."

"Thanks," Fletcher said. "Sorry, go on."

"She insisted I was being reckless. Even though she hooks up with guys she meets at bars all the time. How is that any different?"

She had a point. That was basically Eric's MO: Not being interested in relationships, he only *ever* hooked up with girls he met in the bar. "What time was this date?"

"Three o'clock."

"Okay, and you were at Connie's Coffee Shop, then you were suddenly in a dark room?"

"Yes," Renee said. "I know it sounds crazy, and I don't know how to explain it, but that's what happened."

"When you say 'dark room,' are you talking about a darkroom, like for developing film?"

"No. It was just a big empty room."

"And it was dark."

"Pitch black."

"And to be clear, you didn't leave Connie's?"

"No."

"One second you were sitting at a table in the coffee shop and the next—"

"I was in a dark room," Renee finished for him.

"Just like that?" Fletcher tried not to let the incredulity he was feeling surface.

"Yes."

"And while you were in this room you were a man?"

"Yes."

"But you said it was dark."

"It was."

"So how can you be sure?"

Renee looked at Fletcher with what he thought was a bit of indignation.

"Because I wasn't *myself*. I was... fat. And when I screamed my voice wasn't mine. It was manly. It wasn't exactly deep or anything, but definitely not mine," Renee said. "And my body... my... they weren't... I had a..."

Fletcher waited to see if she was going to finish her sentences, but when she didn't seem to be interested in saying more he said, "Okay. You were in a dark room in a man's body. What happened next?"

"I tried finding a way out of the room but couldn't. Then I was standing in that house."

"How long were you in that room before you—" he wanted to say 'teleported,' but teleportation was impossible and he didn't want to give any credence to it—"found yourself in the Williams' home?"

"I-I don't know."

"Can you give me an estimate?"

"I don't know. I was freaked out. I didn't think to think about how long I was there."

"How about a rough estimate?"

"I don't know. An hour maybe."

"So, just to be clear, you didn't leave Connie's and drive somewhere? You were just at Connie's one minute then the next you were in a dark room?"

"Yes."

"Then—just to make sure I'm understanding you correctly—the same is true about how you left the dark room and arrived at the Williams' residence?"

"Yes. I know it's crazy," Renee said again, "but it's true. I-I can't explain it."

"All right. Now, when you found yourself in the Williams' residence, were you yourself again?"

Renee nodded but then quickly added, "Yes."

Fletcher looked over at Eric and gestured toward the door. "Excuse us for a moment, please," he said.

Renee nodded.

Fletcher stood then, before leaving said, "Can I get you anything? Coffee? Water?"

"No, thanks," Renee said.

"All right. We'll be right back."

"She's cuckoo, if you ask me," Eric said the moment the door clicked shut behind them.

"Yeah," Fletcher agreed. "I'm gonna call Frey. Would you mind refilling my coffee for me?"

"I'm not Alfred," Eric said.

"Alfred?"

"Batman's butler. If I was, I'd be wearing a tuxedo, not these lame-ass Dockers and a button-up shirt."

"I never said you were," Fletcher said.

"You didn't have to."

Fletcher rolled his eyes. "Just get me some coffee," he said as he dialed Frey's cell.

"You could've at least said please."

"Please," Fletcher said as the phone rang. "And if you're unhappy with the dress code, you're welcome to go back on the beat."

"Sergeant Frey," a voice said in his ear.

Fletcher held his empty coffee cup out toward Eric, who begrudgingly took it. "So, she's nuts," he said into the phone. "What have you guys found there?"

Fletcher listened as Frey got him up to speed on the investigation at the house. He jotted a few things down and asked a couple of questions as Frey talked. Eric returned just as they were finishing up. He took his cup back from Eric then said, "Ready to get back in there?"

"What, no 'thanks'?"

"Thanks," Fletcher said dryly.

"You know, sometimes I wonder if you really think of me as your servant instead of your partner."

Fletcher sipped his coffee and said, "Hey, I offered to let you take the lead."

"Well, if I'd known I could just send you off to get me coffee whenever I wanted, I probably would have."

"You're an idiot, you know that, right? Come on," Fletcher said. "I'd like to get home sometime tonight."

They reentered the interrogation room, where Renee sat fiddling with her empty cup again.

"Where were we?" Fletcher said, sitting down. Renee looked up briefly but otherwise didn't indicate she was ready to spill the beans at last. He'd hoped that if he gave her some time to stew, she would come to her senses and drop the charade. Of course, he wouldn't be so lucky. "So, you somehow found yourself in the Williams' house."

"Yes."

"Did you drive there?"

"No. I told you, I was in a dark room and then I was just *there*."

"Ms. Denovan, can you tell me what kind of vehicle you drive?" Fletcher said.

"A Bug."

"A Volkswagen Bug?"

"Yes."

Fletcher sipped his coffee. "What's the license plate number?"

"Um... I don't know."

"That's fine. What color is it?"

"Y-yellow."

"And where is your car now, Ms. Denovan?"

"It's..." Renee started fiddling with her empty cup again.

"Ms. Denovan? Where's your car?"

"Last I drove it, it was to Connie's."

"And where's your car right now?"

Renee didn't answer. Part of getting someone to admit the truth was to find holes in their stories and poke them. Some stories—the really good ones—had only tiny pinpricks that could be easily missed and took a lot of digging to find, while others were as wide as a barn door—and not just ajar, but flung wide open. Renee's story wasn't believable from the start, but the location of her vehicle was as big a hole as there ever was—which was why she didn't want to answer.

"Ms. Denovan, can you please tell me where your car is?" Fletcher said. *Poke, poke.*

Renee tried to look at him but couldn't. "It's, um... at the, uh... at the house."

"Did you drive it there?"

Renee shook her head. "No. I told you, I was just there somehow."

"Right, you did say that," Fletcher agreed. "Then who drove it there?"

"I-I don't know. I've never even been in that neighborhood before."

That might be true, Fletcher thought, but just because she'd never been there before didn't preclude the possibility that she drove there. "Okay," Fletcher conceded for the time being. He glanced at his notes and said, "Let's move on. Do you own a gun, Ms. Denovan?"

"No, sir. I've never owned a gun in my life."

"So the gun found on the living room floor doesn't belong to you?"

Renee shook her head.

"Does the gun belong to you, Ms. Denovan?"

"N-no."

"You do know that when we analyze the gun, the serial

number will tell us who it belongs to, don't you?"

"I swear, Detective, I don't own a gun."

"Did you borrow it from someone?"

"No," Renee said with a shake of her head. "I wouldn't know how to use it even if I did."

"Did you steal it?"

"What?" Renee looked up at Fletcher with a look of incredulity. "Never! I'm not a thief."

"When we complete forensic testing on the gun will we find your fingerprints on it?"

Renee again sat quietly, staring down at her lap. Another hole in her story. She obviously hadn't thought to wear gloves to conceal her fingerprints. Even if she had, and had disposed of them at the scene of the crime—which she would've had to do, since she didn't leave the premises—they would be found.

"Ms. Denovan?"

She gave several small nods in rapid succession.

"Is that a yes, Ms. Denovan? We'll find your prints on the gun?"

"Yes."

"If you didn't shoot Mr. Williams, then why are your prints on the gun?"

"Because when I appeared in the house I was holding it."

Just to probe and see exactly how big this particular hole was, Fletcher asked, "Can you tell me what caliber the gun is?"

Renee looked up at him and shook her head.

"You can't tell me?"

She shook her head again. "No."

"Why not?"

"B-because I don't know. I don't own a gun!"

Even if her story didn't make sense and had obvious holes, she was at least being consistent. "All right. Can you tell me how many times you fired the gun at Mr. Williams?"

Renee looked at Fletcher again, the fear in her eyes evident. "I-I told you I didn't shoot him."

"But earlier you stated that when you... 'appeared' in Mr. Williams' home, you were in fact holding the gun."

"Yes. But I didn't shoot him."

Fletcher took a sip of his coffee, which was now lukewarm, and thought about what Renee had claimed thus far. If she'd murdered Marlon Williams, regardless of what her reason might have been, why would she ever think anyone would believe that she'd somehow teleported there holding a gun but hadn't shot him? He looked over at Eric, who gave him an "I don't know" look.

Fletcher set his cup down and looked back at Renee. "I want to believe that you're telling the truth and that you didn't shoot Mr. Williams, Ms. Denovan, but honestly I'm having a hard time understanding what you're trying to tell me."

I bet her sister put her up to this. The thought entered Fletcher's mind out of nowhere. Abrupt as it was, it was true. Kate's sister never had liked him. But would she really go so far as to convince Kate to divorce him? He pressed a finger into the inside corner of his eye and tried putting Kate out of his mind.

He looked at Renee as he refocused. She stared at her hands in her lap and occasionally wiped a tear from her eye. He didn't really know what else to ask her. Her story was full of holes and made absolutely no sense. Not only did it not make sense, but it was flat out impossible. People don't teleport, and they certainly don't change from a fit woman to an obese man. For the life of him he couldn't understand how she would think they'd believe such an outlandish story. In his years as a police officer, he'd heard his share of outlandish stories—every officer does sooner or later. But he'd never heard anything like this before.

He finished off his tepid coffee and said, "Somebody shot Marlon Williams tonight. Twice." He paused to give the facts she was up against time to sink in. "Several witnesses are on record as hearing two gunshots. Witnesses are also on the record as seeing you exit the Williams home."

Fresh tears began streaming down Renee's cheeks. She

didn't wipe them. Her mascara streaked further.

It was entirely possible someone else had been in the house with Renee, and had gotten away without being seen before the police arrived, Fletcher knew. But there were four witnesses who had seen her come out the front door, alone. It was also possible that a second person had escaped out the back; the other detectives still at the scene of the crime would likely answer that question. But as it stood, the evidence appeared to be stacked against her.

"Is there anything else you'd like to add before we finish up?" Fletcher said.

Renee shook her head.

"What about you?" Fletcher asked Eric.

"I'm good," Eric said.

"All right, then," Fletcher said, turning back to Renee. "Thank you, Ms. Denovan, for your cooperation tonight."

Renee nodded.

"Oh, one more question," Fletcher said. "Did you go on this date barefoot?"

Renee shook her head. "No," she said. "I wore heels."

"And where are your heels now?"

"I-I don't know."

"Hmm," Fletcher said. "Thanks."

Fletcher looked at her questioningly. He picked up his phone and empty coffee cup, then stood. Eric stood as well. Fletcher knocked on the door and Spencer opened it. They walked out, leaving Renee staring at her hands.

"Well, you don't hear that every day," Eric said.

"No, you don't," Fletcher agreed. He checked his phone. Kate had yet to respond to his earlier text that he was going to be late getting home from work.

"What do you make of it?"

"Dunno," Fletcher said absentmindedly. *Doesn't she care that I'm going to be late?* He knew she probably figured it was because of work, but it wasn't that long ago that she had shown an interest in his job.

"It's a lame-ass story, if you ask me," Eric said. "I don't know what was worse: that she teleported or that she turned into a man and back. Who's gonna believe bullshit like that? You gotta at least try."

"Yeah." Fletcher looked through the glass at Renee for a moment. He typed out another text to Kate—*What? Denise got your tongue?*—but deleted it, knowing his sarcasm was evident. The last thing he wanted to do was antagonize her. He called Frey instead.

Fletcher reviewed what they'd learned from the interview and Frey again went over the details of what they'd discovered at the scene of the crime. Surrounding neighbors had also heard the gunshots, but none of them saw anyone else leave the house. The neighborhood was built on a hill so the houses on the next street back, bordering the backyard, were considerably higher and separated by a retaining wall. The neighbor in the house directly behind the scene of the crime was an elderly woman who'd happened to be sitting on her back patio drinking iced tea when she heard the gunshots. No one came out the back door, she said. So far Renee was the only person who'd been seen anywhere near the house.

Fletcher hung up when their conversation ended. He turned to Eric and said, "So, do we have enough to keep her?" Even as mentally distracted as he was about Kate, he already knew the answer, but wanted Eric to think it through himself.

"You're the Wise Guy and all, but if you're asking me—"

"I am."

"Well, we've got four witnesses saying she came out of the house after they heard gunshots. But there very well could have been someone else there as well."

"That'd make her an accomplice at the very least. And Sarge said there's another witness who says nobody exited the back of the house."

"Then, yeah, I think we got enough to hang onto her."

"Good. What do we charge her with?"

"At this point," Eric said, "I'd say we got probable cause, so—manslaughter?"

"Are you asking me or telling me?"

"Geez, Wiz, you don't gotta get all Boyd Crowder on me," Eric said.

"Who?"

"Boyd Crowder, from *Justified*."

"What's that?"

"Only the greatest TV show ever—"

"Whatever."

"Whatever?"

"Eric, I'm not really in the mood and just want to wrap this up, all right?" Fletcher wanted to get home. *I hope I have beer in the fridge.* He usually did, but he couldn't remember for sure. And if he was going to talk with Kate tonight, he was definitely going to need beer.

"Fine, I'm telling you," Eric said.

Fletcher nodded, then called Sergeant Frey again and discussed booking Renee. Frey told Fletcher to make it happen, then hung up. "Sarge agrees to book her," he said to Spencer.

Spencer nodded and moved to open the door to the interrogation room.

"Hold on a sec," Fletcher said. He didn't know why, but for some reason he wanted to be the one to tell her what was about to happen. "Let me talk to her first."

Spencer stepped back and Fletcher opened the door. Renee looked up at him when he entered. *I shouldn't be doing this.* Pulling the door closed behind him, he said, "Ms. Denovan. I want to talk to you about what's about to happen."

Renee sniffed and wiped her eyes with the backs of her hands.

Looking at Renee and, for some reason, feeling bad for her, he said, "Based on your testimony, and the testimony of Mr. Williams' neighbors, you are going to be placed under arrest."

"But... I swear, I didn't kill him." Renee wiped more tears. "I just went to get coffee. That's it."

Fletcher empathized with what she must be feeling. He didn't know why, in this particular instance, but he did. His job required he approach each case objectively, but he couldn't help but think she didn't seem like the type to commit murder. "But you understand?"

Renee nodded.

He turned back to the one-way glass and gestured for Spencer to enter. When the door opened, he turned back to Renee and said, "Officer Barr is going to take you now and get you processed."

"Ms. Denovan," Spencer said, "You are under arrest. Come with me, please."

Renee hesitated for a moment then stood. She followed Spencer out of the room, looking at Fletcher as she passed him.

Fletcher watched her go. Her story didn't make sense. He didn't normally feel particularly compassionate toward suspects, but something made him want her story to be true. It just didn't make any sense. People don't change bodies. They don't teleport around, either. Maybe in movies, but life wasn't a movie, though he was starting to feel like his own life had somehow become a soap opera.

"Are they all this crazy?" Eric said when Fletcher walked out of the interrogation room.

"Huh?"

"Making shit up like that?"

"No. That's a first. But you'd think if she *didn't* kill Williams she would have come up with a more plausible excuse."

"You think she's telling the truth? That she really didn't kill him?"

"I don't know. But part of me wants to believe her."

"Well, I suppose every now and then you gotta earn that name of yours," Eric said with a slap on Fletcher's arm.

"It's not like I picked my name when I got promoted to

detective," Fletcher said, slapping Eric back with more force. "How conceited do you think I am?"

"To pick Wise as a last name, I'd say quite a bit."

"You're such an idiot," Fletcher said. He looked at his phone again, but still no texts from Kate.

CHAPTER 3

Fletcher and Eric sat begrudgingly at their desks—Fletcher just wanting to go home and Eric overdue at whatever bar he went to before CJ's—staring at Fletcher's computer screen. He had it turned so they could both review Renee's interview. It would be a while yet before the other detectives finished their work cataloging the scene of the crime, and he knew Frey would want to go over everything while it was still fresh in everyone's minds.

"Come *on...*" Eric said in a moan. "I'm missing some primetime!"

"It's Monday night," Fletcher said.

"This is a college town, Wiz. Every night's primetime."

"Haven't they figured you out yet?"

"Who? The college chicks?"

"Who else would I be talking about?"

"Nah. They don't care."

Fletcher had been a detective for a long time. He knew that cases required you to stay late from time to time, but he felt the same as Eric. He looked at his phone for the hundredth time, but Kate hadn't replied. Eric was getting a constant stream of texts, whereas he couldn't get even one. He couldn't believe Kate would throw out such an outrageous declaration and then refuse to talk about it.

"The way you keep checking your phone makes me think you're engaged in a little side action with a hottie of your own," Eric said. He wiggled his eyebrows then made a kissy-face.

Fletcher rolled his eyes. "I'm not you, Eric."

"Ouch, Smarts, that really smarts."

Fletcher shook his head and looked back at the screen.

"What? Didn't like the rhyme?"

"It's not a rhyme when you use the same word twice, dumbass."

Eric threw a pen across the desk at Fletcher and said, "Damn, dude. What's your problem?"

"Can we please just focus on this?" Fletcher tried concentrating on what Renee was saying but he had missed the last couple of minutes. Even though it was the fifth time they'd watched the interview, he slid the progress bar back.

He watched the video through again, trying to make sense of Renee's testimony. But each time he watched it, it made less sense. What would motivate a young woman with no prior record to kill someone? And why try to cover it with an asinine story? There were any number of possible reasons for her to be at the Williams' residence, the most obvious, in his opinion, was that she was having an affair with Marlon. Maybe Marlon had threatened to come clean with his wife and she, being young, was afraid of what would happen. Maybe she'd panicked and decided to kill him then try to wiggle out of it under the guise of self-defense. But in reality, the only reason he could think of in his tired state of why she said what she said was that she legitimately thought they were stupid.

The evening dragged on. They could only watch the video so many times before they practically had it memorized, so they sat at their desks doing largely nothing. Fletcher checked his phone several times, typing out several texts to Kate then deleting them, unsent; Eric texted non-stop. The clicking of his phone was obnoxiously loud in the otherwise quiet room. Sergeant Frey and the other detectives finally returned to the station around ten pm, and after nearly an hour of mind-numbing debriefing, they were allowed to leave.

Normally Fletcher reveled in the art of piecing together the many elements of an investigation—he'd voluntarily stayed to work a case on more than one occasion—but tonight all he wanted was to get home and talk with his wife.

Twenty minutes later he pulled into his driveway, keeping to the right edge of the concrete so he wouldn't block Kate from getting out when she left for work in the morning. As the garage door rose, he let out a sigh of relief when he saw that Kate's car occupied the left half of the garage. Piles of junk occupied the right. *At least she came home.*

Fletcher got out of his truck, pushing the lock on the door down as he shut the door, and walked into the garage and through the laundry room, closing the garage door behind him. When he went into the living room, he saw Kate sitting on the floor in front of the couch. Her knees were tucked up to her chest.

"Can we talk?" she said.

"I've been wanting to all day," Fletcher said, sitting on the end of the couch farthest from her, "but you've been ignoring me."

"I didn't want to do it over the phone."

"Sorry I'm late."

"It's fine," Kate said. It was never fine when she said it was fine. "You had to work."

"About last night—"

"Let me start," Kate said, interrupting him.

"Okay."

"I want a divorce."

The words hit Fetcher like a bullet to the chest protector, knocking the breath out of him. "Yeah, you said that," he wheezed. Hearing her utter them again so matter-of-factly left him feeling numb. "What I can't understand is why."

"This," Kate said, gesturing between the two of them, "us—it's not working anymore. It hasn't been for a while."

"I know things haven't been that great…"

Kate shook her head in agreement.

"And that's it? You're ready to call it quits?"

Kate nodded.

"Shouldn't we try counseling again?"

"We've already tried that, Fletch."

"And things got better."

"But it doesn't last. I admit that while we were going, and for a month or so after, it was better, but then you went right back to where you were before."

"Look, I know sometimes I'm not good at—"

"Sometimes?"

Fletcher looked at Kate, who turned her head and stared across the room at the TV, which was on with the volume turned down. "You know what I mean. We've been over this. And we agreed that we would try."

"I try," Kate said without looking at him. A strand of her otherwise neat hair, tied back in a ponytail, was down, partially blocking her face from view.

"And so do I."

"It doesn't feel like it."

Fletcher scooted over and slid off the couch, sitting next to Kate, but with his back to the TV, facing her. He tucked the stray hair back behind her ear, but she didn't move or turn to look at him. He gazed at her for a moment. She wasn't wearing makeup and her eyes glistened. "Kate, I'm sorry I don't always do or say the right things, but I love you."

"Really?" Kate turned and looked at him.

"Yes. Very much."

"But that's the problem, Fletch. I don't *feel* like you do."

Silence hung in the air between them. Kate went back to staring past him at the TV.

He honestly didn't know what to say. They'd been round and round about how he didn't express his love the way she needed him to. Counseling had made him more cognizant of that fact, but unless he was actively thinking about it—which was hard to do day in and day out—he'd forget. It wasn't like he did it on purpose—he would never do that. But with the busyness of their lives, he had other things on his mind. Eventually, he said, "I try."

"I know," Kate said. "But it's not enough." She looked back at him and placed her hand on his cheek. "I can't sit around any longer waiting for you to figure it out."

"So that's it?" Fletcher put his hand over hers.

"I love you, Fletch," Kate said. She wiped tears from her eyes with her free hand. "But I need someone who can give me what I need."

Fletcher wanted to say something, but again, he didn't know what. Instead, he tried sliding his arm around Kate, but she shied away. Their relationship had had its ups and downs. In the ups, it was almost as if they had just fallen in love—always touching, hugging on each other, and plenty of sex—but during the downs they hardly touched at all. In that moment, sitting across from Kate, Fletcher felt a brick wall go up between them. Her mind was made up, he knew. She no longer considered herself to be his wife, or him her husband. She'd already mentally made the break.

They sat in silence for a good fifteen minutes before Kate said, "I'm going to bed." She pushed herself to her feet and walked across the living room without so much as a kiss or a hug. Fletcher watched her go. Before disappearing around the corner to the bedroom she stopped and looked back, causing a glimmer of hope to rise in him. "Do you mind sleeping in the guest room?"

Fletcher stared in disbelief; the hope evaporated. He shook his head.

He didn't know how long he sat there before eventually

going into the kitchen and staring into the fridge. He hadn't had anything to eat, but he wasn't hungry. Instead, he texted Eric. "*I know it's late but you wanna get a beer?*"

"*I thought you went home.*"

"*I did, but I need a beer.*"

"*Sure.*"

"*Meet me at the pub in 20?*"

"*Sure thing, Wise Guy. Slow night anyways.*"

Fletcher retrieved his keys from the shelf in the hallway by the front door. He walked into the garage and hit the garage-door opener with the side of his fist, but then went back into the house.

He knocked on the bedroom door and said, "Kate?" He waited a moment, but there was only silence. "Kate? Can we please talk about this?"

When it was clear there would be no response, he turned and walked away.

Eric was already sitting at the bar when Fletcher walked into Ponderosa's. The renovated historic building with creaky wood floors was a favorite downtown spot for the college kids, but the echoes of their typical din were absent tonight. A lot of locals avoided Ponderosa's because of their ever-present hoopla, but Ponderosa's had been his spot since he was a college kid himself. The walls were covered in coasters from around the world. It was said if you brought in a coaster they didn't already have you'd get a free beer. He didn't know if it'd ever happened and had never asked. By the time he climbed on the bar stool, the owner of the pub, Mac, already had a beer waiting.

"Trouble in paradise?" Eric said.

"You already know there is," Fletcher said. He picked up his beer and took a drink.

"I figured you'd work things out, like you always do."

Fletcher swallowed another mouthful of beer. "Not this time, apparently."

"Weren't you doing counseling or some shit like that?"

"We went for a while but haven't gone in a few months. But now she's set on getting divorced." He took another drink then swirled what was left in his glass around for a bit. "We talked for like ten minutes, then she locked herself in the bedroom. Said she was going to bed."

"Bed my ass," Eric said.

"That's what I thought. She's never once gone to bed that early. She's always up late. She just didn't want to talk anymore." He finished off his pint. "And to top it off, she wants me to sleep in the guest room."

As if on cue, Fletcher's phone buzzed. He picked it up and saw he had a text from Kate: *I decided to stay the night at Denise's instead.*

Of course you did, he thought. He opted against actually replying.

"If she's the one who wants a divorce, shouldn't *she* be the one to sleep in the guest room?"

"You'd think."

"Another beer?" Mac said.

"My wife wants a divorce, Mac."

"So… that's a yeah?"

"Sorry, Mac. I don't know when to turn the sarcasm off— or so I've been told."

"Yeah," Eric said, "he's been a real piece of work today."

Fletcher glared over at Eric. He really wasn't in the mood. He didn't know why he'd even invited Eric. He would have been perfectly content to sit and drink alone, in relative peace and quiet.

"No worries, Fletch," Mac said. "Sorry to hear that."

"Besides," he said, "when have you ever known me to have just one?"

"Well, I didn't want to assume."

"Because you didn't want to be an ass?"

"Just because you're being one doesn't mean I have to be," Mac said.

"Fair enough."

"Do you want another beer or are we gonna sit here and BS all night?"

"If those are my choices, I'll take the beer."

"So what are you going to do?" Eric said while Mac set another beer in front of Fletcher.

"I don't know." Fletcher drank half his beer down in one long pull. "What *can* I do? If she wants a divorce, we get a divorce."

CHAPTER 4

25 days earlier…

G abe fought the excitement that began growing in him
when he saw he had a new email from Your Ideal Mate.
He was currently matched with six women on the dating site,
but none of them were particularly fast at responding when it
was their turn. The site followed a step-by-step process which
gave each person the option to continue to the next stage or to
stop. Maybe it was because they thought he was overly eager—
admittedly, he had a habit of replying the moment he got the
email. He couldn't help it. He had never been popular with girls
and couldn't help getting excited when one showed an interest
in him.

He opened the email and read the brief message: *We're sorry,
but Trudy has closed your match. Even though every match is made using
our patented system, not all of them will turn out to be Your Ideal Mate.
However, we stand by our promise: Everyone is guaranteed to find their
Ideal Mate.*

"*Again?*" Gabe pounded his meaty fist on the desk.

He loaded the website and navigated to his homepage.
Trudy was no longer listed under his Active Matches. He clicked
on the Closed Matches link and scrolled down to the bottom

where her name was now listed. He now had twenty-two closed matches. He scrolled up and down through them, disgusted. *Why won't any of them give me a chance?*

Gabe's finger froze on the wheel of the mouse. He leaned forward in his chair, as far as his stomach would permit, and squinted his eyes. "You're kidding me..." he said. He'd noticed a pattern. Your Ideal Mate had a total of ten stages of customizable back-and-forth interaction. In setting up his profile, he'd selected stage five to share pictures of himself. And he'd only made it past stage five with a few of his matches.

He knew he wasn't what most women considered attractive. He was overweight—had been his entire life—and even though he was in his early twenties, he was already starting to go bald. Unlike meeting someone in a bar, where looks were always the first impression, he'd thought internet dating would be an opportunity for someone to get to know him before they saw what he looked like. And it worked. Women who matched with him seemed receptive to who he was—albeit a little slow in responding at times.

"Superficial bitches," he said, forcefully sitting back in his chair. The springs groaned. Except for—he counted; one, two, three—the furthest he'd made it with any of the women he'd been matched with was stage five, when they saw his picture.

Gabe scrolled down to Trudy's closed profile.

Stage five.

All but three women had closed their match with him after they saw what he looked like.

"Complete bullshit."

He logged off the site and went into the living room, where he plopped into his well-worn recliner. Its stuffing had long since been crushed so it didn't provide much support anymore, but he didn't have the money to buy a new one. He sifted through empty chip bags and candy wrappers on the coffee table until he found the TV remote. He turned the TV on, mindlessly clicked through a few channels, then turned it off again.

Gabe decided he just needed to get out of the house. He heaved himself back to his feet and snapped up his keys. The car's worn-out shocks groaned when he eased himself into the driver's seat. The passenger seat was covered in fast food bags, wrappers, and cups. With a fleeting sense of disgust, he swept it all to the floor, where it joined more of the same. He backed out of the driveway not knowing where he was going. He just wanted to be *away*.

Women didn't give him the time of day. They never had. He got shot down every single time he went out with the few friends he had and showed interest in someone. Women just wouldn't give him a chance. He was convinced that if someone would just take the time to get to know him, they'd realize he was actually a nice guy. Maybe not what they would consider attractive, but looks aren't everything—or so they say. So he'd decided to give internet dating a shot.

He liked Your Ideal Mate because it gave you the most control over what you shared about yourself, and when. He'd set it up so matches had to progress through four stages before they saw his picture, thinking maybe if they got to know him a little before they saw what he looked like, his looks wouldn't matter as much. But that obviously hadn't worked. His matches had proved to be just as superficial as the people he met at bars.

He hadn't consciously realized where he'd been going, but now Gabe pulled into a convenience store with a Burger Mania attached to it. It used to be a favorite spot when he was in college—it was close to the campus and a place he could get a quick bite, plus they had amazing milkshakes. He hadn't been here in over a year, though, because there were places closer to where he lived now to satiate his sweet tooth. He rolled his window down as he drove around the parking lot to the drive-thru on the backside of the building and stopped at the menu.

"Welcome to Burger Mania," a crackly voice said over the dilapidated speaker. "Order when you're ready."

"Large chocolate shake, please," he said.

"I'll have your total at the window."

Gabe pulled up to the drive-thru window on the backside of the building.

"Four seventy-five," said the cashier, a scrawny teenaged kid with emo hair.

I bet he doesn't have trouble with the girls, Gabe thought as he unbuckled his seatbelt. He leaned sideways in order to get at his wallet in his back pocket. His skin began to tingle when he handed his debit card out the window. A weird sort of yearning accompanied the tingling—a feeling he recognized but hadn't felt in years.

He remembered the exact moment he'd last felt it. He had been in high school biology, sitting at his desk and listening to Mr. Driff lecture. What the topic was he couldn't remember. Tanner Johnson, the varsity football quarterback, was sitting at the desk in front of him. Gabe remembered staring at Tanner's back as Mr. Driff droned on, wondering what it would be like to be him—to be the guy all the girls fawned over. Tanner was the homecoming king and his girlfriend, Cindy, was the hottest girl in school. He distinctly remembered the odd feeling that had washed over him as he willed himself to *be* Tanner.

But he hadn't become Tanner, because that was impossible.

Gabe stared at the cashier as the boy processed his debit card, and the intensity of the yearning and tingling grew. The cashier handed him back his card then turned and walked away. He returned a moment later and handed the shake out the window. The yearning was still there, so Gabe willed himself to be the cashier, urged the yearning to grow even more. His heart raced and his vision blurred. For a split-second Gabe was looking down at himself—fat, balding, and sitting in a beat-up car littered with garbage. The shake slipped from his fingers and fell to the ground with a splat. And then he was looking up at the cashier again.

The boy looked down at the mess on the ground then at Gabe. Their eyes locked briefly before he slipped back through the window, visibly shaken, and moved out of sight again.

While Gabe waited for the cashier to make him a new shake, he stared at the steering wheel, trying to process what had just happened. Something *had* happened. It had been quick, but it had happened. He hadn't dreamed it, the cashier's reaction proved that. But it wasn't possible. Was it? He'd thought about it, wanted it so much when he was in high school, but it was impossible. He couldn't change who he was. He especially couldn't become someone else.

"Here ya go," the cashier said.

Gabe looked up. The cashier was holding a new shake as far out the drive-thru window as he could, holding it with both hands, but keeping his eyes averted.

Gabe reached up and took it.

"Sorry about that," the cashier said.

"No worries," Gabe said. He stared up at the cashier, who quickly turned and disappeared. The small rectangular window slid closed automatically. He pulled the spoon out of the shake, licked it off, then left the drive-thru. In the parking lot, he stopped and took a bite.

Gabe pulled out onto the road and headed toward home. His mind was going a million miles a minute. He couldn't stop thinking about what had happened. For just a moment, he'd seen himself sitting in his car. Had he imagined it? Maybe. But he felt the shake slip through his fingers. And the cashier had obviously been distracted by something. And he'd looked away when their eyes met. No, he hadn't imagined it. Something had happened.

Gabe pulled into his driveway. While he finished his milkshake, he thought about the feeling he'd had in the drive-thru. If it truly was what he thought had happened, that meant he could somehow do what he'd always wanted to do. He needed to find out. And if it was true—if he did somehow have the ability to shift into someone else's body—then no one could ever know about it.

CHAPTER 5

G abe turned the car off and went into his house. He sat heavily in his recliner. It was impossible to change bodies with someone else. This wasn't the Twilight Zone or some fantasy world. This was real life. That sort of stuff didn't happen. And yet he distinctly remembered seeing himself sitting in his car, from inside the drive-thru window. It had happened. He knew it.

But how?

Even if it *did* happen, which it did, he had no clue how he'd done it. He didn't *do* anything. He'd just been sitting there waiting for his milkshake.

I imagined it.

No. It happened.

Did it?

He needed to find out if it was just his imagination or if he actually *had* changed bodies with that kid. Which meant talking to him. He pulled his phone out of his pocket and googled Burger Mania. It closed at eleven.

He didn't want to go back there while the kid was working, and it was only eight o'clock. To kill the time, he tried reading. But every time he reached the bottom of a page he realized he had no clue what he'd just read. He couldn't concentrate. Besides, he needed to think. But he also needed to stop his mind from going every which way.

Gabe paced the house for a few minutes, then sat heavily in his recliner again. He really needed to get a new one. He fired up his Xbox. Games were the perfect solution. He could play them without a thought, leaving his mind free to contemplate what he was going to do.

At ten-thirty he changed into a pair of black cargo pants with zippered thigh pockets, and pulled his 9mm down from the shelf in his closet. He removed the magazine and ejected the chambered bullet onto the bed, then put the magazine in the thigh pocket on his left leg. He zipped the pocket closed and walked out of his room. He put on a coat, slipped the gun into the right pocket, and by ten-forty he was driving back to Burger Mania.

At five minutes to eleven, Gabe pulled off the side of the road about fifty yards from the convenience store/burger joint and waited. The Burger Mania sign went off promptly at eleven, but the rest of the convenience store remained open. Twenty minutes later, the cashier emerged from the front of the store. Gabe watched intently as he walked around the side of the building to a bike locked to an electric meter. The teenager rode his bike across the parking lot and onto the largely unlit intersecting road.

Gabe drove after him. He pulled up alongside the teen, rolled the passenger window down, and shouted, "Hey!"

The cashier ignored him at first, but after Gabe shouted again, the cashier looked over at him. "Yeah?"

Gabe pointed his gun through the open window at the boy and shouted, "Pull over!"

"What the…" The cashier's eyes widened. He stood up on his bike and started pedaling faster.

"Shit!" Gabe swore to himself. He pulled ahead of the frantically pedaling teen and veered over onto the shoulder. The shoulder dropped off abruptly into a ditch, so the cashier was forced to stop.

"Get in," Gabe said through the window.

"No way."

Gabe held his gun pointed at the teen. "Do you *want* me to shoot you?"

The cashier hesitated for a moment, but then climbed off his bike. He let it fall to the ground and opened the door. "W-what do you want?"

"Just get in."

The boy climbed in and awkwardly tried to find somewhere to put his feet among all the trash on the floor.

"Shut the door," Gabe said. When the cashier complied, he pulled back onto the road. "Do you have a cellphone?" His question was rhetorical. What teen didn't?

"Yeah…"

"Toss it out the window." When the teenager didn't immediately comply, Gabe pointed the gun at him.

"All right, all right." The boy leaned over against the door and held his hands up. He reached into a pocket and pulled his phone out, then tossed it out the window.

Gabe drove down the dark road, lined by houses on the right and a small lake on the left, until they got to a stoplight. When it turned green, he turned left onto Highway 89.

"What is this?" the cashier said after they'd driven a few miles.

Gabe looked over at the cashier and said, "Do you remember me?"

"Yeah, you're the guy… what was that from before?"

The cashier's question answered Gabe's own. Something had happened. "I don't know."

"Where're we going?"

Gabe didn't answer.

"Dude," the cashier said, "where the *fuck* are you taking me?"

"I don't know," Gabe said. "I… I needed to know."

"Know what?"

"If something happened."

"I could have sworn we—"

"Shut the fuck up," Gabe said. "I need to think."

They drove in silence for about half an hour, through a few neighboring towns, until they entered a wooded area that was in complete darkness. Gabe slowed down and watched the side of the road closely. When he saw a dirt road appear in his headlights, he slowed further and turned onto it. The cashier fidgeted in his seat, so Gabe pointed his gun at him and said, "Don't do anything stupid." He hoped the kid didn't decide to jump. With his gun presently unloaded, Gabe wouldn't be able to stop him even if he tried. And the time it would take for him to stop the car and load the gun would make it almost impossible. He couldn't chase the kid down—with his slender frame he was going to be much faster than Gabe. The moment the kid disappeared into the darkness it would be over; he'd be gone.

After driving for a few miles down the bumpy road—thankfully the kid had sense enough not to jump—Gabe stopped the car and shut the engine off. He kept the headlights on and said, "Get out."

The cashier obeyed. Gabe leaned over and locked the passenger-side door, then climbed out himself. The car rocked and its springs creaked in relief. The cashier was too frightened to run. He probably thought he'd get shot the moment he tried. Gabe pointed the gun at him again and gestured toward the front of the car. "Stand by the hood."

The cashier took a few steps toward the front of the car and stopped by the wheel.

"No, no, between the headlights."

The boy hesitated, but moved when Gabe flicked his gun toward the hood.

"Stay right there."

Gabe walked backwards, away from the car, toward a juniper

tree illuminated by the headlights. He kept the gun pointed at the cashier.

"Come on, man, what are we doing out here?" the teen said.

"I had to think."

"About what?"

Gabe stared at the silhouetted figure of the cashier. *Think, think.* Was the whole thing a fluke? Or could he do it again? He'd always wanted to be somebody else—but until today it'd only been the wistful desire of someone who, admittedly, watched too many sci-fi movies. It wasn't real; it couldn't be.

Gabe clenched his eyes closed and tried to remember that feeling, the one he'd had so many times when he was in high school. Then he opened them, afraid the kid was running. But he was still standing there—either too scared or too stupid. He closed his eyes again and focused on the feeling he'd had at the drive-thru.

He opened his eyes. There it was.

Yes! He focused on it, urged it to grow.

His skin tingled and his heart raced. His vision blurred—just as it should.

The sensation passed and his vision cleared. He was looking at himself, brightly illuminated by the car's headlights.

"Holy fuck!" he heard himself exclaim. Only it wasn't his voice. It was the boy, speaking *as* him.

Gabe looked down at his hands. They were thin. His arms, too. He looked at his body. His chest and stomach were flat. There was a Burger Mania logo on the left side of his shirt. "It worked!" he exclaimed, his voice still that of the cashier's.

"Dude," said the cashier—no, *him*; his body, his voice, with the annoying kind of squeak it developed when he was excited, or panicked—"what the fuck is going on?"

"It worked!" Gabe exclaimed, his voice that of the cashier's. "I can't believe it worked! We switched!"

"Well—" His body pointed the gun at him. "—switch us back."

"Right." If this new skill was going to be useful in any way, he would need to be able to switch back.

Gabe concentrated again, thinking about the feeling, and his skin began to tingle. He urged it forward. His vision blurred and his heart raced again.

He was once again looking at the silhouette of the cashier.

"*Dude.* That's awesome!" the cashier said. The fear in his voice was gone. He seemed excited. "You're like a real-life X-Man!"

"I am," Gabe agreed. A smile blossomed on his face. For once in his life someone thought something he'd done was awesome. It felt amazing.

But no one can know.

"Come on, let's head back." *No one can know.* While the cashier walked toward the passenger door, he unzipped the left pocket of his pants, retrieved the magazine, and slid it into the gun.

No one can know.

"Door's locked," the cashier said.

"Sorry about that." Gabe walked toward the car, racking the slide as he went. He aimed the gun at the cashier as he approached.

The cashier threw both arms up between them and took a few steps back. "W-what are you doing?"

"No one can know."

"I-I-I… I promise I won't—"

Gabe pulled the trigger.

CHAPTER 6

Shifting into someone else's body was like nothing Gabe had ever felt before. He'd spent his entire life hating who he was, wishing he could be someone else—and now he could. The kid was right; he was a real-life X-Man. No longer was he just a fat slob who got pushed around and treated like he was a nobody.

Gabe spent the drive home thinking about how he could use his new ability to his advantage. He had all sorts of wild ideas, but nothing practical came to him immediately. He couldn't do just *anything*. Superheroes had to use their powers wisely. If he was careless, he'd give his secret away, and he certainly didn't want to do that. He didn't want to spoil the party before it ever got started. He got home without a plan, but that didn't bother him. He had time, plenty of time. He fell asleep feeling a sense of deep satisfaction, something he had never experienced before. He was no longer a loser. And soon the world would know.

The next day Gabe had to pull a double shift at work. He didn't particularly like his job and he hated the people he worked with. He loved reading, which was why he tolerated working at Book World, but the shift manager he always got stuck with was a complete asshole. Hank was some sort of wannabe drill sergeant, and ran his shift as such—and he had it out for Gabe for some reason. Probably because Gabe didn't kowtow to Hank's BS. But to punish him—at least, that was how it seemed—Hank always scheduled Gabe to work weekends, which he abhorred. The weekend crowd was the worst. And why would Hank schedule Gabe for double shifts if not to punish him?

"Get the lead out, would you?" Hank said when Gabe passed him on the way from the employee lounge to the registers at the front of the store. "You don't get paid to drag your feet like a sloth."

It's too early for this, Gabe thought with a glare in Hank's direction. He deliberately didn't increase his pace, and Hank folded his muscular arms across his bulging chest and shook his head.

Gabe absolutely hated Hank. He was a condescending piece of shit who found every possible reason to harass Gabe. If Gabe was an X-Man, Hank was his arch-nemesis.

No, Gabe thought as he took his spot behind the register, *that spot is reserved for someone else.* He leaned on the counter, trying to relieve some of the pressure on his feet while he waited for the first customer of the day to come through. It was going to be a long day. Open to close.

The store opened at ten, and with silent contempt, Gabe watched customers trickle in. About ten minutes later, an elderly woman set an Elvis calendar on the counter. He scanned it. While he waited for the woman to write a check he thought, *If I'm going to do anything with this ability, I have to be able to do it at will.* He stared intently at the woman's bluish hair and willed himself to shift into her body.

Nothing happened at first, but then he felt it. The feeling started out small. He recognized the symptoms that accompanied the feeling from the night before: His pulse began to increase, his skin tingled, and his vision blurred. He didn't want to actually become the old woman—that would cause an unnecessary scene in the store and, worse, give away his secret ability—so he pulled back.

"Oh my!" the woman said. She leaned forward and rested her arms on the counter.

"Are you okay, ma'am?" Gabe said. *Shit.*

"I... I'm not sure." She tapped herself on the chest a few times then put a hand to her forehead. "I feel faint."

"Do you want me to send for help?" *Please, god, no.*

"No, no," the woman said, waving him off. "I think it's passing."

Phew. He put the calendar in a bag.

The woman straightened. She finished signing the check and handed it to Gabe. He completed the transaction, then held the bag out to her and said, "Have a nice day."

"Thanks," the woman said, taking the bag from him and mumbling something about calling her doctor.

Gabe tested his new ability throughout the day. For once, he didn't mind working a double shift and having customer after customer parade by him. At first, he tried his ability out on everyone who came through his line. He didn't want them all feeling strange like the old woman had, so he stopped as soon as he felt the process begin. Next, he started picking them at random, only thinking about shifting with specific people. Then he tried on customers across the store. It worked every single time he wanted it to.

This is awesome!

By the end of the long, torturous day, he was still as happy as he had been last night. Even sitting down in front of his favorite games on his Xbox had never made him this happy. Not even Hank's constant badgering brought him down. Along with the other closing employees, Gabe followed Hank's smug ass out of the store and focused his newfound ability on him. The feeling was there. He didn't allow it to progress, but he held onto it, wondering what sort of range he had. He got into his car, ignoring Hank's parting insult about coming to work Monday with less lead in his shoes, and concentrated on the feeling of shifting into Hank's body instead.

I should shift into his body, speed down the road, and crash into a streetlight.

But what would happen while Hank was in my body?

Hank drove off. Gabe closed his eyes and focused his attention on maintaining the feeling. After about five minutes, no matter how hard he tried to hang onto it, the sensation faded. He'd followed Hank out of the mall parking lot numerous times. He always went in the same direction—toward town—so Gabe guessed he lived in Prescott as opposed to Prescott Valley, which was in the opposite direction. Depending on whether or not Hank caught the light leaving the mall parking lot, he could've driven anywhere between three and five miles. It was a good estimate—something to start with, at least.

That night, while he sat in front of the television playing a game, he thought more about how he might be able to use his ability. Gaming for him could either be completely immersive— becoming the Navy SEAL trying to stop the terrorists from deploying a nuclear bomb in DC—or he could play it mindlessly and let his mind wander. Tonight, he let his mind wander.

Magic wasn't real. And neither were X-Men. Switching bodies with someone was impossible. But he could somehow do it. He didn't understand how—right now, all he knew was that he *could*.

Gabe hated who he was—always had. His entire life he'd been made fun of for his weight, been called names, had jokes played on him. What little self-esteem he had was gone before he ever got to high school. It only got worse after that, crueler. During those four long years, he'd hated everyone. He spent his time locked in his room playing video games and reading sci-fi and fantasy novels.

College wasn't better, though people were noticeably less cruel. His freshman roommate joined a fraternity and tried to convince him to join too, but he didn't bother. He'd heard Marls' pledging stories and wanted nothing to do with the humiliation he knew he would have to endure. Who wanted a fat fuck like him in their fraternity anyway? If he'd thought it might get him laid, maybe, just maybe—but what college girl would sleep with him when there were hundreds of other hot guys to be had? No, college wasn't much better than high school. He had, however, managed to make a couple of friends. And one of them was a girl!

Marls was the roommate he'd been paired with, even though their personalities were nothing alike. Marls fit into the "popular" category. Gabe didn't know if it was out of pity—Marls being a frat boy and all—but their friendship seemed genuine enough. Marls even occasionally chose to hang out with him instead of his fraternity brothers. And even though Gabe was always jealous when Marls brought a girl to their room, he never complained. On more than one occasion he'd pretended to be asleep when Marls returned late, and he got to listen in as Marls banged a girl on the top bunk. "Don't worry about him," Marls always reassured them, "he's a sound sleeper."

To this day Gabe still didn't understand how Jenny had ever become his friend. They'd met toward the end of their junior year. He'd seen her around campus before, and had a few classes with her, but they'd never talked directly until she spotted him reading a gaming magazine. She was sitting in the row next to him and leaned over to ask him if he was a gamer. He had been so surprised that she'd spoken to him he'd just stared at her like an idiot. It wasn't until she repeated her question that he realized she was actually talking to him. He told her he was, and almost fainted when she suggested they get together to play sometime.

They spent the next year and a half playing whenever they could. They mostly played online, but every once in a while Jenny brought her laptop over to the house he rented with Marls and they played together. Those were his favorite times, rare as they were.

He knew their relationship was strictly platonic, but despite his best efforts, and no matter how many times he told himself he was being a complete idiot, he couldn't stop himself from falling in love with her. It didn't take long, either. He remembered the tsunami of self-loathing that took over him at the end of their junior year of college. Jenny had gone home for the summer and he spent the weeks in complete misery—even more so than usual. He'd berated himself for being stupid, for thinking that Jenny could possibly love someone like him. They were just friends. She never said or did anything that would have made him think otherwise. Why would he think that? Because he was an idiot, that's why. By the time she returned for senior year he was madly in love with her. He lost count of how many times he'd thought about declaring his feelings for her through the headphones when they played online, or how many times he'd looked at her longingly as she sat on his couch.

Then Marls asked her out and absolutely crushed Gabe. It was a betrayal like nothing he'd ever experienced before. Marls knew he was in love with Jenny—how could he not, as much as Gabe had talked about her over that summer? But he asked her out anyway. And worse, he hadn't even had the balls to tell Gabe. He had to find out when he asked Jenny if she wanted to play and she declined because she and Marls were going to a movie. They'd gone to movies before, but it had always been the three of them. He'd never gone alone with Jenny, which was why he knew something was up with them—and it was. And as far as he was concerned, it was the end of his friendship with Marls.

He couldn't be mad with Jenny, though. What had he expected? Jenny was a beautiful woman—just because she was a gamer didn't mean she would go for a guy like him. It made sense that she would go for Marls. All the girls did. That didn't prevent him from feeling betrayed, though.

Gabe was used to being laughed at, to being made fun of. He was used to being poked—and not in a Pillsbury-Doughboy-type fashion. He'd experienced all this and more numerous times and had long since grown numb to it, but he'd never been betrayed before. Betrayal was new. He'd tried to play it cool, act like he didn't care, but he did. And the longer he kept his feelings to himself, the worse they became. Eventually he got over it—at least, he'd thought he had; maybe he just got used to it—but when Jenny and Marls returned from a date a year later and she had a ring on her finger, he snapped. Not outwardly—he was congratulatory and pretended to share in their excitement—but inside he wanted to kill Marls.

Later, when Marls asked him to be his best man, Gabe actually laughed. "Are you kidding me?" he'd said.

"What? I thought you were happy for us," Marls said.

Gabe had shaken his head and left without another word. He'd immediately started looking for somewhere else to live and found a house to rent by the end of the week. He moved out a few days later. He couldn't live with someone who had so easily betrayed him. Especially someone who was without remorse. Gabe never talked to either of them again, despite Jenny begging him to come to the wedding. He simply couldn't watch her marry someone else, especially not his former best friend.

After a while he didn't think about them anymore.

Until now.

He'd fantasized about what it would be like to sleep with Jenny even before he had fallen in love with her. She was an attractive woman and he was young and, well... he thought about it a lot. Now he realized that if he shifted into Marls' body his fantasy might finally come true.

But he didn't want to sleep with Jenny as Marls. He wanted her to *want* to sleep with him—with Gabe, as himself.

That would never happen, though. Not so long as she was married to Marls.

Then it hit him.

He knew exactly what he would do.

The idea came to him as clearly as if his subconscious had been preparing for this day since he'd first felt that odd sensation in high school.

Gabe tossed his controller and headset onto the floor, not bothering to turn the Xbox or television off, and went into his room. He sat at his desk and fired up the internet browser. *This is perfect*, he thought as he waited. He clicked on his saved link to YourIdealMate.com when the browser was up and running, and set to work.

It was two o'clock in the morning when he finished.

Gabe sat back in his chair and looked at the screen.

Is this really what you want to do?

His meaty hand gripped the mouse, moving the cursor over the website's "activate" button.

Yes, he decided. *It is.*

He clicked.

CHAPTER 7

It didn't take long for Gabe to get his first match. It was all he could do to not reply immediately when he saw the YIM email. He didn't want to seem too eager. That was what popular people did, right? They were aloof, nonchalant. But his new alias, Sam Gilkons, hot guy popular with the ladies, wouldn't be so eager. Sam would give Renee Denovan—one of the many women who had closed her match with Gabe after she'd seen his photo—the opportunity to initiate communication with him.

And a few hours later, she did.

"Sam" waited three days before responding. Gabe wondered if waiting for a response built as much anticipation in her as it did in him. When they arrived at stage five, where Sam showed a picture of himself—a photo of a physically fit man standing on a beach—Renee didn't close the match.

Bingo.

Gabe—or rather, Sam—continued interacting with Renee. After a few more steps, he asked her if she wanted to meet in person. Following YIM's suggestion for the first date, he suggested Connie's Coffee Shop. Connie's was a local favorite. It was very public, but more importantly, it was within range of his house.

When the day for their first date arrived, Gabe was nervous. Apart from the countless hours he'd spent gaming with Jenny over the years, he'd never been on a date before. Even though he and Jenny had started gaming together online, interacting only by voice with their headsets, he remembered being nervous the first time she came over to play at his house. He tried settling his nerves by telling himself he wasn't actually meeting Renee, but it didn't help. He was a mess: pacing his house, unable to eat—which, for him, never happened.

She's just a character in a game, he told himself. *Your game.*

He showed up to Connie's about half an hour before the scheduled time and ordered a coffee. Connie's peppermint mocha was his favorite—and not that non-fat wannabe version. His role in his game was to order a drink, sit down and enjoy it—or at least pretend he was enjoying it as best he could without an appetite—while nonchalantly tinkering on his phone, then leave without seeming suspicious.

Renee showed up ten minutes before their scheduled date.

Early. I like that.

Too bad it wasn't real.

Gabe watched Renee intently as she ordered a drink. He tried his best not to follow her with his eyes while she got her coffee and looked for an empty table. From his glimpses of her, it became readily obvious that she was even more beautiful than her profile picture gave her credit for. She dressed modestly, which led him to believe that she wasn't planning on sleeping with Sam. But he imagined their conversation going pleasantly and, later, her agreeing to go somewhere for dinner.

Gabe studied her, largely out of the corner of his eye. He watched her fidget when the appointed time of the date came and went with no Sam. He watched her for another ten minutes, then slid his chair back, lumbered to his feet, and walked as nonchalantly as he could toward the exit. He looked directly at Renee as he passed her. She looked back at him briefly, but didn't show any sign of recognizing the person she had rejected because of his appearance.

He reached toward her mentally until he started to get the feeling. He stopped himself when he felt it, keeping it right on the surface, and tossed his empty cup into the trashcan by the door.

Gabe sat heavily in his car and drove home. His desire to shift into Renee itched at his skin like a thousand bug bites. He got home, grabbed a piece of tape, and made his way down the basement stairs as quickly as he could. He entered the new, personal cell he'd made while he waited for his first match—a room with cement walls, linoleum floors, boarded up storm window, walls painted black, and a newly installed sturdy door. He locked the deadbolt with a key, then felt his way to the corner. "Shit," he said as he fumbled and dropped the key while trying to put the tape on it. He knelt down, felt for it, and thankfully found it. He pushed himself back up, then, standing on his tiptoes, taped the key as high up on the wall as he could reach.

The room was completely dark. Just as he'd designed it.

He felt his way around the room and sat heavily on the ground, his back against the wall. He closed his eyes, even though he couldn't see anything, and focused on his itching skin.

His breath grew short.

His heart raced.

He felt his sitting position change and the inside of his eyelids grew red. Gabe opened them. He was sitting at a table in Connie's Coffee Shop.

It worked!

CHAPTER 8

It was all Gabe could do to stop himself—or herself, as the case may be—from exclaiming out loud in the middle of Connie's. He was absolutely elated that he had shifted successfully. Until now he hadn't been certain whether he could shift if he wasn't in direct sight of the person. But it worked! A second ago he'd been locked in his basement and now he was sitting in Connie's Coffee Shop as Renee Denovan!

He looked down and smiled at the sight of cleavage. The urge to grab Renee's breasts and squeeze them was nearly unbearable. The last thing he wanted to do was cause a scene. He pushed the urge away—for now. He dropped her phone into her purse, which was hanging on the chair, then stood up. He grabbed the purse and took an awkward step. He looked down after a second wobbly step and saw that Renee was wearing heels. It would seem Renee's skills didn't stay with her body. *How do women walk in these things?* He leaned against the table and lifted his heel—something he wasn't flexible enough to do himself—and took off the shoe. He removed the other one, then nimbly walked out of Connie's.

As the door closed behind him, Gabe reached into the purse hanging on his shoulder and felt for keys. Not finding them right away, he held the purse open with both hands to get a better look. After locating them, he pushed the unlock button and scanned the parking lot for the car. The lights of a yellow VW Bug—one of the newer ones, not the classic Super Beetles he'd grown up liking—flickered off to his right.

Gabe walked over to it, feeling light as air, opened the door, and slid into the leather seat. He tossed the shoes onto the floor in front of the passenger's seat and fired the Bug up. He exited the parking lot onto Sheldon Street, turned left, and drove a few blocks up the hill to Pawn Paradise. After parking, he found Renee's wallet in her purse. Inside, he found a mess of various gift cards, credit cards, old college IDs, and her driver's license. He checked her license and saw it had a local address. *Excellent.* He would need that.

Gabe looked at the neon "Open" sign flashing behind a window covered in iron bars, and caught a glimpse of Renee in the rear-view mirror. He angled it to get a better look. Renee's vivid blue eyes greeted him. He reached up and ran her petite hands over her smooth face. In stark contrast to his own round and well-padded face, the bones of her cheeks and jaw were easily discernible beneath her skin, which was covered by a thin layer of foundation. His heart quickened when he saw her chest in the reflection. He took a quick look around the parking lot, verifying he was the only one there, then sat back in the driver's seat. With both hands he pulled the top of Renee's dress away from her body. He felt a wave of heat rise in his face at the sight of breasts so close. He'd never seen any in real life, let alone touched one.

Tentatively, Gabe reached a hand into the dress and grabbed one. It felt soft and yet, at the same time, firm. He detected a small protuberance beneath the lacy bra material and took a slow, shuddering breath. He wanted to slide his hand beneath the thin layer of clothing, but he didn't dare. *Maybe later*, he thought. Right now, he had lives to destroy. He took a couple of deep breaths, grabbed the purse off the passenger seat, and opened the door. He left the heels behind.

A bell heralded Gabe's—or rather, Renee's—entrance to the pawnshop. He took a quick look around, then walked up to the glass counter. He scanned the contents, making his way from one end to the other, until he arrived at the guns. He knew where they were—he'd bought his own 9mm here a few years back—but the chances of Renee also being familiar with the store were not high. He didn't want to be obvious.

"Can I help you?" a voice said.

Gabe looked up at the overweight, unkempt man behind the counter, and was reminded of himself. "I'm looking for a gun," Gabe said, hearing Renee's silvery voice for the first time. It made his own wheezy voice even more disgusting.

"What kind of gun?"

Gabe stared down at the assortment displayed beneath the glass. "Oh, I don't know. My boyfriend wants me to get one for protection. Something with stopping power, he says."

"You have any experience?"

"No, but he said he's gonna teach me."

"Well, it really comes down to personal preference."

Gabe looked at the man who was leaning on the counter, similar to how Gabe himself stood behind the cash register at work. He batted Renee's eyes and said, "What do you recommend?"

"Hmm…" The man looked Renee up and down. "Well, if you're asking me, I'd probably go with a .380 or 9mm. Both are friendly calibers for someone like yourself."

Gabe wanted to smile coyly at the obviously sexist remark, but he had no idea how to do that. He batted Renee's eyes again instead. But he did agree—9mm was his preferred caliber. "Um…" he said, as if he was thinking. "Well, a 9mm sounds good to me. I think that's what my boyfriend has anyway."

"All right. Any particular make?"

Gabe shook his head. "I really don't know much about guns."

"Hmm..." the man said again. He unlocked the sliding glass door on the back side of the counter and pulled a gun out. He set it on the glass counter with a solid clunk. "I'd go with this one."

Gabe picked up the gun, smaller than his own, and tested the weight in his hand as if he knew what he was doing. He did, of course, though he tried not to look too adroit in his handling of the firearm. The size and weight felt good in Renee's dainty hands. He turned it over a few times, set it on the glass, and declared, "I'll take it!"

The man nodded. Taking the gun with him, he walked back to a messy desk. He returned a moment later and set a form on the counter. "First I'll need you to fill this out."

"What's this?" Gabe said.

"Standard background check."

"Do I have to come back or something while you run that?"

"No waiting time in this fine state—so long as you pass," the man concluded with a wink.

"How long's that gonna take?"

"A few minutes is all." He took a pen from behind his ear and offered it to Renee.

Gabe nodded and took the pen. He pulled Renee's driver's license out of her purse and set to answering the questions. Having bought a gun before, he knew what sort of questions they asked. One of the trickier parts of his plan was learning where the women he planned to use had been born. Turned out it wasn't that hard: Renee had easily told him what city she was born in. All he'd had to do was ask her. He glanced inconspicuously at Renee's license as he filled out the application for her personal info. "I move around so much," he said as he wrote, "sometimes I forget what my current zip code is." When he finished, he slid the form across the glass.

The man scooped it up along with Renee's ID and said, "It'll just take me a few minutes to run you through the system."

Twenty minutes later, Gabe walked out of Pawn Paradise

with a gun and a box of ammo. Before pulling out of the parking lot, he looked around, ensuring no one was nearby, then unpacked the gun. He nimbly loaded the magazine, slid it into the gun with a click, and chambered a bullet by pulling the slide back. He insured the safety was on, then slid the gun into Renee's purse.

Gabe backed out of the parking lot and made his way down Sheldon toward Gurley. He turned onto Gurley and stayed left when the road became Highway 89. As he drove toward his destination, his heart started beating faster. He felt a rush similar to the one he got when he was closing in on the boss at the end of a game.

Gabe knew his target would be home. Even though he didn't keep in contact with Jenny or Marls anymore, Jenny still emailed him, keeping him up on what was going on in their lives. And a couple of months after they'd gotten married, Marls was laid off from his job. Unable to find work, Marls sat at home collecting unemployment while Jenny supported them. He'd scheduled Sam's date with Renee for a time he knew Jenny would be at work, leaving Marls alone at home.

Fifteen minutes later, Gabe pulled to a stop in front of the house he used to share with Marls. He grabbed the purse, holding it in his lap, and took a moment to consider whether he really wanted to go through with his plan. He could still pull the plug on the operation. There were plenty of other ways he could ruin Renee's life without killing someone. He laughed at the thought of stripping down and running naked through the mall. But anger quickly replaced the amusement.

Marls had known that Gabe loved Jenny. Yet he'd married her anyway. Gabe had never actually objected, but his reaction when they got engaged should have told Marls everything he needed to know. But Marls wouldn't have backed out anyway. He probably would have thought Gabe was being selfish. Marls betrayed him—and worse, he'd had the gall to ask Gabe to be his best man!

Gabe had gone round and round over whether he should forgive Marls, but as far as he was concerned, Marls didn't need forgiveness... he needed to pay. Jenny would be hurt, for sure, but maybe she would reach out to him for comfort. And with Marls out of the way, he could, at the right time, make sure Jenny knew exactly how he felt.

Gabe got out of the Bug, slid the purse over his shoulder, and confidently strode barefoot up the driveway. He stopped on the front step and tested the brass doorknob. It turned. He pushed the door open and walked in.

Marls walked out of the kitchen, confused, and said, "Hello?" He was drying his hands on a towel.

"You shouldn't have betrayed me," Renee said.

"I'm sorry, do I know you?"

"She was mine and you knew it." Renee reached into the purse and pulled out the gun.

Marls dropped the towel and held up his hands. "Whoa, whoa, whoa."

Renee lifted the gun toward Marls, clicking the thumb safety off in the process, and fired.

CHAPTER 9

Gabe felt his way around the dark cell to the corner where he'd hidden the key. He reached up, his hand throbbing for some reason, and pulled the key from the wall. It took a moment for his eyes to adjust when he unlocked the door and stepped out of the room. He rubbed his hand while he waited. The feeling of absolute power numbed the pain.

When he could see without it hurting, he made his way up to his bedroom. The blackout curtains he used to prevent glare while gaming made the room almost as pitch black as his "dungeon." He flipped on the light and mindlessly picked his phone up from the dresser by his bed. He checked the time: 4:45 pm. He flipped the light back off and flopped onto the bed, which groaned with the sudden burden.

He closed his eyes, glad he didn't have to work today, and mentally replayed what had just happened: the feeling that had accompanied shifting into Renee; opening his eyes and finding himself sitting in the coffee shop; seeing and touching real breasts for the first time in his life—*Oh. My. God*; standing face to face with Marls for the first time since his betrayal; pulling the trigger and watching Marls fall to the ground.

I can be anyone I want. I can do *anything I want.*

When this was over—he didn't even fully grasp what "this" was yet—he would never have to be himself again. He could come up with a plan to shift permanently into someone else's body and live the rest of his life as whomever he wanted, leaving his fat fucking body behind forever.

Becoming Renee had been magical. It was almost as though he'd been playing another first-person RPG. His mind kept playing it over and over as he slowly drifted further away from himself and fell asleep.

The ringing of a phone ripped Gabe from his dreams like an alarm blaring full blast at four in the morning. He sat up, disoriented, and looked over at the ringing device. He picked it up and saw that Jenny was calling. He stared at the phone, coming straight to his senses, but didn't answer. This was exactly what he'd wanted. She was reaching out to him. But suddenly, he was afraid. He decided to let the call go to voicemail instead. But his phone started ringing again the moment he set it back down. He watched it ring until it stopped. It immediately started ringing for a third time. This time he answered.

"Hello?"

"Oh, Gabe!" Jenny wailed into the phone.

"*Jenny?*" Gabe said. He tried his best to sound surprised. He hadn't talked to her for over a year.

"I'm sorry for bothering you so late but I didn't know who else to call..."

"What do you mean?" He held his phone away from his ear and saw that it was 10:13 pm. *I must have fallen asleep.*

"Gabe? I... I'm sorry to bother you but I... I just need somewhere to go."

"Why? What's going on?"

"It's Marls..."

Gabe waited a moment, but when she didn't say anything more, he said, "What about him?"

"He... someone... someone shot him, Gabe."

"*Shot him?*" Gabe's voice squeaked the way it sometimes did when he got excited. "Is he... okay?" Gabe heard Jenny crying into the phone. "What? What happened?"

"Can I just please come over, Gabe?"

"I don't know..."

"I know things ended badly between us, and I'm sorry, but you're the only one I know here. And I don't want to be alone."

"You certain there's no one else?"

"Gabe..."

He already knew what he was going to say, but he paused so he wouldn't sound too eager. He was always too eager. "Of course," he finally said. "You're welcome to come over any time."

"Where do you live?"

"Oh, uh..." He realized that he'd never given them his new address when he moved. He gave it to her then said, "See you in a bit."

"Thanks, Gabe. This really means a lot to me."

"Sure." He hung up and got out of bed, mind racing. Jenny reaching out to him was exactly what he'd hoped would happen when Marls was no longer a factor, but he hadn't expected it to happen so soon. He'd figured she would go through the whole burial and grieving process, then try to reconnect with an old friend. If she was calling him wanting to be with him on the very night her husband was murdered...

No, Gabe told himself. *She doesn't have feelings for you.* It would be amazing if she did—it was something he'd long fantasized about—but he'd only ever been a friend. *But what if she* does *have feelings for you?* What then? He couldn't possibly act on that, could he? *No*, he told himself. *Not tonight.* Tonight, and in the days to come, Jenny would need a friend. And that was exactly what he was going to be. It might seem suspicious if he was too eager, so he would wait. That's what Sam would do. And that's what he was going to do from now on.

He turned the lights on and went to the bathroom to clean up. His shirt was damp with sweat—and his apartment was a disaster. He wasn't expecting company. He tried not to think about Jenny while he worked. He'd spent so long trying to get over her and bury his feelings for her that he knew if he thought about it too much, he'd ruin things with her when she arrived. Instead, he focused on his experience of being Renee.

The feeling had been unbelievable. It was certainly not something he'd ever experienced before. First and foremost, he'd felt full of energy. He spent most of his waking hours tired. Work absolutely killed him. Every day he counted down the minutes until his allotted breaks. And god forbid he was even a minute late clocking back in; Hank made sure he didn't hear the end of it for the rest of the day. But when he was Renee, he felt bubbly, ready to run a race—assuming he had something better to wear than those cursed heels. And the view... He stopped himself from following that train of thought. Instead, he considered his newfound power over other people. He'd had absolute control over Renee. She was powerless to stop him. He could have done anything he wanted with her—to her. And he'd chosen to singlehandedly ruin her life. *It's your own damn fault. You shouldn't have been such a superficial bitch.*

Gabe's stomach grumbled. He realized he'd fallen asleep without eating. When he finished washing up he went to the kitchen in search of food. He found nothing appealing in the fridge. He opened the freezer to see if there was anything he could nuke real quick, but shut it immediately.

He had an idea.

He would order pizza.

That had been his and Jenny's thing. They always ordered pizza when she came over to game. He got on his phone and looked up his favorite pizza place, ensuring it was still open, then called and ordered a pizza. He heard a knock at the door the moment he got off the phone.

Gabe's heart raced. He hadn't seen Jenny since he'd moved out of the house he shared with Marls over a year ago. And now that she was standing at his door, his feelings for her came flooding back like a beer bong he wasn't ready for. He took a few deep breaths as he walked to the front door. He placed his hand on the knob, took one more deep, shuddering breath, and opened the door.

Jenny crashed into his chest, wrapping her arms around his thick neck. "Oh, Gabe!" she cried.

Gabe didn't know exactly what to do, so he gently wrapped his arms around her and patted her back. Her smell instantly registered with his senses, and the feel of her body against his consumed him. He closed his eyes and reveled in the moment, letting her cry into his chest. The moment dragged on but was never awkward—and he typically hated physical contact.

Eventually, she stepped back, and Gabe reluctantly let go. As she wiped her eyes with the backs of her hands he said, "Please, come in."

Gabe turned to let her by and became acutely aware of the mess the house was still in. Dirty plates and empty chip bags littered the room. He hurried past her and gathered up the plates and garbage, making a spot for her to sit on the couch. It wasn't something he'd had to worry about for a long time, since he never had anyone over. Jenny waited while he worked, then sat heavily on the plush couch cushion.

An awkward silence hung in the air. Not knowing what else to say, Gabe said, "I ordered pizza."

"I'm sorry to bother you so late, Gabe, but I didn't have anywhere else to go. I couldn't be home, not with... what happened."

"No worries," Gabe said. He sat next to Jenny—not too close, though—and patted her on the back. "I can't believe someone would... who?"

"I don't know. Some woman named... um..." Gabe stopped himself from blurting out Renee's name. "...Renee Denovan. I don't know who she is or how she knew Marls, but she walked into our home and shot him."

"Do the cops have any idea why?"

"No, not yet."

"Did they at least catch her?"

Jenny nodded. "Apparently after she… um… she just went outside and sat in the middle of the driveway and didn't move until the police showed up."

"That's crazy," Gabe said. *Bitch got what she deserved.* "I can't believe someone would up and do that."

Jenny turned and leaned into Gabe, burying her head in his chest. She started sobbing again. "It doesn't make sense…"

"I know, I know," Gabe said, rubbing her back. "But I'm sure they'll figure it out. That's what they do, right?" He hoped they didn't figure it out. How could they, though? His plan was perfect because it was impossible. Renee would go to trial—unless she took a plea deal—and nobody would believe whatever she might try to tell them. Then she'd go to prison. Two birds killed with one stone: Both Marls and Renee got what they deserved.

Gabe continued consoling Jenny as she cried. He excused himself when there was another knock on the door heralding the pizza's arrival. Jenny wasn't hungry, which suited him perfectly. He didn't really want to share anyway. She talked while he ate and listened and did his best to care.

The night wore on. At two in the morning, Jenny finally said, "Do you mind if I stay the night? There's no way I can go home."

"Sure, sure," Gabe said gleefully. He'd always dreamed of Jenny staying the night at his place. Maybe not under these circumstances, but he'd take what he could get. "You can have my bed if you want."

"That's sweet," Jenny said, "but the couch is fine."

Sweet? She'd always thought he was sweet. But he didn't want to be sweet. Women didn't sleep with guys they thought of as "sweet." He let it go, though. Too soon. "Let me get you a pillow and blanket."

"Thanks again, Gabe. I know it probably doesn't matter, not now, but neither of us wanted to hurt you."

Gabe froze and looked down at Jenny. A pang of anger rose in him. He pushed it down—he'd already had his vengeance. He shook his head and said, "You're right. It doesn't matter."

CHAPTER 10

October 20th

Fletcher rolled over in bed. The light shining in his eyes made him open them and sit up with a start. "Shit!" he said. He looked for his phone on his nightstand, but it wasn't there. He didn't need it to know he was late, though. The light gave it away.

He rolled out of bed and turned on the shower. Then he went and looked for his phone. Not finding it on the couch, he got down on his knees and looked under it—he had the habit of putting it there when he watched TV, which he vaguely remembered doing when he got back from Ponderosa's. It wasn't there either, so he went into the kitchen, where he found it sitting on the island. He snatched it up and pushed the side button to make the time show. 8:48. "Shit," he said again.

He went back into the bedroom, plugged the phone in—its power was at ten percent—and climbed into the shower.

It was 9:45 when he walked into the station.

"We weren't out *that* late, AO, were we?" Eric said when Fletcher approached his desk.

Fletcher sat down, rubbing his temples. "AO?"

"Astute One."

"You have to break out a dictionary for that one?"

"Testy, too. Damn. Lighten up."

"Sorry. I overslept and haven't had any coffee yet."

"I figured. What with Kate being..."

Fletcher stared at Eric for a moment, and when Eric looked back at his own computer, Fletcher booted his up.

"So," Eric said, "what are your thoughts?"

"About what?"

"About whether Renee's telling the truth or not."

"What did you say about Kate?"

"I..."

"What?"

"Nothing."

"Do *you* think Renee's telling the truth?" Fletcher said.

"Hell no. Her story's cray-cray." Eric spun his finger around his ear while his eyes made loops in their sockets, then started typing on his computer.

Fletcher watched him expectantly, then said, "Eric?"

"What?" Eric replied, without looking at Fletcher or stopping whatever it was he was typing.

"Important email?"

"Huh?"

"What were you going to say before?"

"What are you talking about?"

"I wouldn't be very astute if I couldn't tell you were dodging right now, would I? Spit it out already."

"Fine. You really want to know?"

"Yes."

"After you went home, I saw her."

"Who?"

"Kate."

"Where?"

"CJ's." Fletcher furrowed his brow. "She was with her sister and..."

Fletcher held his hands up and slightly out as though to say, "And?"

"They were with a couple of guys."

Fletcher stood abruptly and shoved his seat back, making it crash into the cubicle partition. He shook his head and walked away.

"That's why I didn't want to say anything!" Eric called after him.

Fletcher's head throbbed. He needed coffee before he could even begin to think about what Eric had just said. He went to the break room and thanked the caffeine gods when he saw that the pot was steaming and full. He poured himself a mug of the black nectar and returned to his desk. He decided not to jump to any conclusions until after he talked with Kate. He took a few blessed sips then said, "Has Renee been arraigned yet?"

"Yeah, she saw Judge Sinclair this morning," Eric said.

"Dammit. I meant to call Scott this morning."

"I took care of it, but Sarge wants us on this case, so you need to make sure problems with Kate don't interfere with the investigation."

"They won't," Fletcher said. There was no way he could know if that was true, though.

"You sure?"

"I said they won't. Get back to whatever you were typing so furiously, would ya?" Fletcher turned to his own computer and keyed in his password, but before it was finished booting, his mind had already drifted to who Kate might have been out with.

"Hey," Eric said.

Fletcher looked past his monitor at Eric. "What?"

"You've been staring off into space for like five minutes."

He looked at his computer. The screen had gone blank. He drank more coffee, in bigger gulps now that it had cooled below scalding temps, and woke his computer back up. He clicked on the necessary folders to dig through the network until he found the folder titled *Marlon Williams*. He opened it and found several files, including the video of Renee Denovan's interrogation.

Fletcher sifted through the files from the scene of the crime.

The witness affidavits were pretty solid. A total of four neighbors had seen Renee emerge from the house shortly after they'd heard two gunshots and a woman scream. And, as Frey had indicated over the phone, there were also two neighbors from the next street up, whose backyards abutted Marlon's at the top of a twelve-foot retaining wall. They also made statements about hearing the gunshots and scream. The owner of the house immediately behind the Williams' residence was outside at the time and didn't see anyone emerge from the back of the house. The investigation revealed that the back door was locked and all the windows in the house were latched. The only means of egress from the premises was the front door. The door Renee Denovan was seen exiting from.

Fletcher clicked on the file titled *Gun*. He looked at the pictures first, then the file containing the written description. Not finding anything surprising, he picked up his phone and called the ATF. When a voice on the other end answered he said, "Hello, this is Detective Wise with the Prescott Police Department. Could you run a serial number on a gun for me?" He waited until the operator on the other end was ready then read the number in the report. He asked for a rush trace, the operator saying they would do what they could, then he hung up.

"What are the odds the gun's hers?" Eric said.

"I'm not going to be surprised when we find out it is. I'm more interested in learning how long she's owned it."

"Right," Eric said.

"It's one thing if she already owned the gun, but something entirely different if she bought it specifically to kill Marlon."

"Right," Eric said again.

Fletcher could tell Eric had no idea why that would be important. "Because…"

"Because…" Eric echoed.

"If she bought the gun specifically to kill Marlon that would show… I'm thinking aloud to help you, Eric. Which is something you need to start doing."

Eric tapped his forehead and said, "I do all my thinking up here, thank you very much. Besides, you don't want to know half of what goes on up here."

"You're right," Fletcher agreed. "I don't. But sometimes saying what you're thinking out loud so you can hear it does wonders for helping you work through things. So..."

"So... what?"

"You know, I'm really beginning to wonder if you have the aptitude for this."

"Dude, I know you're hungover and all, but that doesn't mean you need to be a dick."

"Having a headache is not the same as being hungover."

"Headache hangover, to-may-toes to-mah-tos, po-tay-toes po-tah-tos, caramel carmel, creek crick, pillow pellow..."

Fletcher rolled his eyes. "Are you finished?"

"Let me think..." Eric looked up at the ceiling, tapped his chin a few times, then said, "Yup."

"You're an idiot, you know that?"

"That's not what the chick from CJ's said last night."

"Spare me, would you?"

"Since you asked so nicely."

"And I thought you said it was a slow night?"

Eric shrugged. "Late night rush."

"If it turns out Renee lied about the gun, what else did she lie about?" Fletcher said. He already had a list prepared in his mind, despite his headache, but as a trainer, he wanted to see what Eric came up with.

"Uh... did you forget the whole teleporting-and-turning-into-a-man thing?"

"I meant besides that."

"Like what?"

"You tell me. What other questions should we be asking?"

"How does she know the victim?"

"What else?"

"Why'd she kill him?"

"Right. To get the right charges, we need to find out what her motive for killing Mr. Williams was," Fletcher said. "More important, if she specifically bought the gun to kill Williams, then that would show—"

"Intent!" Eric exclaimed.

"Exactly. And it's about time." Speaking of time, it was time to go out and do a little legwork. "I'm going to go talk to Renee's roommate." He should really be taking Eric with him—god knew he needed the practice—but he wasn't in the mood. "Will you put together a warrant for her apartment, as well as for Connie's Coffee Shop?" Those were tasks Eric didn't need his hand held for.

"Sure thing, Smarty Pants."

"Really?" Fletcher said. He pushed his chair back and stood up. "Are we in grade school now?"

"I know you are but what am I?"

"I'll never understand how you get so many women to sleep with you." Fletcher walked out of the detectives' area, stealing a glance over at Tina when he passed the dispatchers' area. She was busy talking on the phone and didn't see him. *Does she ever notice when I pass by?* He briskly shook his head, knowing he shouldn't think about her like that.

Fifteen minutes later he pulled into the Pinetop Apartment complex, climbed the four flights of stairs, and knocked on the door of apartment 412 B. A dog inside the apartment started barking. He heard a muted woman's voice shushing the dog, then the door opened.

"Renee?" said a young woman with disheveled hair, expectantly. She held an enthusiastic black and white border collie by the collar. Her face turned sour when she saw it wasn't Renee.

"Elizabeth Warner?" Fletcher said.

"Yeah." A worried look crossed her face. "Who are you?"

"My name is Detective Wise," Fletcher said, holding up his

badge, "with the PPD. You're Renee Denovan's roommate, right?"

"Oh God," Liz said. She backed away from the door and accidently let go of the dog. It shoved its way through the opening to sniff at Fletcher.

Fletcher reached down happily to pet it. He really did love dogs.

"I told her not to go," Liz said.

"Ma'am, do you mind if I come in and ask you a few questions?"

"Is she… please don't tell me she's dead."

"No, ma'am, she's not dead," Fletcher said. "May I come in so we can talk?"

"What about?"

"She's gotten herself into a bit of trouble."

Liz wrapped her arms around her stomach. She was wearing what looked like a sorority t-shirt and flannel pajamas. "What kind of trouble?"

"That's what I was hoping to talk to you about."

"Sure," Liz said with a nod. She opened the door farther. "Please, come in. Ollie," she said tersely, "get in here."

Fletcher stepped into the apartment and, when Ollie followed him in, closed the door.

"Just let me go put the dog away," Liz said.

"Sure." Fletcher watched Liz lead the dog by the collar down the hallway and usher it into a bedroom. She closed the dog into the room and walked back down the hall.

"What's happened to her?" Liz said.

"Please, sit," Fletcher said, gesturing to the futon to his right. While Liz walked around the coffee table covered in magazines, beer bottles, and empty energy-drink cans, he grabbed a chair from the dining room table to his left, positioned it on the other side of the coffee table, opposite the futon, then sat. "Renee is fine, but she's been arrested."

"*Arrested?* For what?"

"Do you know someone named Marlon Williams?"

Liz shook her head. "No."

"Does Renee?"

"Not that I know of."

"She uses a dating site, right? Your Ideal Mate?"

"Yeah."

"Could he possibly be someone she knows there?"

"What's this about?" Liz said.

"Last night Renee was arrested for murdering someone by the name of Mar—"

"Murder!" Liz exclaimed, almost rising off the futon.

Fletcher nodded. "Marlon Williams was murdered in his home last night and Renee is our prime suspect." Liz stared at him with mouth agape. "The reason I'm here is because I need your help corroborating her story."

"I-I don't understand. Renee would never kill anyone."

"You're under no obligation to talk to me if you don't want to, but I want to believe that you're right. So anything you can tell me will help me figure out exactly what happened yesterday."

"Yeah, sure," Liz said.

"Do you mind if I record our conversation?" Fletcher said. He pulled a recorder from his jacket pocket and held it up for her to see.

Liz shook her head. "No. Go ahead."

Fletcher pushed the record button and set the device on the table between them. "Can you start off by telling me your full name?"

"Elizabeth Irene Warner."

"How do you know Renee?"

"We met in college a few years ago. We've been friends ever since."

Fletcher nodded. "Can you tell me what happened yesterday?"

"What do you mean?"

"Well, why would you think Renee was dead?"

"She had a blind date with a guy she met online."

"Tell me about that," Fletcher said.

"She started doing this online dating thing, even though I told her she was crazy, and yesterday she was going to meet someone for the first time."

"Who was she going to meet?"

"Sam something-or-other, I can't remember his last name."

The dog barked a few times from the bedroom. Fletcher looked over his shoulder in that direction, then said, "Do you know where they were meeting?"

"At CC's."

"CC's?" Fletcher said. The dog continued barking.

"Sorry," Liz said. "He doesn't like being locked up when he knows someone's here."

"Feel free to let him out."

"You sure?" Liz said.

"If you think he'll be happier out here, it'll be easier to talk," Fletcher said.

"Okay." Liz got up and went down the hall.

Fletcher turned in his chair and greeted the dog when it jumped up into his lap. He petted it around the ears. "Ollie, you said?" he said when Liz appeared around the corner.

"Yeah." Liz grabbed at Ollie's collar and said, "Get down."

Ollie jumped down and quickly found a spot on the couch.

"Sorry about that."

"It's okay," Fletcher said. "He yours?"

Liz sat back down next to Ollie. "Renee's."

"You're such a good boy," Fletcher said to Ollie in a baby voice. "Where were we? Oh yeah. CC's?"

"Connie's Coffee Shop. That's what she calls it. She said they were just meeting for coffee. For an hour, and that she would text me as soon as their date was over. But I've been up all night trying to contact her. She texted me a few times from the coffee shop but then suddenly stopped. She was supposed to text me when the date was over but when she didn't, I called the police."

"Why would you call the police?" Fletcher said.

"Because I didn't like the idea of her going on a date with someone she met on the internet."

"Why not?"

"Because. There's no way she could know whether or not the guy was a serial killer."

"All right, so you called the police because you thought she might have been abducted or something?"

Liz nodded.

"That's a yes. So she texted you during the date but—"

"Actually, no," Liz said.

"I'm confused. You just said she was texting you but then suddenly stopped."

"The guy never showed up. She was sitting there alone and texted me to tell me she thought she got stood up. Here," Liz said, digging her phone out of her pocket. She opened the messaging app and held the phone out over the table. "See for yourself."

Fletcher took the phone and read the exchange between Renee and Liz. Renee sent the first text to Liz at 3:30 pm.

Renee: *I think I'm being stood up.*

Liz: *Maybe he got caught in traffic...*

Renee: *Traffic? Seriously?*

Liz: *I'd say text him, but you don't have his number.*

Renee: *I told you that's for safety. YIM doesn't recommend sharing personal contact info at first.*

Liz: *Because of serial killers...*

The last text from Renee was at 3:34 pm. After that was a series of texts from Liz, beginning at 3:47 pm and spanning a couple hours:

Liz: *How's it going?*

Liz: *Did he show up?*

Liz: *Renee?*

Liz: *Could you please text me back?*

Liz: *Renee!?!*

Liz: *Okay, now I'm starting to get worried.*

Liz: *Renee, PLEASE ANSWER!*

"Mind if I take a picture of these?" Fletcher said.

Liz shook her head and said, "No, go ahead."

Fletcher set Liz's phone down on the table and used the camera on his own phone to take several pictures, making sure to capture the entire conversation.

Looking at the texts made Fletcher think of Kate. He'd be lying if he said he hadn't ever looked through her texts. He had never been the jealous type—he was always okay with her having guy friends—but when things had really started going south between them, he couldn't help but wonder. He'd never found anything, so he'd been surprised by what Eric said this morning about seeing her out with her sister and a couple of guys.

He shoved the thought of Kate away, remembering that he'd said his relationship problems wouldn't affect this investigation. "Did you call her?"

"I tried to, but she never answered," Liz said.

"May I look at your call log?"

"Sure."

Fletcher switched apps on Liz's phone and took pictures of the call log. Liz had tried calling Renee about a dozen times, beginning at 5:51 pm yesterday and continuing throughout the night, until just about twenty minutes ago.

He handed the phone back to Liz and said, "Thanks. And this was the last time you heard from her?"

Liz nodded. "As you can see, she didn't answer any of my calls or texts."

"Did anyone else know about her date? That you know of?"

"Can't think of anyone. I tried calling her work, but she wasn't there."

"What about her parents?" Fletcher said. "Could she have gone to see them?"

"Her parents live back east."

"Why didn't you call them? Maybe they knew where she

was."

"Honestly? I didn't want to worry them until I knew more."

Fletcher nodded. Shifting gears on his line of questioning, he went back to the actual murder. "So Renee didn't know anyone named Marlon Williams?"

Liz shook her head. "Not that I know of."

"You sure? An old boyfriend, perhaps?"

"I've never heard the name before. If he was an old boyfriend, she would have mentioned him. We talk about pretty much everything."

"Does she own a gun?" Fletcher said.

Liz shook her head again. "No. She doesn't."

"You sure?"

"I mean, I'm pretty sure." Liz fidgeted on the couch. "Do you mind if I get something to drink?"

"No, no, go right ahead," Fletcher said, leaning back in the seat.

"Would you like anything? Water? Or I could brew some coffee."

"No, thanks."

Liz went into the kitchen and Fletcher watched over the breakfast bar as she retrieved a cup from a cupboard and filled it at the sink. Was she lying about Renee owning a gun? Why would she be? She seemed genuinely concerned about Renee's well-being. And if Renee did own a gun, that didn't necessitate Liz knowing about it. Maybe Liz was anti-gun and so Renee didn't feel the need to share that part of her life with her.

Liz returned to the couch and took a drink. Fletcher discarded the thought that she was covering for Renee. He didn't have any reason to suspect it yet, and the ATF report would answer the question soon enough. He shifted gears again. "Can you think of anyone that Renee might have had a disagreement or a fight with?"

"No," Liz said. She took another sip of water. "Renee is one of the nicest people I've known. I've never known her to have a problem with anyone."

"An old boyfriend?"

Liz shook her head. "I mean, she's had boyfriends she's broken up with, but they weren't the dish-throwing kind of breakups."

"Is there any reason to believe any of them might have wanted to hurt her?"

"None that I can think of. And if she was in any way worried about one, I'm sure I would have known."

"Why's that?"

"She's my best friend."

"What about a co-worker?"

"Not that she's ever mentioned."

"Where does she work?"

"She's a waitress at Tex's."

Fletcher nodded. It claimed to be the finest steakhouse in the state. He'd shared many a dinner there with Kate. It was one of her favorite places to go if they were looking for a nice meal. He turned his thoughts back to the whole internet dating thing. "So, Renee was meeting someone she'd met online?"

"Yeah. I warned her not to, but she always says meeting someone online is no different than meeting them at the bar."

"Well, she has a point." Liz looked at him as if he were crazy. "What can you tell me about internet dating?" He was genuinely curious as it hadn't come along until after he'd met and started dating Kate.

"There's any number of apps to choose from; you just pick one and fill out your info, then you get matched up with people," Liz said.

Fletcher nodded. He knew he was going to need to access the site, but not until he got a warrant. "Had she been using it long?"

"Not long. She broke up with her boyfriend a few months ago and decided for whatever reason to start doing it. I don't know why. She's never had a problem meeting guys. I mean, have you seen her? Guys fawn over her left and right."

"Had she met many people? On the site, I mean."

"No," Liz said. She took another sip of water then said, "I mean, she says she's talked to several guys on the site but yesterday was the first time she actually went to meet someone in person."

"And you said he didn't show up?"

"That's what she said."

"Are you certain his name wasn't Marlon Williams?" Fletcher said.

"I'm certain. It was Sam something."

Fletcher couldn't think of any more questions to ask at the moment, so he picked up his recorder and stood up. He turned the recorder off and put it back into his jacket pocket, then he retrieved a business card and handed it to Liz. "Here's my card. If you can think of anything else that might be of interest, please don't hesitate to call me. I hope you can believe me when I say that I'm as interested in finding out what happened to Renee as you are." She took the card from him. "Does Renee have a computer?"

Liz nodded. "She has a laptop in her room."

"Okay. Well, there's a good chance I'll be back to pick it up, all right? We may need to search the apartment as well."

Liz nodded again.

"Thanks for your help today, Ms. Warner." He moved toward the door. Before opening it, he turned back and said, "Again, please don't hesitate to call me if you think of anything else that might be helpful to Renee."

Back in his car, Fletcher didn't start the engine right away. He closed his eyes and thought about Kate. He still couldn't believe she wanted a divorce—to just throw it all away. And she went out with her sister and a couple of guys? He wanted to text her about it, but didn't want to sound accusatory. Besides, how would he even know she was out with someone? She'd most likely think he was spying on her. He couldn't help but be curious, though. Maybe he could text her sister. But Denise would surely tell Kate, so that wasn't an option. In the end, he pulled his phone out of his coat pocket and sent Kate a text: *I missed you last night.*

He waited to see if she would reply, but after several minutes of radio silence, he started the car and left.

CHAPTER 11

Fletcher called Eric as he drove back to the station. "You get the warrants?"

"What kind of a sidekick would I be if I hadn't?" Eric said.

"Sidekick?"

"Yeah, you know. Every Sherlock has a Watson."

"So, like I'm Batman and you're Robin?" Fletcher said.

"No, you idiot," Eric said.

"Why not?"

"Because they're superheroes," Eric said, "and we solve crimes."

"All right, name one other crime-solving duo, then."

"Uh. I'll get back to you on that." Eric ended the call.

Fletcher checked his phone before he got out of his car. He had the ringer volume all the way up so he already knew Kate hadn't texted him back, but he checked anyway. Nothing. *What? She won't even talk to me now?* The wall Kate had erected when she'd told him she wanted a divorce was solid. He shook his head and got out of the car.

Eric greeted him immediately when he stepped into the detectives' room. "How 'bout Andy and Barney?"

"So long as you're okay with being Barney," Fletcher said.

"Crap. Didn't think of that."

Fletcher saw the warrants on his desk and scooped them up. He also grabbed a photo of Ms. Denovan and another one of Williams, then turned to leave.

"That's it?" Eric said.

Fletcher stopped. "What?"

"Not even going to tell me about your conversation with Renee's roomie? Is she hot?"

"You're disgusting, you know that?"

"What? It's not like she's under investigation or anything."

Fletcher didn't even know how to respond to that. "I recorded it so you can listen to your heart's content."

Fletcher got back in his car and texted Kate before starting the engine: *Come on, Kate. Please don't ignore me.* He waited a moment then turned the key. The Crown Vic roared to life. He put the car into reverse and heard his phone chime. Keeping his foot on the brake, he picked his phone up from the center console. He had a new text message from Kate.

Kate: *I'm not ignoring you.*

Fletcher: *Then why haven't you been texting me back?*

Kate: *Because I don't have anything to say.*

He shook his head and set his phone back down. He rubbed his middle finger and thumb together, thinking, then picked the phone back up: *Who were you out with last night?*

He regretted it the moment he hit the send button. He got no response initially, but then she texted back.

Kate: *You're unbelievable, you know that?*

He snorted, then shot back: *I'm unbelievable?* His anger rose within him when Kate didn't text back right away. Impulsively, he sent another: *Well?*

Kate: *Not that it's any of your business, but I was out with Denise.*

She wasn't lying, but she wasn't being completely forthcoming either. *Should I press the issue?* No. At least not right now. He needed to concentrate on work and he knew he couldn't deal with whatever path that conversation might go down right now.

Fletcher put his phone down and took his foot off the brake. After driving down the alley behind the police station, he turned left, then at the second light, turned right onto Montezuma. He passed the courthouse, then looked longingly over at Ponderosa's as he crossed Gurley. He pulled into the strip mall at the corner of Montezuma and Sheldon and parked in front of Connie's Coffee. He grabbed his phone and the envelope with the warrants and pictures and got out of the car.

The coffee shop was decorated in various shades of pink. On the rare occasions he solicited this particular boutique coffee shop, he always thought of bubblegum. The atmosphere was, for the lack of a better word, bubbly.

A bell announced his arrival. He got in line behind the two patrons waiting to order and looked up at the menu. So many choices. He knew what he wanted but was pleased to see that there were security cameras in the corners. "Welcome to Connie's," a chipper voice greeted him when it was his turn. "What'll it be?"

"A small drip, please," he said. Only on the rarest of occasions did he treat himself to the frou-frou drinks.

"Sure thing." The cashier wore a pink apron with fancy double C insignia on it. She tapped the touchscreen of the register and added, "Can I interest you in a scone? Or perhaps a muffin?"

"No, thanks." He placed the folder under his arm as he took his wallet out and handed the cashier his debit card. He waited while she processed his order and filled a light-pink coffee cup. She slid a dark-pink sleeve on it and set the cup on the counter. He picked it up and said, "May I please speak with the manager?"

"Is something wrong?" the cashier said, looking up at him.

Fletcher shook his head. How could she think there was anything wrong? He hadn't even taken a sip yet. "Just need a quick word."

"Sure. Just a moment." She disappeared through a door

behind the counter.

Fletcher picked up his coffee and walked over to the condiments stand. He removed the lid and added a little cream. The cashier returned with another woman and pointed toward him.

The woman made her way over to him and said, "Can I help you?"

"Are you the manager?"

"Owner, actually. I'm Connie." She extended a hand to him.

Fletcher shook it, then unclipped his badge from his belt and held it up. "I'm Detective Wise, with the PPD. Is there somewhere we can speak in private?"

Connie looked startled, but said, "Yeah, sure. Come around here." She gestured to the end of the counter. "We can talk in my office."

Fletcher stepped around the counter and followed Connie into her office. It was quaint, not decorated in the same glam that brightened the shop. There was a desk, filing cabinet, and desktop computer. The only decoration was a picture of the inside of the store, showing the tables largely full and a line reaching all the way to the door.

"Our grand opening," Connie said.

"Looks like a big success."

"It was." Connie shut the door and said, "What can I help you with?"

Fletcher slipped the envelope from under his arm and pulled the pictures out. He handed the picture of Ms. Denovan to Connie and said, "Do you recognize this woman?"

"Renee?" Connie said, nodding. "Sure."

"You know her?"

"Yeah. She used to work here."

"Really?"

"She quit a year or so ago. Good worker. Didn't have the problems with her that I usually have when I hire college kids."

"What sort of problems?"

"Missing shifts, mostly."

"Hmm." That did *not* remind him of when he was in college, *at all.* He handed Connie the picture of Marlon Williams and said, "And what about him? Do you recognize him?"

Connie shook her head. She handed both photos back to Fletcher and said, "What's this about, Detective?"

"Renee has gotten herself in a bit of trouble and I need your help corroborating her story."

"Sure, of course. Trouble, though? Doesn't sound like her." She went behind her desk and sat down. "How can I help?"

Fletcher put the photos back in the envelope and pulled the warrant out. He handed it across the desk to Connie. "I went ahead and prepared a warrant."

Connie took it and looked it over.

"Renee indicated she came here yesterday for a date and I need to know if she was telling the truth. Do you have a receipt, maybe, that shows she was here?"

"Let me check." After about five minutes of sifting through credit card receipts, she said, "If she was here, she didn't use a card."

"All right," Fletcher said. "What kind of memory does your security camera have?"

"I don't know its exact capacity, but it's state of the art."

"So, it'd have yesterday's footage?"

"Oh, yeah. I usually keep a month's worth. I can bring it up on the computer if you like."

"That'd be great." While she worked, Fletcher sipped his coffee.

Connie turned the monitor so Fletcher could see it. "What time are we looking for?"

Remembering Renee said her date was at three, he said, "Let's start at two fifty."

Connie dragged the cursor until the time stamp in the lower left corner said 2:49:59 pm, then clicked play. The video started. At 2:51:23 pm, Renee entered. She was wearing the same yellow dress she'd been wearing last night. She ordered a coffee, paid with cash, put what looked like a couple of dollars in the tip jar, then sat at a table. She started out looking pretty composed for someone on a first date. It made Fletcher think of when he'd first met Kate.

He'd been twenty-five, and she was twenty-two. His friend Trevor knew her sister Denise and they thought—for whatever reason—it would be fun to play matchmaker. He was initially interested when Trevor first told him about Kate—he hadn't had a date in a while—but had balked when Trevor confessed that she was fresh on the market after ending her engagement. Trevor joked that it was just a date; it wasn't like he was going to marry her. He finally agreed.

To Fletcher's relief, they kept the date casual and met for drinks at Ponderosa's, Fletcher's home away from home. Even though it was supposed to be a casual meeting over drinks, Fletcher remembered being more nervous than he'd been in a long time—nowhere near as composed as Renee seemed to be in the video he was watching now.

She sat rather still in her chair, watching customers come in and go out, sipping on her coffee. She did fidget with the lid a bit, but it was nothing compared to his bumbling self the night he'd met Kate.

He had a habit of talking with his hands, sometimes with great animation. And he remembered how excited he'd been when he met Kate. She looked absolutely stunning in the white tube top and black mini skirt she was wearing. So, naturally, in his excitement, he accidently spilled his beer all over her. Obviously, and with much embarrassment, the date came to a rather abrupt end. Why Kate had agreed to go out with him again he'd never fully understood, even to this day.

At 3:10:05 pm Renee took her phone out of her purse. She fiddled with it on and off until 3:45:58 pm, at which point she put her phone in her purse. She stood up, grabbed her purse off the back of the chair, and took a couple of stumbling steps.

Fletcher watched as Renee rested a hand on the table, bent her knee, and removed her shoe. She took the other one off too, then walked out the door with her heels in hand, leaving her empty coffee cup on the table. *That explains why she wasn't wearing shoes.*

The video confirmed that portion of her testimony. As both she and her roommate had claimed, it appeared that she had in fact gone to Connie's. The 'date' part was yet to be determined, however, as she'd entered the coffee shop alone and left alone less than an hour later. She'd claimed she was there to meet someone, but the video itself didn't corroborate it. That didn't mean she was lying about it, but it would have to be verified by another means.

However, the congruity between her testimony and the video ended with the fact that she had indeed been there. Where her testimony and the video did *not* agree was how she left Connie's. She hadn't teleported from Connie's as she'd claimed. The video told a realistic story, a sane and logical story, grounded in reality. She'd simply gotten up and left.

Why would you make up such a story?

What sort of game are you playing?

"Can I get a copy of this?" Fletcher said.

"Yeah, sure," Connie said. "Give me just a moment."

Fletcher sat back in his chair while Connie dug a thumb drive out of her desk. He sipped his coffee while she transferred the file.

No one in their right mind would believe Renee's story—assuming she was crazy enough to stick with it. The evidence was clear. He began to suspect that the rest of the evidence, as it came in, would tell a similar story. He highly doubted the case would ever make it to trial. By now she had likely lawyered up, and he couldn't think of a single local defense lawyer who wouldn't sit her down after they learned her motive for killing Marlon—and they would—and explain to her exactly what she was up against. Her lawyer would convince her to take whatever plea might come her way.

Connie pulled the thumb drive out of the computer and held it over the desk. "Here you go."

Fletcher leaned forward and took it. He shoved it into a coat pocket and stood. "Thanks for your help."

"Sure," Connie said.

"I may be in touch again if I have any more questions."

Connie nodded. "I'll do whatever I can to help Renee. She's a sweet girl. I hate to see her in trouble."

Fletcher nodded, then excused himself. He ordered a refill on his way out of the coffee shop.

He started his car and called Eric before pulling out of the parking lot.

"What's up, Wizard?" Eric said.

"Want me to grab you something to eat before I head back to the office?"

"What were you thinking?"

"Dunno. Not really hungry, just thought I'd ask." His stomach had felt wonky ever since Kate had dropped the divorce bomb on him. The beer and coffee hadn't helped either.

"Well, I could stand to get out of the office for a bit. How 'bout we go to the Burger Mania over by Supermart?"

"Really? It's halfway to Prescott Valley."

"Got anything better to do?"

"Prepare for Renee's hearing."

"That can wait until after lunch. Come pick me up."

"Naturally," Fletcher acquiesced. "I don't know why you even have your own cruiser."

"Just quit being a dick for one second and come pick me up."

Fletcher sighed. "Be there in ten."

CHAPTER 12

Fletcher pulled his all-white cruiser to a stop in front of the police station. He was tempted to keep driving when he saw Eric standing there with his thumb out like an idiot. Eric opened the door and slid into the passenger seat. He pulled the door closed and said, "Bonnie and Clyde, off to get burgers and fries!"

Fletcher looked over his shoulder to ensure the road behind him was clear, and made a U-turn. "You do realize Bonnie and Clyde were gangsters, right?"

"Of course."

"Do you?"

"Yeah...?"

"Then in what capacity are we Bonnie and Clyde? Was it the bank robberies? Or the cop-killing?"

"Fine. It was a bad example."

Fletcher stopped at the light, then turned right onto Gurley. "I was closer with Batman and Robin, though it's more like Batman and the Joker."

"Damn, Mr. Can't-ever-have-a-little-fun..."

"I just don't see the point in pretending to be some sort of crime-fighting duo. And I *do* know how to have fun."

"Prove it," Eric said. "Come out to CJ's with me tonight."

"How would that be fun for me? I'm married." He would rather spend his time trying to convince Kate to reconsider than watching Eric hit on girls who were way too young for him.

"So. What's that saying?"

Fletcher looked over at Eric, who was looking at him expectantly. "What saying?"

"The one about looking at the menu but not eating... or shopping but not buying..."

"You mean 'look but don't touch'?"

"Yeah! That's it. If you come out with me you can do that."

"That might sound like fun to you, but not me."

The conversation lagged and Fletcher's thoughts went to Kate. Had things really gotten *that* bad?

"So..." Eric said after an awkward silence filled by nothing but the sound of the car driving down the road and the annoying clicking of Eric's phone as he fired off text after text. Fletcher had never understood why anyone left the phone's keyboard sound on. It bugged the hell out of him. "What'd you learn?"

"About what?"

"Hello? About what you've spent the morning running around doing. Renee?"

"Oh. She's lying."

"Duh."

"But part of her story's true."

"Yeah? Which part? Being a dude?"

"I've yet to verify the veracity of that claim."

"You being serious?"

"Well, I haven't gotten that far in the investigation yet."

"But you *do* think she's lying, right?"

"Duh," he said, echoing Eric. "But at least part of her story's true. She was at Connie's. Whether she was there to meet someone, I don't know yet. I mean, she says she was there for a date, and her roommate said the same thing, but no one showed up."

"Didn't she say that though? That she got stood up?"

This was probably the longest he'd seen Eric go without texting. He was, for once, actually engrossed in the conversation. "Yeah. But she also said that she somehow teleported to a dark room and from there to the Williams' house, but the surveillance clearly shows her getting up and walking out of Connie's of her own volition."

"Well, it's a slam-dunk if you ask me," Eric said. "No judge is going to buy the whole teleportation thing."

Fletcher snorted in agreement. "I've heard some crazy stories, but that has to be the most outlandish by far."

"No, remember that time… no, you're right. She was a man!" Eric said with a laugh. "The complaint will be a breeze. We should be able to bang it out and maybe clock out a little early and hit the end of happy hour at Ponderosa's. Oh, shit, it's Tuesday—are you gonna ride your bike?"

"Not today," Fletcher said. He usually brought his bike to work with him on Tuesdays and Thursdays, and left work early to ride Highway 89 where it wound its way down the backside of the Bradshaw Mountains. "With the shit between me and Kate, I honestly didn't even think about it. Hitting happy hour at Ponderosa's sounds like a plan to me."

"Sweet!" And then Eric was gone, back into his phone, the annoying *click click click* once again filling the silence.

When the road split, Fletcher followed it to the right, toward Prescott Valley. The mall and Supermart were situated halfway between the neighboring towns. Even though he didn't have much of an appetite, he started salivating when he pulled into the parking lot of the Burger Mania and caught a whiff of the aroma emanating from the restaurant. As much as Fletcher enjoyed hamburgers, what he really loved was fries. Burgers were burgers, in his opinion—it was really hard to mess one up—but fries… There was a whole spectrum of fries. Just as he thought salsa defined a Mexican restaurant, it was the fries that defined a burger joint. And Burger Mania had awesome fries.

The line was long but moved quickly. When the attendant

set the basket of fries and burger in front of Fletcher, he started on the fries first. Only when they were gone did he pick up his burger.

"You always do that," Eric said, holding his burger close to his mouth.

"Do what?"

"Eat all your fries first."

"That's because they're best when they're hot."

"Whatever floats your boat," Eric said through a mouthful of burger.

When he was done eating, Fletcher leaned back in his seat, took a sip of his lemonade, and said, "You ever use a dating site?"

"You already thinking of putting yourself back on the market?" Eric said through the fries he was chewing.

"I was just thinking of Renee's case. She claims she doesn't know Marlon, but do you think it's possible they knew each other through the site?"

"Why would he be on a dating site? He's married."

Thinking of his own marital problems with Kate, Fletcher said, "Maybe things weren't so great in paradise."

"So, a match gone bad?"

"It happens. Certainly gives us a motive."

"You think she's lying about knowing him?"

"She lied about what happened to her at the coffee shop," Fletcher said, "so why should we believe that she doesn't know Marlon? Besides, why would she kill someone she doesn't know?"

"Maybe she's crazy. I mean, she claims she teleported into a man's body."

Fletcher gladly let Eric finish eating in silence, then they returned to the station. Fletcher spent the afternoon on the phone with Scott Stephens, the county prosecutor assigned to the case, and pieced together the complaint. With the evidence they already had, even this early in the investigation, it wasn't hard to conclude that they needed to keep Renee in jail throughout the judicial process. In order to do that, they had to convince the judge to set a sufficiently high bail. They weren't worried, as they'd both had great luck with Judge Sinclair agreeing with their suggestions. Eric worked on getting a search warrant so they could access Renee's profile on Your Ideal Mate.

"So?" Fletcher said when Eric got off the phone with the dating site.

Eric sat back in his chair and said, "Finished."

"Now all we can do is sit back and wait. Places like that can be notoriously slow about responding to warrants."

"So what you're saying is that we should bust outta here early?"

Fletcher looked at the time on his phone: 4:02 pm. He couldn't think of any other pressing work he had on any of his other cases, so he said, "Yeah. Let's get out of Dodge."

"Ooh, ooh!" Eric said. "How 'bout Wyatt Earp and Doc Holliday?"

Fletcher reached up and scratched his chin. Nodding, he said, "Now *that* I think I can get behind."

"Who's Earp and who's Holliday?"

Fletcher turned his monitor off, slid his phone into his pocket, and said, "You know I hate all these stupid nicknames. But..."

"*But?*"

"If we're gonna be Wyatt and Doc, I'm definitely going with Doc."

"Exactly what I was thinking," Eric agreed. As they passed the dispatchers on their way out, Eric called, "Hey Tina! What time you get off?"

Tina looked up over the top of her cubicle and said, "Five."

"Wanna join us at Ponderosa's?"

"Yeah. That sounds great, actually."

"Sweet! See you there," Eric said. When they entered the hallway on the far side of the room, Eric swatted Fletcher on the arm and said, "There ya go, Doc."

"What'd you go and do that for?" The last thing Fletcher needed right now was to hang out with Tina.

"You weren't gonna do it."

"No, I wasn't." He might have wanted to, but he certainly wouldn't have done it.

"Yeah, so I did it for you."

"Why would you invite her to join us for me?" Fletcher said. "I'm married."

"You're getting divorced, though, right?"

Fletcher looked around. "Would you keep it down? I don't need the whole department knowing."

"Geez. Sorry, man. Didn't know you were so sensitive about it."

He wasn't sensitive, per se, he just didn't want his dirty laundry aired publicly. It was going to get out—there was no getting around that—but he should at least have the right to make that call himself. Besides, he hated the idea of becoming a statistic. It went against his preference of staying below the radar.

They made it the rest of the way out of the station in silence. "Meet you there?" Eric said when the heavy exterior rear door slammed shut.

"Yeah." Fletcher sat heavily in the worn seat of his S-10. He closed his eyes and took a slow, deep breath, then dug his phone out of his pocket and looked at the last few texts he'd exchanged with Kate. He contemplated what, if anything, he wanted to say. He didn't like the idea of just giving up.

The sound of a horn made him look up. Eric had pulled up next to him and was waving for him to follow.

Fletcher put his phone back in his pocket and started the truck. When he turned onto Gurley, he looked for an open parking spot in front of the shops running the length of the block—rock-star parking, as he liked to think of it. He always felt that the beer gods were shining their countenance upon him whenever he found one right in front of the pub. There wasn't one today, though, so he turned the corner at the end of the block and pulled into the parking lot behind the building. On a really bad day, beer-god-wise, this lot would be full as well, but he breathed a sigh a relief when he found an open spot.

He entered the old building via its back door. Ponderosa's was one of several tenants located in the old three-story building. Fletcher hated shopping, so he'd never been into any of the other shops. He passed the patio area of Ponderosa's—a section of the pub located in the building's large atrium—and walked down the creaky wood floor to the entrance. He smiled at the hostess who greeted him, and pointed past her toward the bar. He found Eric sitting at a table in the corner by the archway leading out to the patio. There was already a beer waiting for him.

"That was fast," Fletcher said, sitting across from Eric. He picked up the beer and took a swig.

"The Doc should never have to wait for beer."

"I appreciate it," Fletcher said. The malty flavor hit the spot, and the stress he'd been feeling all day instantly began to melt. "But the more I think about it, there's no way you can pull off Wyatt Earp."

"I was just about to apologize for inviting Tina, but since it appears that Dick showed up instead of Doc, never mind."

Fletcher waved him off. "It doesn't matter." It did, though. He really didn't want to see Tina right now.

"I guess, never having been married, I didn't put much thought to how you might be feeling."

"And here I was beginning to wonder if you ever thought at all."

"I'm always thinking."

"About something other than who you're going to bang next?"

Eric stopped typing mid-text and set his phone down. "Have I ever told you that you're an ass?"

It was true that Eric had never been married. In fact, Fletcher had never known him to be in a steady relationship at all. He made his rounds, for sure, and without much care for his reputation. There were women who considered him gross and would never sleep with him, but Fletcher had never known Eric to go home alone if he didn't want to.

Eric made it through exactly one sip of beer before he impulsively picked his phone back up.

Fletcher sipped his own beer. He knew exactly what Eric was doing by asking Tina to join them—and it wasn't that Eric was hoping to get lucky. He'd overheard Eric ask Tina out once, and she'd made it perfectly clear that she wasn't interested in him. So he knew she hadn't agreed to join them for a beer just because Eric was here. And even though he had no interest in thinking about Tina like that—hell, he didn't want to think about getting divorced either—he liked the idea that the only reason she'd agreed to come was that he would be there.

"I ordered wings, too," Eric said without looking up from his phone.

"Good call."

"I know you don't want to hear it, but if Kate's serious about wanting a divorce, you gotta move on."

"You do realize that she literally just told me yesterday? We haven't even filed paperwork yet."

"Shit," Eric said, setting his phone down again.

"What?"

"I forgot to tell you."

"Tell me what?"

"While you were out this morning, I had to pop on over to the courthouse..."

"Yeah?"

"And I ran into Kate."

"At the courthouse?"

"I was on the elevator and the door opened on the library level. I was as surprised to see her as she was to see me." He picked up his beer, took a drink, and said, "That elevator ride was the most awkward I've felt around a woman since... well... ever."

"The library, you say?"

"Look I know what you're thinking—"

"She was getting divorce papers." Fletcher sat back in his chair. "Fuck." He picked up his glass and drank it down.

"I'll get another round." Eric stood just as their waitress, Mary, approached with two plates of wings. He sat back down and asked, "Can we get another round?"

"Sure thing," Mary said, setting the plates on the table. "Hey, Fletch," she added before turning away.

"Sorry, man," Eric said. "I probably should have told you. But by the time I got back to the station I was thinking of something else and forgot."

"No worries," Fletcher said. It was probably better that he hadn't found out during the day. That would have ruined any chance he'd had of getting any work done. Mary returned with two more glasses of beer. "Thank you," he said, then picked one of the glasses up and took a healthy drink.

"Eat your wings or that'll go straight to your head," Eric said.

Fletcher shook his head. "Whatever appetite I might have had's gone now."

What other reason could Kate possibly have for being at the courthouse library? It wasn't somewhere her job would require her to be. As far as he knew, she'd never even been inside the courthouse. *I can't believe she's actually moving forward with this.* He dug his phone out of his pocket and started typing out a text: *Why were you...*

"Put that away, man," Eric said.

Fletcher ignored him and kept typing: *at the courthouse today?* He pushed send, then picked up his glass and took a drink while he waited for a reply. It came a few minutes later.

Kate: *I wanted to get the ball rolling.*

He shook his head and took another drink. "I can't fucking

believe it," he said after swallowing. He typed his response: *So you seriously want to go through with this?*

Kate: *We've been over this, Fletch.*

Fletcher set his phone down, not knowing what else to say. A minute later he received another text from her.

Kate: *I came home early today if you want to go over it.*

He picked his phone back up. *You've already got the paperwork filled out? That was fast...*

Kate: *Denise helped me.*

Kate: *It's pretty straightforward, actually.*

Fletcher: *She would help...*

Kate: *So are you going to be home soon?*

Fletcher stared at his phone. He decided against answering right away and drank more beer.

Kate: *Fletch?*

Kate: *I would really appreciate if you didn't make this harder than it needs to be.*

"This is unbelievable," Fletcher said. Eric looked up from his own texts, his phone in one hand and a wing in the other. Fletcher took a drink before replying: *I don't know what time I'll be home.*

Kate: *Well, I'm spending the night with Denise again, so if you aren't here when I leave, I'll just leave the papers on the table.*

"What?" Eric said. He held his chicken wing with his thumb and finger.

Fletcher set his phone down and picked up a wing. "Apparently she's already got the paperwork filled out."

"That was fast."

Fletcher raised his eyebrows as he bit into his chicken. He wasn't particularly hungry, but he ate anyway; it gave him something to do during breaks from drinking beer. He was licking his fingers when, through the archway leading out to the patio, he saw a familiar head of brunette hair walk by. He looked down at his phone. It wasn't quite five.

"Hey guys," Tina said when she walked up to them a minute

later. Their table wasn't big and was pushed up against the wall, so it had only three chairs. She pulled the third chair out and took a seat.

"You're early," Eric said.

"It was slow, so I managed to escape."

"Couldn't wait to see me, eh?"

"It was Fletcher, actually," Tina said. She looked Fletcher in the eye and said, "Sorry."

"About what?" Fletcher said.

Tina looked over at Eric, then back at Fletcher.

"You *told* her?" Fletcher said, with a glare that suggested 'I'd really like to punch you in the nose right about now.'

"Sorry?" Eric said with an innocent smile.

"You're a dick, you know that?"

Mary appeared and greeted Tina. "Can I get you something to drink?"

"I'll have the Blonde," Tina said.

"I'll take another one as well," Fletcher said.

"And what about you?" Mary said, looking at Eric.

"You're damn right."

"Be right back," Mary said, turning on her heel.

"Anyway, I hope you're not mad," Tina said.

"Not at you." Fletcher glared at Eric again.

"Well, for what it's worth, I really am sorry. And not just for being here."

"Thanks." Fletcher took another drink of his beer. He didn't like it that Eric had invited Tina, but he'd be lying if he said her presence hadn't improved his mood. He looked at her over the top of his glass. There was no doubt that she was hot; he'd thought so for as long as she'd worked at PPD. He tried not to think about her like that, but it was hard.

Mary brought the next round of drinks on a tray and, after depositing them on the table, asked, "You guys interested in anything else to eat, or just drinks?"

"I don't know about them," Tina said, "but I'm hungry."

"I'm starving," Eric said.

"I'll be right back with some menus," Mary said.

Fletcher didn't have an appetite, but since Eric and Tina were both ordering food, he decided to order something as well. Though he still felt sick to his stomach, his mood improved a little. Tina had two beers, then switched to water, but he and Eric kept drinking. He was going to regret it, he knew, but he'd regret it if he didn't drink, too. Lose-lose.

Occasionally he stole glances at Tina. He couldn't help it. He didn't know what it was about her, but ever since she'd joined the force—which had been back when things were still good between him and Kate—there had been something about her that had captivated him. So he'd avoided her as much as possible. He loved his wife and hadn't wanted to do anything to ruin his marriage.

But was the same true of Kate?

Fletcher ran his finger across the top of his half-empty glass and looked at Eric, who had put his phone away for once and was bantering with Tina. He and Tina had left Fletcher alone with his moroseness when they'd realized he wasn't very talkative.

He finally let his mind circle back around to what Eric had said this morning: Last night he'd run into Kate with her sister, out with some guys. Was that a date? Or was it just a casual meet-up for drinks such as he was doing now? But this was two guys to one woman, and it was against his wishes—Eric had invited Tina even though he knew Fletcher wouldn't want her here.

He looked over at Tina again and let his mind slip. She certainly was beautiful. Were he not married, he could see himself with her. Did she like him? Or was she only here out of pity for him, since Eric had told her about his forthcoming divorce? What would he say if she invited him to go home with her? *Would it be cheating? Kate already said she wanted a divorce...* No. He couldn't think about that and he mentally berated himself for even letting his mind go there. He didn't want to get divorced.

And he couldn't understand how Kate could so easily throw their relationship away. If she would only give him the chance, he would fight.

"I think it's time to call it a night," Eric said.

"Huh?" Fletcher said. He looked at the time on his phone. They'd been there for three hours? "It's only seven thirty."

"And we have to go to work in the morning. Besides, you haven't said a thing for the last hour."

Fletcher pressed his thumb into his forehead, between his eyes. "I probably shouldn't drive." He looked up at Eric and said, "Mind if I crash at your place?" It was within walking distance of the pub. There was a time where he would've killed to live within stumbling distance of Ponderosa's. Maybe if Kate followed through with the divorce, he'd find something close to downtown instead of living way out in Prescott Valley.

"Well, seeing as how Tina here has rebuffed my every advance, I figured I'd wander down to CJ's. You're welcome to join me, though."

Fletcher shook his head. "Nah. I'm done."

"You know where the key is."

He didn't want to stay the night at Eric's. He knew what going down to CJ's meant: Eric was on the prowl.

"I can take you home," Tina said. "Or you're welcome to crash at my place, too, if you want."

The thought of walking into an empty house to find divorce papers didn't appeal to him. "If you don't mind, I think I'd rather not be home right now."

What are you doing, Fletcher?

Eric waggled his eyebrows at him.

This is the exact opposite of what you should be doing.

"No, I don't mind at all," Tina said. "I wouldn't have offered if I didn't mean it."

"Thanks," Fletcher said. He swirled the last bit of his beer in the glass then polished it off. Was she inviting him to spend the night, or to "spend the night"? *Stop it, Fletcher. You can't think like that right now.*

It was only seven thirty. Every seat and barstool in the pub was occupied—most of them by a younger, hipper crowd. It took a few minutes for Mary to make it back to their table with their respective bills. After they'd paid their tabs, they stood up to leave.

Fletcher said, "Welp, I wish I could say this was fun, but I can't."

"Hey!" Eric said.

"Yeah, I thought it was nice," Tina said.

"He's just being an asshole," Eric said. "Should probably take back your offer and leave his drunk ass to find his own way home."

"I'm not drunk," Fletcher protested, "just probably shouldn't drive."

Another loitering group immediately took their table as the three of them moved away.

They walked toward the front of the pub; in the atrium outside the entrance, Eric said, "See you two in the morning." Fletcher waved him off as he exited the building through the front door, and he followed Tina toward the back exit. He couldn't help but notice how her blue jeans accentuated her backside. A pang of guilt washed over him, so he turned his head and looked through the windows of the other shops.

Outside, Fletcher followed her through the parking lot to her car. "This is really nice," he said as he slid into the leather seat. He still drove his old beat-up S-10—a deliberate choice. It was the first vehicle he'd bought and paid for himself. Kate's car was nice and newer than his, but it wasn't sparkling-leather-seat nice.

"Oh, you know, we dispatchers really rake it in," Tina said.

Tina didn't live far away, Fletcher knew; the ride wouldn't last long. It was dark out, so he stole a few glances over at her. Focused on the road, she didn't notice. A long-forgotten feeling washed over him—a feeling of timidity. He was bad at reading women, but he knew she had agreed to go to Ponderosa's because of him. Even though he knew it would be wrong, knew he wanted to work things out with Kate, in that moment he wanted her. He wanted to cast aside all hesitation and reach over and place his hand on hers where it rested on the gear shift. Or maybe he would be bold—slide his hand under her arm and rest it on her thigh.

Memories of this exact feeling flooded his drunken mind: the first time he took a girl on a date in high school, and how he'd wanted so badly to reach across the gap between the seats in his parent's minivan and hold her hand; the first time he'd taken Kate on a date—just the two of them—in his beat-up truck and wanted to do the same, the feeling accompanied by fear because it was their first real date. He hadn't even known if she liked him. Sure, she'd agreed to go out with him after their awkward first meeting, but that didn't mean she was romantically interested in him. Fletcher had always been incredibly dense when it came to women, so it took him forever to make his first move. Even now, he didn't know if Tina was actually interested in him or just along for the pity party. But he knew he couldn't do anything right now anyway. As much as he might want to, deep down he felt it would be cheating—whether Kate felt the same or not.

He shifted uncomfortably in his seat, knowing he shouldn't be in her car, and stared out the passenger window for the rest of the drive. Tina didn't offer up any conversation, and he was perfectly content with the silence. Strangely, it wasn't awkward. Was that wrong?

Tina lived in the Willow Condos, a few miles north of downtown. The condominium wasn't too far from one of the local colleges and was an uncomfortable blend of retired people and students. He'd responded to numerous noise complaints there back when he'd patrolled the streets.

Fletcher followed Tina inside.

"The couch pulls out if you want," she said.

"Thanks, but I'm good," he said. "Can I use the bathroom?"

"Yeah." Tina pointed at a doorway and said, "Through the bedroom."

"Thanks." Fletcher went where she had indicated, feeling a little weird about being in another woman's bedroom. He relieved himself, then returned to the living room to find a pillow and blanket on the couch. Tina was in the kitchen filling a glass of water at the sink.

"Here," she said. She held out a glass of water in one hand and a couple of ibuprofen in the other.

Fletcher took them both and said, "Thanks." He popped the ibuprofen into his mouth then guzzled the water. "You didn't have to do this, you know."

"I know. You mind if I watch a little TV?"

"No, of course not."

Tina sat in the recliner next to the couch and turned the television on. Fletcher lay down on the couch, and was asleep before Tina settled on a channel.

CHAPTER 13

October 21st

Fletcher woke with a throbbing headache. He reached around on the ground in the dark for his phone and found it under the couch he was laying on. He turned it on, and the time displayed 4:42. It took him a moment to remember where he was, but then the car ride with Tina replayed itself. He scrunched his eyes closed and rubbed his temples with the heels of his hands.

He searched the browser on his phone for a taxi and selected the first one that popped up. When a voice answered on the other end he said quietly, "Can I get a pick-up at Willow Condos?"

"Sure thing. We'll have someone there in ten minutes."

"Thanks."

Fletcher put his phone into his pocket, then felt around for the glass Tina had given him before he fell asleep. Not finding it, he stood up and walked as quietly as he could to the kitchen. He found the glass on the counter and filled it with water from the faucet. He drank it down, refilled it, and started on the second glass. From where he stood at the sink, he could see the door to Tina's bedroom. He considered going and joining her—

something told him she would more than welcome him—but dismissed the thought almost as quickly as it occurred. After finishing the second glass, he set it down and made his way to the front door.

Fletcher locked the door before pulling it shut behind him, and stepped out into the crisp autumn air. He ran his hands up and down his arms vigorously, working some warmth into them, and walked toward the condos' entrance. He wondered when one of those new rideshare services would finally start serving the area. A taxi pulled in just as he walked past the front office. He stuck his hand up and the taxi pulled to a stop.

"Where to?" the driver said when Fletcher sat down in the back.

"Ponderosa's."

The driver didn't offer up any conversation, so Fletcher sat in silence as the taxi made its way downtown. He figured the driver thought he was returning from some sort of a tryst, but that didn't bother him. He wished he *was* returning from a tryst. He certainly wanted it—just couldn't bring himself to do it.

Thirty minutes later Fletcher found himself leaning on the island in his kitchen with both hands, staring down at a stack of legal papers with a Post-it affixed to it. The top one said, "DECREE OF DISSOLUTION OF MARRIAGE WITHOUT MINOR CHILDREN." Katherine Wise was listed as the petitioner and he was listed as the respondent. The boxes for self-representation were checked, as well as the box indicating the dissolution was one of consent.

"Consent? Really?" he said. "Cause I don't remember consenting."

Fletcher read the note Kate left on the Post-it, then flipped through the papers. She wants it to be simple and without a lot of fighting. Every page was filled out. When he turned to the page itemizing their possessions, he was surprised to find that Kate had put the house in his column. *Really?*

He shook his head and went to the bedroom. Without

bothering to undress, he flipped the covers back and climbed in. Within moments he was asleep.

* * *

Fletcher knew he was late for work the moment he woke. He didn't care, though, because he had no intention of going in. He grabbed his phone from the nightstand and glanced at the time as he slid his finger across the screen to open it—9:10. He texted Eric, telling him he wasn't coming in today.

Eric: *You make it home OK?*

Fletcher: *Yeah. Crashed at Tina's but came home early this morn.*

Eric: *You dog!*

Fletcher: *It wasn't like that. I slept on her couch.*

Fletcher: *Anyway, like I said, I'm taking a personal day.*

Eric: *No worries. I'll let Sarge know.*

Fletcher plugged his phone in to charge then took a shower. When he finished, he dressed in cycling clothes. He'd always hated exercising, but cycling was different. He needed to think, and there was nothing better than riding his bike to facilitate that.

Even though he'd told Eric he was taking a personal day, he realized he didn't really want to. What would he do? Sit around and mope all day? So he grabbed a pair of work clothes, figuring he could go for a ride then still put in a few hours at the station. He really wanted to find Renee's motive before they went to the grand jury.

Fletcher went to the kitchen, laying his work clothes on the couch, and made himself a couple of bottles of water with energy powder mixed in, as well as a protein shake. He glanced at the papers on the island a few times, but otherwise ignored them. He went out to the garage, set the water bottles and shake on the roof of his truck—which he'd parked in Kate's spot in the garage; no sense parking outside if she wasn't planning on coming home—then lifted his road bike off its wall-mounted rack. He took the front tire off and fitted the front fork to the mount in the bed of his truck. When he finished, he placed the two water bottles in the bottle racks on the bike, put his helmet and gloves on the passenger seat, then went back inside to get his work clothes.

Twenty minutes later Fletcher was riding down the alley between the employee parking lot and the station, his earbuds in and his cycling playlist on random. He turned right at the end of the alley, rode the block and a half to Montezuma Street, then turned left onto Montezuma and followed it as it wound its way south out of town. He was glad to be making up the ride he'd missed with his cycling buddies yesterday. Nothing else gave him the sense of calm he felt when he rode.

The chilly air blowing across his body gave him goosebumps. This time of year, he was tempted to wear warmer clothing, but after a couple of minutes' riding he no longer felt the chill. He'd made the mistake of over-dressing one too many times.

As he settled into his cycling rhythm, his mind turned to Kate. 'Dissolution of marriage'—the fancy, or legal, way of saying divorce. He couldn't believe their relationship was where it was. How could something that had started out so good end up so bad?

Things moved pretty quickly after their first date—at least for him. At the ripe old age of twenty-five, he had never been in a serious relationship. He'd known it was serious when, after only a couple of months, they started talking about a future together. He wasn't ready to get married—and at the time, she claimed she wasn't either—but he didn't mind talking about it. He knew she was the one he wanted to marry. He loved her, he knew that. By the time their relationship was six months old they had moved in together. They were happy.

Although there was a lot of talk about marriage, he wasn't ready nearly as soon as she was. He was still new to the force and wanted to get a few more years under his belt, and hopefully build up a little savings. He knew with marriage would come additional financial responsibilities—especially if children were in their future, which they were—so he wanted to be more prepared. Looking back on it, as the wind whistled past the music playing in his ears, that was probably the first of the cracks in their relationship that would eventually cause it to break.

For two and a half years Kate had expressed her desire to marry. After a year, he finally broke down and bought a ring. He didn't propose for another six months, but she knew he had it, so it seemed to satisfy her a little. Thinking about it now, it sounded silly. He chuckled at the thought that he "broke down" and bought a ring.

Fletcher's legs started to burn as the grade shifted to a steady climb. His thoughts naturally gravitated to focusing on maintaining a steady rhythm with his legs as well as his breathing. He reached down and grabbed a water bottle from its rack and took a drink. As the grade leveled out, his mind began to wander again.

He and Kate had hit a few rough patches after he'd bought the ring; they always started with an argument about why he wouldn't commit to her. Kate had friends who'd met someone and gotten married in less time than they'd been together. He remembered explaining that he wasn't them and that he *did* want to marry her. He didn't remember exactly how many arguments there had been—five or six—but he finally decided to propose. He still wasn't ready to get married, but he wanted her to know he loved her and was committed to her.

The engagement went off flawlessly, not that it was anything special or required a lot of pieces to fall together. Even though he loved cycling, Kate had never been into it, but one thing they did enjoy together was hiking. So he planned a routine hike up to the top of Granite Mountain—the mountain that stood guard on the west side of the valley. At the top, for those who persevered the switchback trail—it wasn't for the casual hiker— was the reward of a picturesque view of Prescott, Prescott Valley, the Bradshaw Mountains that cradled the southern end of Prescott, and, in the distant northeast, Mingus Mountain.

Even farther to the northeast, the San Francisco Peaks were visible in the crisp air. It had been early fall when he had taken her up there, and the tops of the distant peaks were already blanketed with snow.

The simple act of getting down on one knee with the valley spread out behind them served as a reset for their relationship. Their once-passionate lovemaking, which had tapered off when the fighting began, found a new life. But it didn't last.

Kate started planning their wedding almost immediately, and when he indicated she was moving too fast, the fighting began anew. Her sister's nosiness didn't help, either. It drove him crazy when she meddled in their affairs. He grew to loathe Denise before their wedding day even arrived. He was convinced that were it not for her, they wouldn't have had half the trouble they did.

Finally, in the summer of 2004, they got married. All their previous problems had evaporated when he saw her walking down the aisle. In that moment, he knew he was the luckiest man in the world. He couldn't understand why he'd waited so long. He loved her so much and wanted nothing but the best for her—for her to always be happy.

Fletcher crested the final rise before the road started its winding descent. He took another drink of water and thought about turning around and heading back to the station. He replaced the water bottle, but instead of turning around, he shifted his hands from the top of his handlebars to the drops. He positioned his pedals so they were parallel to the ground, one foot forward and one back, tucked his knees in against the frame, and let gravity do its job.

He accelerated until his velocity matched the speed limit of the winding road. No longer having to worry about cars passing him, he drifted away from the shoulder and used the entire lane, leaning left and right to follow the road's sharp curves. He reached up with one hand, found the mic on his headphones, and paused his music so he could listen to his bike humming beneath him. God, he loved that sound.

Fletcher had always thought their marriage was great. They were both happy and they didn't fight—at least not like they had before they were married. They had disagreements from time to time, but they were never over anything serious. They both wanted children, and after their first anniversary he finally felt he was in a position to support a family. The irony was that, where he had been in no rush to get married, Kate turned out not to be in a rush to have kids. As the next few anniversaries came and went, she never seemed to be getting any closer to being ready. He began wondering if she really wanted children, despite her earlier assurances that she did. He didn't want to pressure her, figuring she would be ready when she was ready.

It wasn't until after their eighth anniversary that things really started getting bad. Truth was, though, their relationship had been going slowly downhill for a few years. He hadn't recognized that it was heading in that direction until Kate had approached him with the desire to go to counseling. It was then that he realized their respective expectations of what marriage should look like were different.

Sitting in front of the counselor, Fletcher learned what Kate's expectation was: She wanted the feeling of newness. He argued that that wasn't realistic, that it wasn't practical to expect that the nature of their relationship would never change. Relationships go through phases, and as far as he was concerned, the newness phase was over. That didn't mean he loved her any less; it was just different. She claimed she didn't feel loved anymore. He had reassured her that he *did* love her, and went away from counseling vowing to try harder to express his love the way she needed him to. But it didn't come naturally to him. If it had, they never would have found themselves going to counseling—she wouldn't have felt unloved.

Over the next couple of years their relationship oscillated between good and bad. It was good immediately after she reminded him he was becoming complacent, and bad when he drifted back to being his natural self.

"I shouldn't have to buy you fucking flowers every damn week just so you'll feel loved," he shouted, interrupting the peaceful hum of his bike. Anniversaries, of course; at random, sure—but every goddamn week? Who actually does that? Flowers were superficial. They wilted and died, then you threw them away. Was their relationship really so shallow that it required constant meaningless gestures? They weren't meaningless to her, she said, but he just didn't get it. Maybe they weren't meant to be together. Better suited for other people, she'd said.

I'm never going to be who she wants me to be.

Fletcher's mind went blank. It was the first time he'd thought that, and he immediately realized the truth of it.

He didn't know what to think. He didn't know what to do. So he just rode.

He listened to his bike, to the wind. When he got to the bottom of the winding descent, he crossed the road and turned his bike around. Standing on the side of the road, he pulled a water bottle from its rack and took a healthy drink.

It's so easy when things are going well, he thought, and you can cruise effortlessly. But sometimes you find yourself in a valley and you have to dig in and climb back out. Maybe Kate was okay with giving up, and they faced a difficult climb, for sure—but *he* wasn't willing to give up.

Fletcher replaced his water bottle, turned his music back on, and started pedaling. From here on, there would be no wind in his face, no easy glide or smooth curves. There was only work—hard work. But in the end, he knew, he would be rewarded with great satisfaction.

The climb back to his life varied in difficulty. For large swaths of it he sat on the saddle, his hands gripping the horns on the outer ends of his handlebars. For portions of it, when the grade was such that he couldn't pedal while sitting, he stood and used the weight of his body to help. At times, he moved almost as slowly as he would if he got off and walked. But he kept pumping. He wouldn't give up.

At the top, he got his reward. The grade shifted from a steady climb to a gradual descent. The last few miles weren't as easy as the steep descent on the back side of the Bradshaws; he still had to pedal to help himself along. But it was a satisfying level of work—the speed at which he moved brought with it a level of satisfaction greater than the work required. He was willing to make the same level of effort to save his marriage—if Kate would only give him the chance.

Fletcher turned into the alley leading to the employee parking with a new resolve not to give up on his marriage. He loved Kate too much to simply let her go. He would have to convince her that their marriage was worth saving.

As Fletcher approached his truck, he saw Eric standing by it. He pulled his earphones out of his ears as he rolled to a stop. "What's up?" he asked, knowing Eric wouldn't be standing outside for no reason.

"I was about to head down to the mall when I saw your truck," Eric said. "Did you get any of my texts?"

Fletcher reached around to his back to pull his phone from the pocket on his cycling jersey. "I told you I was going for a ride. What's going on?"

"There's been another murder," Eric said. "At the mall."

"Really?" Fletcher lifted his tired leg over his bike then bent over his handlebars to unlock the front tire.

"Another woman shot someone."

"Okay…"

"And she's telling the same wild-ass story as Renee."

Fletcher looked up. "*Really?*"

"Yeah. Come on, we gotta go."

"What's she saying?" Fletcher said as he worked at removing the front tire.

"That's she didn't do it, and that she was a man."

"Really…" Fletcher furrowed his brow. He pulled the tire

free from the bike frame and lifted the bike into the bed of his truck.

"Hurry the fuck up," Eric said. "Sarge wants you down at the mall stat."

CHAPTER 14

Between Jenny sleeping on his couch—the first time in his life *any* girl had stayed at his house—and the complete elation he'd felt at being Renee, it was hard for Gabe to fall back asleep. He wasn't in a hurry, though. He spent much of his waking hours in other worlds—both on screen and in print—because he hated his life and hungered for any opportunity to escape it. But he didn't have that same desire now. In fact, he wanted the opposite. If it weren't for Jenny's request to go to sleep, he would have sat with her the entire night. For the first time in his life, he had no desire to escape reality.

With Jenny asleep on his couch, Gabe turned his full attention to what remained of his high. He was glad his nap hadn't completely ruined it. The memory was still there, but the crisp vividness was beginning to fade. Not wanting to miss its dwindling effect completely, he climbed into bed. With the lights off and the curtains drawn, he closed his eyes and replayed the day's events over and over.

Gabe brought to mind the moment he shifted into Renee. He could almost feel his heart racing and his skin tingling again. He was still amazed he had this ability. For the first time he wondered what Renee had felt, what she thought. Was she afraid when she'd gone from sitting in the coffee shop to suddenly being in his dungeon? What about when she discovered she was in his body? What he would have given to be a fly on the wall when she tried explaining the whole thing to the police. Had they laughed? He hoped they had.

His thoughts shifted to the power he'd felt over Marls when his former friend had walked into the living room—a room Gabe hadn't been in since he'd moved out of the house—and seen a stranger in his house. He imagined the confusion Marls had felt when he was accused of betrayal. Had he thought of Gabe? Had he pissed his pants when the attractive woman pulled a gun out of her purse and aimed it at him? He hoped so. And the *power* he'd felt as he stood over Marlon's bleeding corpse—he'd never felt anything like it. In that moment Gabe had known he was unstoppable. He could be anyone. He could do *anything*.

Unfortunately, the feeling was completely gone when he woke the next morning. He almost felt hungover. He pressed the heels of both hands into his temples, hating that he felt like himself again—fat and weak. "I gotta do that again," he said.

After lying on his back for a few minutes remembering the awesomeness of the previous day, he rolled over in bed and grabbed his phone off the nightstand. It was 9:30 am. He also had a new text message from Jenny.

Jenny: *Thanks so much for letting me stay with you last night. I have so much I need to do but I'll be in touch.*

Gabe smiled as he texted her back: *Let me know if there's anything I can do to help.*

He checked his email next, and exclaimed "Yes!" when he saw he had a new one from Your Ideal Mate. He clicked the link in the email, which loaded the mobile version of the site. Nicole Henricks had agreed to meet for coffee at Connie's, as he'd suggested. She wanted to know if Wednesday at eleven worked. Another text from Jenny flashed across the top of the screen.

Jenny: *Thanks, Gabe. That really means a lot.*

Gabe smiled again and he eagerly typed his reply to Nicole. He was already pining for that feeling of elation again. He told Nicole that Wednesday would be great and that he was looking forward to meeting her. Before logging off, he navigated to his match with Renee and said, "This time *I'm* the one closing the match."

A thought occurred to him while he got ready for work—something he hadn't planned on: Would Jenny interfere with his plans for Nicole? What if she asked to stay at his house again? Now that Marls was out of the way, he really hoped Jenny would realize, after all the years they'd known each other, that she actually loved him. But at the same time, he couldn't very well have Jenny hanging around the house with a woman trapped in his body screaming in the basement.

The rest of that day crawled by as he contemplated his conundrum. Planning his day around someone else wasn't something he'd had to worry about before. Each time his manager, Hank, came by to harass him he greeted Hank with a smile.

"What in God's name do you have to smile about?" Hank said as he made his way back to the registers after his break.

Gabe's smile broadened, which he could tell further annoyed Hank, and he said, "Nothing." He was laughing inside, though.

Hank was completely clueless that he was about to die.

"Then wipe that smug look off your face."

Gabe's hatred of Hank flared. His desire for tomorrow became almost unbearable. He couldn't wait. It was the eve of eves.

His shift continued to drag until a customer said, "Did you hear about the murder?"

Gabe looked up from the books he was scanning and, feigning ignorance, said, "Murder?"

"Saw it in the news this morning," said the customer, a middle-aged woman.

"What happened?"

"All they said was a woman murdered a man in his home."

"Did they say who it was?"

"The identities haven't been released to the public yet."

"Crazy," Gabe said.

"I know."

"That's the kind of stuff that happens down in Phoenix, not here."

"Yeah. Prescott is supposed to be a sleepy retirement community. That's why I moved here—to get away from the craziness of living in the city. But I guess you never can tell these days."

"I guess not." Gabe finished ringing her up then said, "Have a nice day."

A couple of hours later Gabe got a text from Jenny: *I know we haven't been in touch lately, but it would really mean a lot to me if I could stay with you again tonight. I just can't bring myself to go back to my house.*

Gabe hadn't arrived at a solution yet, so as he stood at the register, he thought over what he wanted his answer to be. He wanted her to stay. He wanted her to continue reaching out to him for support. His date wasn't until eleven—that was plenty of time to get her out of the house, wasn't it? But what if she didn't leave?

He'd just have to make sure she did.

Gabe texted her back: *You're more than welcome to stay again if you want.*

Jenny: *Thanks so much, Gabe. I can't tell you how much this means to me.*

Gabe: *The door's locked but I get off at nine.*

Jenny: *Okay. Thanks again.*

Gabe spent the rest of his shift trying to come up with a way to ensure Jenny was gone by eleven. He also spent quite a bit of time reflecting on how satisfying it felt to know that Renee's life would never be normal again. He felt no remorse for what he had done to her, or to Marls. They both deserved what they got.

People like them didn't deserve to live happy-go-lucky lives.

Gabe left work with a smile on his face—something that rarely happened. Jenny was parked in his driveway when he got home, which made him even happier. They spent the evening talking and playing video games, just like the good old days. When there was a lull in the conversation, he turned his attention to what he was going to do tomorrow. Each time he shot somebody in the game, he pretended it was Hank.

"You look happy," Jenny said at one point. "What're you thinking about over there?"

"Huh? Nothing..."

"Gabe? I don't remember you ever being so upbeat. It's like we've switched roles—I'm the downer and you're the..."

"The what?"

"Nothing. After what happened between you and... it's just good to see that you're happy."

Happy? She had no clue what she was talking about. He wasn't happy. He was miserable. He hated everything about his life. It was only yesterday that he'd felt happy, for the first time in his life. But he obviously couldn't tell her that. "I really missed this," he said.

"Me too," Jenny said. "Things should never have gotten the way they did. I'm sorry."

"You don't have anything to be sorry about," Gabe said. He looked over at Jenny and gave her a quick smile. "It wasn't your fault." He really didn't want to talk about this right now. He had been having a good time but now the conversation was turning sour. "I have somewhere I need to be tomorrow morning so I should probably get to bed."

"Oh, sorry. Didn't realize you had to get up early."

"I don't, really, but I'm tired." He turned the TV off. "What are your plans tomorrow?"

"I'm meeting with an attorney," Jenny said.

"Oh? What time?"

"Ten."

Perfect. "What do you need an attorney for?"

"They said I was likely going to have to testify if this goes to trial, so they recommended I get one."

"I guess that makes sense. Anyway, you're welcome to stay here just as long as you need to."

"Thanks," Jenny said. She grabbed the blanket and pillow from the end of the couch where she'd folded and placed them this morning. "See you in the morning?"

"Yeah," Gabe said. "See you in the morning."

CHAPTER 15

G abe ate breakfast with Jenny and was at Connie's forty-five minutes early. He ordered a large Connie's Confection—a frozen blended coffee with lots of sugar and whipped cream on top—and sat at a table with a book. He wasn't really reading it, but he turned the pages every few minutes to give the impression he was. Nicole arrived right on time, wearing a tight red blouse and black yoga pants. *Dear God*, he thought when she stepped up to the counter and he saw her ass.

He watched Nicole until she had her drink and sat at a table. She sat facing him, and looked in his direction a couple of times. She didn't recognize him, though, despite having been matched with him. *What did you think when you first saw what I looked like? Huh?* He tried to imagine what her reaction had been when she'd received notification from YIM that Gabe Snyder had responded, opened the site, and seen his photo. He'd made it to stage five with her—the stage where he chose to share a picture of himself—before she closed the match. *How long did it take you to decide you were superficial and only cared about looks? Doesn't matter now.*

Gabe concentrated on Nicole, focusing on the now familiar feeling that accompanied a shift. With practiced ease, it took only a moment before he felt it. His eyes locked with Nicole again, and he looked away with feigned embarrassment. With the yearning building inside him, he slurped down the remainder of his Confection, then got up and left.

Minutes later Gabe was locked in his new dungeon. He sat on the ground with his back against the wall and allowed the yearning he'd been holding at bay grow. It overflowed him, causing his heart to race and skin to tingle. He felt the buzzing—which would be his vision going blurry, if he'd been able to see—then he was sitting in Connie's Coffee Shop. He looked down and smiled at the sight of Nicole's ample chest directly below his nose.

Gabe's hatred of Hank pushed its way ahead of his sexual desire. He stood up and left Connie's. Thankfully, Nicole wasn't wearing heels. Once outside, he dug through Nicole's purse, found her car keys, and located her car, a sporty red number with leather seats and tinted windows. He pulled out of the parking lot and headed to a pawnshop—a different one than he'd visited when he was in Renee's body, in the opposite direction. He purchased a handgun under Nicole's name and made his way back through town toward the mall.

At stoplights, he looked down and admired the scene mere inches from his face. The seatbelt nestling between Nicole's breasts held the blouse close to her skin, blocking his view down her shirt, but it was cut low enough that he could still see the tops of each mound. A thought occurred to him as he drove, *Why rush?* He had all the time in the world to enjoy himself before he put a couple of bullets in Hank. As he continued toward the mall, a different sort of yearning built in him—one of desire. A desire he had never been able to satiate before.

With his new gun tucked safely in Nicole's purse, he strolled into Book World and made a beeline toward the bathrooms. He entered the family bathroom, clicked the lock, then turned to admire himself in the mirror.

The woman staring back at him was gorgeous. She was

someone who would never go out with a guy like him, not in a thousand years. She'd proven that when she closed her match with him. Gabe turned around and looked at Nicole's ass in the mirror. He reached around, sliding his hands up and down the smooth material. He squeezed with both hands, feeling her tight muscles. Next, he admired Nicole's chest. He stepped closer to the mirror and bent forward. The view down her shirt made the face in the mirror smile back at him, with perfectly straight white teeth.

Gabe stood back up and said, "Now let's see what you've got."

He worked at unbuttoning the blouse, revealing a lacy black bra. When he got the last button open, he pulled the blouse back and admired the view. He pulled the shirt closed, then open, then closed again. Then he opened the shirt and shimmied out of it, letting it fall to the ground. Gabe turned a few times, admiring the bra and yoga pants from different angles. Then he reached behind him with one arm and felt for the clasps on the bra. With his complete lack of experience, he fumbled, but finally managed to get it undone. Then, with bated breath, Gabe crossed his arms across Renee's chest, took hold of the straps on opposite shoulders, and slid them down.

Gabe stared as the bra fell to the floor. He studied the reflection in the mirror then looked down, seeing real breasts for the first time in his life. He reached up tentatively to grab them, but someone jiggled the doorknob, making him jump.

"Uh... just a minute," Gabe called out in Nicole's voice.

"Shit," he said to himself as he bent over to pick up the bra. His heart pounding from the interruption, he slipped his arms through the straps and fitted the cups into place. He reached around to secure the band, but he couldn't for the life of him fit the tiny hooks back together. In a moment of panic, he said, "Screw it," and slid the bra off. He shoved it into Nicole's purse then put the blouse on. After buttoning the shirt, Gabe flushed the toilet and ran the water in the sink. He slid the purse back over his shoulder and opened the door. "I'm so sorry," he said to the woman waiting outside with a baby in a stroller.

"No worries," the woman said.

Gabe took a moment to gather his wits, looking around the store as he walked slowly. *That was awesome. Now, where are you, you dumb fuck?*

He spotted Hank helping a customer by the eBook display. He made his way over, reaching into the purse as he went and finding the gun with his hand. He squeezed the grip and conjured his hate for his supervisor. When Hank was just a few feet away, he said with the sweetest voice he could manage, "Excuse me, sir?"

"Yes?" Hank said, looking over at Nicole.

Gabe let the purse slide off his shoulder, keeping a grip on the gun. As the purse fell to the ground, he leveled the gun at Hank and, as coolly as if he were playing a video game, pulled the trigger.

CHAPTER 16

L et me get changed," Fletcher said to Eric. He secured his bike to the mount in the bed of his truck, then unlocked the door and grabbed the duffle bag sitting on his seat.

In the station he took a quick shower to rinse off, foregoing shampoo or soap, then got dressed. Ten minutes later he was driving to the mall in his cruiser, with Eric in the passenger seat. "Why is it that I always have to drive?" he said in annoyance. He was tired and hungry and could have used a chance to cool down more.

"Because Batman would never let Robin drive the Batmobile, you idiot," Eric said.

"We're back to that?"

"Yeah, well, you rejected my Wyatt and Doc idea, so..."

Fletcher ate a protein bar as they drove to the mall, but knew it wouldn't hold him for long. The improvement to his mood was fading quickly.

He followed Highway 69 toward Prescott Valley and exited at the mall entrance. The road curved right, following the curve of the excavated hill on which the mall sat. At the top, he turned into the parking lot and followed the road around the mall. He found an open spot near the entrance to Book World, where several patrol cars were parked, their lights flashing. Crime scene tape was wrapped around the cement posts at the entrance of the store and a group of officers stood just outside the door. Fletcher shut off the car and reluctantly got out.

"It's about time, Wise Guy," Sergeant Frey said as Fletcher and Eric approached.

"Sorry, needed a little time to clear my head," Fletcher said. "What do we have?"

"Something eerily similar to the Williams case."

"That's what Eric was telling me."

"A gal identified as Nicole Henricks walked into the bookstore and killed a Mr. Hank Michaels. She claims she was meeting someone for coffee then somehow ended in a dark room—as a fucking man."

"I'm assuming you've already questioned her?"

"No. I'm making it up. You okay, Smarts?"

"I'm fine. But if you already questioned her, then what's with the big rush for me to get down here?"

"Because I want you to tell me what the fuck is going on here. I've got two murders in less than a week's time, with both suspects telling the same wild-ass story."

"What do we know about the victim?"

"He was the on-duty manager here at Book World."

"And did…"

"Nicole."

"Did Nicole know him?"

"Claims she didn't."

"Witnesses?"

"She shot him in the middle of a fucking bookstore, Wise, so what do *you* think?"

"All right. How many?"

"At least a dozen."

"What do they say happened?" Fletcher said.

"By the sound of it, Ms. Henricks walked in the store, spent a little time in the family bathroom, then walked up to Hank and shot him. Though, just like the other one, she claims she *didn't* shoot him."

"Did she try to run?"

"One of the witnesses—a big guy, six foot five and two-twenty if you ask me—was standing a few feet away and tackled her when she started backing away. He held her on the ground until the first officers arrived."

Fletcher shook his head and ran a hand through his hair.

"So what do you think?" Frey said.

Holding onto the back of his neck, Fletcher said, "Don't look at me. I'm just as confused as everyone else. Renee's story is a mix of truth and lies. Her roommate's on record corroborating that she was in fact internet dating and that she met someone for a blind date at Connie's, but she denies owning a gun or shooting Williams. I haven't heard back from ATF yet but I'm sure forensics will confirm that it was her who shot him."

"And now we have two women telling the same ridiculous story."

"Could they be working together?" Fletcher said.

"You're the wizard," Frey said.

"Yeah, Sherlock," Eric piped up.

"Is Nicole still here?" Fletcher said.

Frey pointed over to the clump of patrol cars and said, "Yeah, she's over in Barr's car."

"Again?" Fletcher said to himself. As he walked over toward the cars, he thought about what he wanted to say. It didn't sound like there was much of a mystery as to what happened, but how could two women be telling the exact same fantastical story? The only logical explanation was that they were working together. But why?

"Sup, Holmes," Spencer said.

"You too?" Fletcher said.

"Eric told me to call you that."

"I know Eric's a boy stuck in puberty, but don't you think this whole name thing is getting a little old?"

"Nah, man."

Fletcher shook his head and peered into the rolled-down rear window of Barr's car. Nicole had blond hair, and was wearing black yoga pants and a tight red blouse. Her mascara was smeared across her cheeks and her eyes were red. Just like Renee, she wasn't dressed to kill.

"So, you gonna tell us what the hell is going on?" Barr said.

"Your guess is as good as mine." Fletcher studied Nicole. She was staring straight ahead, not moving, and seemed to not notice his presence. He was trying to think of something to ask her, something the other detectives wouldn't have thought of, but he couldn't really come up with anything. From what he'd just been told, it didn't sound like there was really any question whether she'd shot Hank Michaels or not. The only real thing they needed to figure out was motive—and why she was telling the exact same story as Renee. Maybe he could try to link them together. He pulled out his pocket recorder, turned it on, then leaned in toward the rolled-down window. "Miss Henricks?"

Nicole looked over at him but didn't speak.

"My name is Detective Wise. Do you mind if I ask you a few questions?"

"I've already told them, it wasn't me," Nicole said.

What if they are *telling the truth?* Fletcher thought. *No. Don't be an idiot.* "They tell me you say you were meeting someone for coffee?"

Nicole nodded. "It was a blind date."

"Blind date?"

"Yeah, I was meeting this guy I met on Your Ideal Mate."

Fletcher cocked his head back. "I'm sorry?"

"Your Ideal Mate," Nicole said. "It's a dating site. Only the guy didn't show."

Holy shit. They were *working together!* Or at least he was beginning to think so. "Where did you say this date was?"

"Connie's Coffee Shop over on Sheldon."

"And the guy didn't show?"

Nicole shook her head.

"Do you mind giving me a verbal answer?" Fletcher said. "Did the guy show for the date?"

"No. I sat there waiting for him then next thing I knew I was—"

"In a dark room," Fletcher said, breaking from protocol of never interrupting a subject during an interrogation.

Nicole nodded then said, "Yes."

"Just like that? Poof. You were sitting at the coffee shop then you were in a dark room."

"I know it sounds crazy…"

Yes. Yes, it does. But what was crazier was that she was now the second person in just three days to use the same exact story. It couldn't be a coincidence.

"…but I'm telling the truth."

"They also told me that you, uh, weren't yourself. Could you explain that part to me?"

"I don't know what to say except that I wasn't me."

"What does that mean?"

"That I was someone else."

"Who?"

"I don't know… I was… I was in a man's body."

The odds of two separate women telling the same story after murdering someone in the same city two days apart were next to zero. "Can you describe this man for me?"

"Well, it was dark, so I don't know what he looked like."

"Is there anything at all that you can think of?"

"Only that he was fat."

"Fat, you say?"

"Yes."

Fletcher reached into his coat pocket and pulled out his small notebook. He flipped through it, read over some of his notes, and said, "What was the name of the guy you were going to meet?"

"Sam Gilkons," Nicole said.

Yup. They're working together. Now to prove it.

"Detective?" Nicole said.

"Yeah?"

"What's going on?"

"I don't know," he lied. Well, it was mostly a lie. He didn't know *exactly* what was going on yet, but he had a pretty good idea: Renee and Nicole were working together to murder people. What he didn't know was why. His phone started buzzing in his pocket. He slipped his hand in to silence it. "Miss Henricks, do you know a woman by the name of Renee Denovan?"

Nicole shook her head. "No. Never heard the name before."

I'm sure you haven't... "Did you know Mr. Michaels?"

Nicole shook her head. "I mean, when I saw him, I recognized him, but—"

"Recognized him how? From where?"

"From the store. I read a lot so I'm in Book World often."

"But you didn't know him?"

"No."

"You ever talk to him?"

"Maybe once or twice. He's helped me find a book before."

Certainly not much motivation for killing someone in cold blood.

"Ever heard of someone by the name of Marlon Williams?"

"No," Nicole said with a shake of her head.

Did Marlon and Hank know each other? he wondered. He stared Nicole in the eyes, trying to think of any more questions that might further link her with Renee. She returned his stare for a moment, but then looked down. "Miss Henricks." Nicole looked back up. "My job is to determine what happened today, so I want to stress how important it is that you be perfectly honest with me."

"I *am*," Nicole said. Her tears were flowing freely now, further smearing her mascara.

"Anything you can think of that might help prove you're telling the truth will greatly help me."

Nicole nodded and said, "Thank you."

Fletcher turned off his recorder and waved to Spencer and Eric, who were chatting a few feet behind him, to follow him toward the front of the car.

"You don't believe that yarn, do you?" Spencer said.

"Yeah, what a load of crock," Eric said.

"No. But what are the chances two women would independently kill someone and tell the exact same story?" Fletcher said.

"They're probably working together."

"She said she doesn't know Renee."

"She's obviously lying."

"True," Fletcher said pensively. "She mostly likely is. But what if she's not?"

"What are you saying?"

Fletcher didn't know what he was saying. He didn't believe them. How could he? "What if they're telling the truth?" he said anyway.

Spencer laughed out loud. "You actually think they somehow became men? Even if they did, that doesn't explain how it wasn't them that pulled the trigger."

"You're right. Just thinking aloud. Most likely they're colluding. But even if they are, something's not right here." Fletcher's phone buzzed again. He pulled it out of his pocket and saw he had a missed call and voicemail from Kate. He shoved his phone back into his pocket, looked up at Spencer, and said, "Just go easy on her, all right?"

"Sure, Smarts. Yeah."

Leaving Eric to chat with Spencer, Fletcher walked back to the group of officers standing by the entrance to Book World. "Sarge," he said as he approached them.

"Yeah," Frey said, turning his attention toward him.

"I'm going to head back into town. I think I might have a lead on what's going on here and I'd like to look into it."

"By all means, Sherlock. We've got things covered here."

"Seriously?"

"You gotta admit, it's perfect. The two of you together, you're just like Sherlock and Watson."

"Give me a break," Fletcher said as he walked away from Frey back toward his car.

"Hey!" Eric called from behind. "Where're you headed?"

"To the jail."

"What for?"

"I want to talk to Renee."

"Because…?"

"Because I want to figure out if they're working together," Fletcher said as they walked.

"How so?"

"Both Renee and Nicole were using that dating site, and they were both going to meet the same person." They approached Fletcher's car and he dug his keys out of his pocket and unlocked the door.

"That Sam guy?" Eric said over the roof of the car.

"Yeah," Fletcher said before sliding into his seat. "They won't admit to knowing each other"—he paused until Eric was seated beside him—"but maybe I can prove they do, through Sam Gilkons."

"We find him, we find the link between them."

"Exactly. And maybe even motive. But first I need access to that dating site."

CHAPTER 17

Gabe couldn't think of any way to describe how shifting into someone else made him feel other than that it was like being on some kind of drug. Being someone else—controlling their body, their life, their destiny—gave him a high better than anything he'd ever experienced before.

He had a couple of hours yet before he had to be at work—which was going to be awesome today—so he climbed into bed and covered himself with a sheet. He lay with his eyes closed, savoring the feeling of killing Hank and destroying Nicole's life. The look on Hank's face was emblazoned in his mind.

Gabe's phone rang and yanked him out of his trance. He rolled over onto his side and picked it up. To his surprise, almost two hours had passed.

It was work.

Gabe answered the phone. "Hello?"

"Gabe," a warbly voice said, "this is Karen."

Karen? Gabe pushed himself up. Why would the store manager be calling? "Uh, I'm not late, am I?" he said, suddenly unable to remember what time he was supposed to be at work.

"No, you're not late, Gabe. I was just calling..."

He could hear Karen begin to cry on the other end of the

phone. He waited for a moment, then said, "Karen?"

Karen sniffed loudly. "I'm sorry, Gabe. I was just calling to tell you that... that you don't need to come in today."

"I *don't?*" He tried to sound surprised.

"The store's closed for the day." Karen sniffed loudly again.

"It is? Why?" He knew, but he wanted to hear her say it.

"Because someone... someone came into the store and shot..." In a wail, she exclaimed, "she shot Hank!"

Gabe smiled. "*What? Why?*" His voice squeaked like it always did when he got really excited about something.

"I... we don't know," Karen said. "I was just calling to let you know the store's closed for the rest of the day."

"Thanks. What about tomorrow?"

"I don't know yet. We'll let you know as soon as we know anything."

"All right," he said. His face stretched into a grin.

"We don't know the details yet, but we're planning a store meeting at some point."

"Okay."

"I'll see you then." Karen sniffed loudly again.

"Bye."

Bummer. For once he'd been looking forward to going to work. He loved books and reading, and didn't really mind the work, but he had hated being there ever since Hank had become a manager. And he'd been really looking forward to seeing the other employees' reactions. Since that would have to wait until tomorrow, he decided to turn his attention to his next fix. It had only been a few hours since he'd shifted from Nicole's body back into his own, but he was already pining for the next one.

Gabe climbed out of bed and sat at his desk. He woke the computer from its hibernation and sat back to think about who he wanted to get revenge on next. A name popped right into his head: Tanner Johnson.

He had endured four years of agonizing abuse from Tanner and his friends in high school. He'd hated every single day of the four years it had taken to graduate. He should add every single person who'd ever laughed at him or helped Tanner to his list, but that wasn't feasible. So Tanner would have to do. He was the high school jock, the one the girls fawned over and the boys emulated—the one he wanted to be. The other kids would probably have left Gabe alone had there been no Tanner. The girls wouldn't have paid any more attention to him, but at least he wouldn't have been subjected to constant ridicule.

It took some sleuthing to locate Tanner but social media made it all too easy. Tanner was still in the area, working for JR's Construction. With a little more digging, he discovered JR's current projects.

Gabe got into his car and started driving. He stopped by Burger Mania on the way to get a shake and by four forty-five, he was sitting in the middle of an entire neighborhood of houses being built. He watched the workers intently as he noisily sucked the last of the shake through the straw.

He spotted Tanner and said, "There you are."

He dug his phone out of his pocket, having to shift his weight to get to it, and checked his email. He didn't have anything new from YIM, so he opened the app instead. He clicked on the active matches tab and looked at the list. It wasn't his turn to interact with any of them, nor was he close to the stage where they would meet. He frowned when he realized he wouldn't get his next fix right away. Even though he didn't want to—Sam was supposed to be nonchalant—he decided he needed to increase his pace with them.

He sat and watched Tanner until the construction workers began dispersing toward their vehicles. He shifted his car into drive and left, not wanting Tanner to see him. It had been several years since he'd last seen the former jock, and he was not about to give Tanner the chance to make fun of him again.

He was a victim no longer.

CHAPTER 18

Fletcher drove to the county jail, where Renee was being held without bond. In their complaint, they had successfully argued to the judge that if she could walk into someone's house and kill them, seemingly without motive, she was someone he and Scott Stephens, the city prosecutor, did not want out on the streets. But as he drove, he entertained the idea that she believed she was telling the truth, as ludicrous as it sounded.

Doing so, however, made him feel conflicted. As the lead detective on the Williams case, it was his job to objectively assist the prosecuting attorney in proving beyond a reasonable doubt that Renee was guilty. The evidence was stacked against her. Her grand jury hearing was in two days, and he would aid Scott in arguing that her case should move to trial. But he also knew she was innocent until proven guilty. It wasn't his job to prove she was innocent, though; that was her attorney's job. His job was to ensure both Marlon and his wife received justice.

But for some reason his emotions kept trying to finagle their way into her case. It happened to every detective at some point in their career, he knew, but it wasn't something he'd ever really had to deal with yet. He always approached the cases assigned to him with professional objectivity. He had to. If he didn't—if detectives let their emotions affect their jobs—his feelings could skew his interpretation of the evidence. He might inadvertently read things into the evidence, things that weren't there, or ignore what the evidence was obviously trying to tell him.

"Talk to me, Astute One," Eric said.

Fletcher looked over at Eric and shook his head. *Enough with the stupid names.* "About what?"

"What're you thinking."

"You don't want to know."

"Why? You thinkin' dirty thoughts about you-know-who?"

"*No.* I just have this feeling..."

"What feeling?"

"That maybe they're telling the truth."

"You know what it means if you think that, don't you?"

Fletcher looked over at Eric. "What?"

"That you're crazy."

"Why?"

"Listen to yourself. You really think they switched bodies with some fat dude?"

"No, I know," Fletcher said. And he did—he knew it sounded crazy. Deep down he also knew it wasn't true. But he *wanted* it to be true. They drove in relative silence—interrupted only by Eric clicking away incessantly at his phone—then he said, "I just want to talk to Renee."

"What about her lawyer?" Eric said.

Renee's lawyer, Timothy Davis, was an impediment. They'd sat on opposite sides of the courtroom enough for Fletcher to know that Tim prided himself in making the prosecutor's job as difficult as possible. If he went through Tim to get access to Renee's YIM account, Tim would make them get a warrant, and he'd worked enough cases to know that websites could be notoriously slow in responding to warrants. He also knew that if he had to get a warrant, his chances of finding a motive before the grand jury hearing would go down significantly. "She's not obligated to talk to me," Fletcher said.

"But does *she* know that?"

"She's been read her rights, hasn't she?"

"Playing hardball. Maybe I should start calling you Billy Beane."

"Billy Beane?"

"Yeah, you know, that guy Brad Pitt played in that baseball movie? He used algorithms or something to win."

"That was *Moneyball*, you idiot."

"Oh. Wasn't there a movie called *Hardball*?" Eric said, diving back into his phone.

"Yeah, that was the one with Keanu Reeves where he coached the inner-city kids."

"Oh. What was the name of the guy he played in that one?"

"I don't remember. The moment has passed anyway."

"What moment?" Eric said.

Fletcher pulled into the county jail parking lot. "The moment where your're tossing out a stupid name as if you'd just thought it up might have made it seem like you actually had an ounce of wit and didn't simply waste the city funds paying your salary to scour the internet looking for them."

"Damn. That was harsh."

When Fletcher got out of the car, he remembered he had a missed call and voicemail from Kate, so he clicked the voicemail icon and pushed play.

"Hey, Fletch," Kate said, *"I stopped by today and saw the papers were still where I'd left them. Was just wondering if you had a chance to look them over and what you thought. Anyway, I'm sure you're working, so I'll try again later. All right."* After a few seconds of silence, she said, *"Bye."*

His and Eric's footsteps echoed in the cement-walled corridor. He shoved his phone back into his pocket, replaying her message in his mind.

Stopped by. She stopped by? Did she already feel that their home was no longer hers? She had put the house under his name, leaving a Post-It on the papers saying she wanted it to be as simple as possible and figured giving it to him outright would prevent unnecessary fighting.

Papers. How could she be so cavalier about this? Papers? They weren't papers. It was a fucking DECREE OF DISSOLUTION OF MARRIAGE.

What I thought. What did she think he thought?

"Who was that?" Eric said.

"Kate." Fletcher shook his head as he un-holstered his gun and set it in a lock box. He looked over at Eric, who was doing the same, and said, "You mind waiting out here?"

"No. That's fine."

"Just, I don't want her to be defensive."

"Sure, sure." Eric reclaimed his gun and holstered it. "I have emails to get caught up on, anyways."

"Really?" Fletcher said with a raised eyebrow.

"Fine. This chick from CJ's has been texting me."

Fletcher shook his head. "You should've stuck with 'emails.'"

He knew he was lying to himself when he sat down at the visitor's box. He knew exactly why he wasn't able to keep his emotions under their typical tight reins: Kate. Every time he thought about her his mind went haywire. And while he waited for Renee to take her seat behind the glass facing him, he couldn't help but want her to be innocent. Nicole, too. He'd never felt that way about suspects before. He tried his best to put Kate out of his mind, but the churning in his stomach wouldn't let him forget her completely.

Renee sat on the opposite side of the glass a few minutes later wearing an orange jump suit. She wore no makeup, and her hair was disheveled. Feeling pity for her, Fletcher picked up the phone. Renee lifted hers as well and placed it against her ear.

"Hello, Renee," he said, choosing to forego formalities.

"Hi," she replied.

"Do you remember me? My name is Detective Wise."

She nodded.

The sight of her made the feeling stronger: He wanted her

to be innocent. He wanted to believe her.

"I know it's completely within your rights to refuse to talk to me," he began. He clenched his jaw, fighting the temptation to tell her—the last thing he wanted to do was give this obviously distraught girl false hope. "But I wanted to talk to you. Feel free to not answer my question if you don't want to."

"Okay."

"I'm the lead detective on your case. The evidence we have against you is very convincing. One thing we're lacking, though, is motive. I can't for the life of me figure out why you would walk into Mr. Williams' home and... do what you did."

"Because I didn't."

"I—" Fletcher stopped himself. "So far we have found nothing to dispute your claim that you didn't know Marlon Williams."

"I didn't," Renee said. "I'd never seen him before that day."

Fletcher nodded. "Do you know someone by the name of Nicole Henricks?"

Renee's mouth turned downward. "No."

"The name isn't familiar?"

Renee shook her head.

"At all?"

"No."

"You're sure?"

"Yes. Why?"

"Look," he started, feeling the urge to go out onto a limb, "I would get into a lot of trouble if anyone found out I'm telling you this, but I think it is pertinent to finding out exactly what happened." Fletcher took a breath, knowing that if she told Tim he would be in hot water. "Nicole walked into Book World at the mall earlier today and shot someone."

Renee's eyes went wide. "Oh my God."

"She told the exact same story you did."

Renee stared at him, mouth agape.

"The *exact* same story. She said she went to Connie's for a date, that she somehow ended up in a dark room, that she, uh, wasn't herself, and that the next thing she knew she was standing over a man bleeding from the chest with a gun in her hand."

"But how can—?"

His belief that she was telling the truth evaporated when he'd said it out loud to Eric. The very notion was ludicrous. It had to have somehow stemmed from being distracted by Kate. Instead, he found himself wanting to tell her that the reason they were telling the exact same story was because they were obviously colluding with each other. But he bit his tongue. If he was going to find his motive, he needed her to believe that he was trying to help her. "That is exactly what I want to find out," he said. "But I need your help."

"Sure. How?"

"I was wondering if you would be willing to give me access to your profile on Your Ideal Mate?"

Renee furrowed her brow. "You think that has something to do with it?"

"I'm not sure." He didn't want her to realize that he knew she was working with Nicole, so he held back the Sam Gilkons connection. "But I have this hunch I want to look into, so I thought I'd come ask." He would go through the formal channels if he had to, but he wanted to give her the chance first. That, and he really needed to find the motive before her grand jury hearing.

"Yeah, sure. If you think it'll help."

Fletcher flipped open his notebook and took his pen out of his shirt pocket.

"My username is Den456 and my password is cafebreve19."

Fletcher wrote as she spoke. He held the notebook up to the glass for Renee to see. "Did I get it right?"

Renee looked it over and said, "Yeah."

"Like I said, I'm not exactly sure what I'm looking for"—that was only partially true—"but if I find something, I'll be sure to tell you right away."

Renee nodded. "Sure."

"Thanks again, Renee."

Renee nodded again and hung up the phone.

Well, that was easy. Fletcher watched as she stood up and was led away by the guard. Fortunately, she hadn't put two and two together. If she knew he was aware of the Sam Gilkons connection, she'd probably have made him go through her lawyer.

The whole thing still didn't make sense. For one, they had to have known that any decent detective would figure out the Sam connection. And two, he still didn't understand why they would use such outlandish stories.

Tim was going to be pissed when he found out about Fletcher's visit with Renee, and would most likely try to block his access to the site until he got a warrant. He needed to work fast if he was going to find their motive and prove that the women were working together.

CHAPTER 19

Eric climbed out of Fletcher's patrol car and shut the door. "I'll catch up with you later," he said over the top of the car. "I'm gonna head back to the mall and see if there's any more help I can offer there."

"Sounds good," Fletcher said. He could use some peace and quiet anyway. "I'm going to take a look at Renee's profile to see if there's anything of interest before Tim cuts me off."

"Let me know if you find anything."

"Will do."

After Fletcher parted ways with Eric, he headed into the station and grabbed a cup of coffee before proceeding to his desk. He looked up when he heard a familiar voice call his name as he passed the dispatchers' area. Tina was walking toward him.

"Hey," he said when she drew near.

"Hi," Tina said. "Just wanted to see if everything was okay."

"What do you mean?"

"It's just, you hardly said a word last night. I could tell you weren't your usual self and you were gone before I got up this morning."

"Sorry. I've just got a lot on my mind." He didn't really feel like talking to Tina about his marital troubles. And he certainly didn't want to talk about how inappropriate whatever it was he was feeling for her was. The metaphorical wall he'd built between himself and her was already crumbling, and he didn't want to tear it down completely by opening up to her and confiding in her. Not while there was still a chance for him and Kate. But just as he was about to continue to his desk, their eyes locked. *God, she's gorgeous.* Images of him gathering her into his arms and kissing her flashed into his mind. He forced himself to break eye contact.

"Well, I just want to let you know I'm here if you ever need someone to talk to."

"Thanks. I appreciate that." He didn't know what else to say, so he turned and continued on his way.

When he sat down at his desk, he fired up his computer. While he waited for it to boot, he checked his voicemail. He had a new message from ATF, which he listened to with great interest. Turns out Renee had bought the gun from Pawn Paradise over on Sheldon the same day she'd murdered Marlon Williams. *Another thing she lied about,* he thought as he hung up the phone. He was glad the ATF's rush was indeed rushed. This fact would give him that much more ammo, so to speak, at her upcoming grand jury hearing. He would need to visit the pawnshop later.

He keyed in www.youridealmate.com. After it loaded, he found himself looking at a smiling man and woman holding hands on the left side of the screen and an advertisement on the right side stating it was free to sign up and view matches. The ad included a large sign-up button. There were also several tabs across the top of the page. One was titled "About," another "Testimonials," and third "How YIM works." A login button in the top right corner was the last item. He clicked on it and entered Renee's username and password.

A photo of Renee appeared in the top left corner. She was wearing shorts and a zipped up purple windbreaker, sitting on a large granite rock with Ollie, the black and white border collie, sitting next to her. Pine trees surrounded the rock, creating a picturesque backdrop. He recognized the setting: She was somewhere in the Granite Basin Recreation Area.

Below the photo were a few thumbnail photos of her, which he clicked on individually to see the larger version. The first one was a selfie of her face, neck, and shoulders. It looked like she was wearing the same purple windbreaker and was leaning against the trunk of a pine tree. The next one was a closeup of her and Ollie. It looked like a selfie as well. The third photo was of her leaning against a building—he recognized it as the front of CJ's on Montezuma Street—wearing a tight-fitting black mini-skirt that showed off plenty of cleavage. She had one leg bent slightly with her foot pressed back against the building, stretching the skirt material and making it ride up higher on that leg, showing plenty of thigh.

Next to the photos of Renee was a window titled "About Me." He clicked on it and started reading:

A brief description of myself: a nature-loving, animal-loving, enjoyer of life

Occupation: waitress

Do I want kids: yes

Do I already have kids: no

Religion: none

Smoke/drink: no/yes

What I care about most: animals and nature

What I am most thankful for: my dog and the outdoors

My friends would describe me as: happy-go-lucky

In 5 years I see myself: married to my ideal mate

Describe my ideal mate: someone who enjoys the outdoors as much as I do

The first thing people notice about me is: my smile

What I do for fun: I like to be outdoors as much as possible. When I'm not outdoors I like to be curled up with a good book.

When Fletcher finished looking over Renee's profile, he scrolled further down the screen. Below her profile information the page was divided into three sections: New Matches, Active Matches, and Closed Matches. She had ten new matches since October 19, the day Marlon was killed. All but three of them had a picture. The three that didn't were simply empty silhouettes. Two of them had a ribbon next to the picture, indicating the person had interacted. The only other information given was a name.

He clicked on the first profile, a man named Victor, and the icon expanded on the page to reveal his profile. He read over the information Victor provided about himself, then studied the buttons at the bottom. There were three available: Interact with Victor, Send Victor a message, and Close Match. He contemplated clicking on the first button to see how the site worked but decided against it—at least for now. Instead, he clicked the X in the top right corner and shrank Victor's profile back down, which made his picture move from the New Matches column to the Active Matches one.

Fletcher scrolled through the rest of the new matches and clicked on one of the matches that didn't have a picture. Eric was his name. Eric's profile expanded and looked identical to Victor's minus the photo. He scanned Eric's information then closed his profile. His icon moved columns as well.

Fletcher moused over the Active Matches column and scrolled down. He counted twelve active matches. The first four, after Eric and Victor, which were now at the top, had a little ribbon next to their photo indicating that they had sent a message. He didn't click on any of them; instead he moused over the Closed Matches.

"Aha," he said when his eye saw a particular name. The icon had a picture of a shirtless man—cropped about mid-chest—who looked muscular. He had bright blue eyes, straight teeth, and wavy dirty-blond hair. He was, Fletcher figured, the type of guy women would gawk over. The picture wasn't what interested him, though. It was the name: Sam.

Before opening the profile, Fletcher scrolled through the

rest of the closed matches—twenty-two of them in all—and saw that there were no more guys named Sam.

He clicked on Sam's icon to expand his profile. At the top of the expanded page, to the right of Sam's picture and above his profile information, there was a message in large black font: **Match closed by Sam on 10/20/15 at 9:41 a.m.** The day after Marlon was killed, Fletcher noted.

He read through Sam's profile more carefully.

A brief description of myself: I'm shy at first but open up once I get to know someone.

Occupation: salesman

Do I want kids: one day

Do I already have kids: no

Religion: agnostic

Smoke/drink: no/yes

What I care about most: loyalty

What I am most thankful for: being able to get out and enjoy nature

My friends would describe me as: someone that is fiercely loyal

In 5 years I see myself: I would like to be married and possibly have kids

Describe my ideal mate: someone who accepts me for who I am

The first thing people notice about me is: people say I have captivating eyes

What I do for fun: I like hiking and reading

The bottom of his profile had the same three options as the others, though the "Close Match" button was greyed out. He clicked on the "Interact with Sam" button. Another window opened and displayed a message: *We're so sorry, but Sam has chosen to close the match.* There was also an arrow pointing left in the bottom left corner of the message, so Fletcher clicked on it. This time there was a question from Renee: What's your idea of a perfect date? Sam answered: a day out in nature followed by an intimate dinner.

Fletcher clicked the back arrow again and got a similar page, only this time the question was from Sam and the answer from Renee. He clicked back a few more times and after one more question from each with written answers, the questions turned to multiple choice. They were all tied one way or another to relationships, questions people who just started dating might talk about.

After reading through the questions—six in total—he closed the window and clicked on the "Message Sam" button. A new window popped up that looked like a series of emails. It opened at the end, a message sent on October 18, in which Renee agreed to meet Sam at Connie's Coffee Shop at 3 pm the next day. He scrolled through the exchange—which was quite extensive—scanning the content. Nothing in particular stood out to him. He went back to the beginning of the profile and saw that Sam had matched with Renee on September 30. Renee initiated the first interaction on October 1, and Sam first responded on October 4.

Fletcher sat back in his chair. So they'd matched and seemed to move along pretty quickly, interacting back and forth, culminating in him inviting her to meet for coffee. She agreed, then he didn't show. That didn't make sense. Did it?

He retrieved the USB drive Connie had given him and put it in the computer, then brought up the surveillance video. He started it at the beginning, which was ten minutes before Renee arrived. He scanned all the patrons who came in or went out, as well as those sitting at tables, looking for someone who resembled Sam Gilkons. However, over the entire duration of the video, he didn't see anyone who resembled him. He'd need a larger sample of video if he wanted to definitively determine that Sam hadn't been there.

Something told him he needed to dig a little deeper. Why would two women get stood up by the same guy for a date, then go out and kill someone they didn't know? At this point, Sam was the key connecting the two murders.

Fletcher dialed the number for Judge Walter Sinclair.

"Judge Sinclair."

"Hey, Walt. It's Fletch."

"What can I do for you, Fletcher?"

"I need a couple of warrants. One for Pawn Paradise and another for Connie's Coffee."

"Another for Connie's?"

"Yeah. The girl who shot the guy in Book World was also on a date at Connie's right before."

"Oh?"

"Yeah. I think they might be related."

"*Really?* Then sure. I'll get them for ya."

"Can they be expedited? I'd like to head over there as soon as I can."

"Well, you actually caught me right as I was about to leave..."

"Please, Your Honor. If these cases are related there's a good chance it could happen again."

"All right," Walter said, "I'll make it happen."

"Thanks," Fletcher said. He hung up the phone and looked at the video on the screen. He dragged the location bar at the bottom until it showed Renee sitting at the table looking at her phone. He'd hoped there would be a phone number for Sam on her phone when he'd reviewed it after it had been turned in to Evidence, but there hadn't been. Now, having read through their online interactions, he knew all their communication had occurred through the dating site.

Fletcher closed the video program, unplugged the USB drive and stuck it back in his desk, then logged off his computer. It was almost five, and as much as he wanted to go get a beer, he couldn't quit yet. That was how he was—whenever he got something on his mind, he couldn't stand to not see it through to resolution. It drove Kate crazy, especially if it had to do with something he wanted. She always complained that he was hard to buy gifts for because whenever he wanted something, he just went out and bought it.

He called Connie's Coffee on his way out of the station to his car. Before he drove over, he wanted to make sure someone was there who could actually help him.

"Connie's Coffee," a peppy female voice said.

"Hi. This is Detective Wise with the PPD. Is Connie there?"

"She is. Just a moment."

The line was silent for a bit then another female voice said, "This is Connie."

"Hi, Connie. This is Detective Wise."

"Hello, Detective. What can I do for you?"

"I was just checking to see if you were there. I need more video, so I wanted to make sure you were in before I headed over." Fletcher's stomach rumbled. He became acutely aware of how hungry he was. His ride had done wonders to bring his appetite back.

"Well, I'm here. Is there something specific you were looking for? I can have it ready when you get here," Connie said.

"That'd be great, actually. I'd like a larger version of what you already gave me, starting about an hour before Renee Denovan came in to about an hour after."

"Okay. Remind me what time again?"

"From two o'clock to four o'clock on the nineteenth."

"Okay."

"I also need a video of earlier today, from about ten o'clock to noon. I'll have a separate warrant for that one."

"All right."

"About half an hour good?" Fletcher said. He needed to stop and get something to eat after he swung by the courthouse.

"Yeah, I'll have it ready."

"Thanks, Connie. See you in a bit."

Fletcher hung up the phone and got into his car. He drove the few blocks over to the courthouse, retrieved the warrant from Judge Sinclair, offering him effusive thanks, then made his way to Connie's. Fortunately, there was a burrito joint right next door. When he pulled into the parking lot his phone rang. He pulled it from his pocket and looked at it. It was Kate. He let it ring a few more times then decided to answer. "Hello?"

"Oh, hey Fletch. I didn't expect you to answer," Kate said. Fletcher didn't say anything—he didn't really know what to say. "Are... are you going to be home soon?"

"Why?"

"I wanted to... I just thought we could go over the papers together."

"Kate—"

"I know what you're going to say, Fletch, and the answer is yes. I *do* think this is best. I didn't come to this conclusion lightly, but ultimately I think it's for the best."

An awkward silence hung in the air. Fletcher remembered how there never used to be awkward silences between them— at least not until the first time Kate had suggested they go to counseling. A feeling of resignation washed over him. If she didn't want to be married to him anymore, there really was no point in even trying. "I'll sign them," he conceded.

"Do you want to go over it together?"

"What's the point? I already looked at them and I just said I'll sign them."

"You don't have to get snarky."

"*Snarky?*" Fletcher said, his voice betraying the anger rising in him. "You're asking me for a divorce, Kate. You don't really have a say in how I may or may not respond."

"I'm not going to argue with you over the phone."

"Then don't. I gotta go." He hung up the phone and immediately received a text from her: *Can we sign them tomorrow?*

Un-fucking-believable, he thought. He texted her back: *Whatever.*

When he got out of his car and shut the door, he got another text: *How about 9?*

He stepped up onto the curb and texted back: *Why are you in such a hurry to do this?*

Kate: *I just want to move on.*

Move on? When he thought about it, though, she was acting exactly like he would. If he had settled it in his mind that he wanted a divorce, he would try to move things along as quickly as possible as well. Once he decided on something, he wanted immediate resolution. He'd just never thought it would be this.

He shook his head and texted: *Where?*

Kate: *What do you suggest?*

Fletcher: *You're the one who wants to do this, Kate. You figure it out.*

Fletcher shoved his phone into his pocket. He bypassed the burrito joint, his appetite suddenly gone, and went into Connie's instead. Connie was behind the counter steaming milk when he walked in. She looked up at him and said, "Oh, hey, Detective! I'll be with you in just a sec."

Fletcher nodded, then got in line behind the two patrons waiting at the counter. Connie's bubbly atmosphere was the exact opposite of what he needed right now. He ordered a small drip coffee when it was his turn, then waited at the end of the counter. His phone buzzed incessantly in his pocket.

Connie finished the coffees she was making, then said, "Be right back." She went back to her office and returned after only a moment. "Here you go," she said, holding out another USB drive.

He took the drive from her, then retrieved the envelope holding the warrant from his pocket. Handing it to her, he said, "Thanks."

"You're welcome."

He turned to leave but stopped when she said, "Detective?"

"Yeah?"

"Does this have to do with what happened earlier today?"

"I... Sorry, but I'm not at liberty to say," he said.

"Oh. I just... I saw on the news about Renee. Then with what happened earlier... I thought they might be connected. And if there was something I could do to help—"

"I appreciate the offer. And I promise, if there is something you can do to help me, I won't hesitate to ask."

Connie nodded.

"Thanks again." This time he left, sipping the coffee as he pushed the door open.

He sat in his car and finally pulled his phone from his pocket to see who had texted him so many times. He already knew before he even woke his phone.

Kate: *Being a jerk isn't going to help, Fletcher.*

Kate: *We could do this at any notary. Do you have a preference?*

Kate: *Fletch?*

Kate: *Fletch?*

Kate: *Fine. I'll pick one and let you know.*

In a considerably fouler mood, he made his way up Sheldon to Pawn Paradise.

"Detective Wise-guy," said Phil, the owner of Pawn Paradise, when he entered. It wasn't the first time a case had required him to visit the pawnshop.

"Hi, Phil."

"What can I do ya for?"

Fletcher held up the picture of Renee and said, "Do you recognize this woman?"

Phil picked up the narrow glasses hanging around his neck on a thin chain and placed them on the end of his nose. He took the photo from Fletcher and said, "Yeah, I recognize her. Bought a gun from me the other day." He handed the picture back to Fletcher, pulled the glasses off, and said, "She in trouble?"

"Wouldn't be here if she wasn't."

"That was rhetorical, you know."

"Can I see her records?"

"Sure, sure." Phil turned and walked to the seventies-style metal desk. A mono-chrome computer sat half buried in a pile of paper. He sifted through the paper and returned with one in hand. "You want the bill of sale, too?"

"Please."

"Just a sec." Phil returned to the desk a second time.

Fletcher looked over the paper Phil gave him. It was the background report.

Phil returned shortly and handed Fletcher a receipt. "I don't suppose you got a warrant?"

Fletcher pulled the warrant out of the manila envelope and handed it to Phil, saying, "Thanks."

"Sure, sure." When Fletcher turned to leave, Phil said, "That it? No small talk?"

"Sorry," Fletcher said. "Not really in the mood."

"What? Trouble in paradise?"

Fletcher snorted. "See ya, Phil."

He sat heavily in his car. The motivation he'd had when he'd left the station was gone. Now he wanted nothing more than to just go home. He was tempted to go straight there, but he realized he had his bike in the back of his truck and didn't want to leave it there overnight. Before pulling out of the parking lot, he tapped on his phone to bring up his texts with Eric and typed out: *How are things going on your end?*

The reply came within moments: *Good. We're pretty much finished up.*

Fletcher: *All right. I got some more surveillance video from Connie's and was gonna look it over, but I think I'm just going to call it a day.*

Eric: *See you in the morning?*

Fletcher: *Yeah, but I'm not sure what time.*

Fletcher: *Kate wants to sign the divorce papers tomorrow.*

Eric: *Damn.*

Eric: *All right, I'll see you when you get in.*

Fletcher set his phone on the center console then put the car in reverse. "Fucking papers," he said as he backed out of the parking spot.

He drove back to the station, parked his patrol car, and went straight to his truck. He shook his head and cursed to himself the entire drive home. When he pulled into his driveway and saw that Kate's spot was empty as the garage door went up, he drove into the garage and parked.

He hadn't heard back from her yet, but he knew that in the morning he would be signing papers, under the supervision of a notary, to dissolve his marriage. He walked straight to the kitchen and opened the fridge, peering inside with a hopeful eye. He counted nine beers.

Fletcher took two out of the fridge and popped both caps off with an opener.

If this was his last night as a married man, he was going to enjoy it.

CHAPTER 20

October 22nd

Fletch," a voice in the distance said. "Fletch," the voice
repeated, this time with a gentle nudge on the shoulder.

Fletcher came to with a thudding pain in his head. He lifted
the pillow off his head and saw someone sitting next to him on
the edge of the bed. "Kate?"

"We agreed to go sign the papers, remember?" she said.

"Huh?" His head hurt too much to think.

"You agreed that today we would go get the divorce papers
signed. You didn't answer any of my texts this morning so I
decided to come over and see if you were home. By the looks of
it, you had quite the time last night."

Fletcher rolled onto his side and squeezed the pillow back
onto his head with his arm. When it was yanked away, he rolled
onto his back and said, "Hey!"

"We're doing this," Kate said. "Here," she said, holding out
both hands, one palm up and the other clutching a glass of water.

Fletcher sat up and placed his thumb in the corner of his eye
socket, against his nose, and pressed. With his other hand, he
took the ibuprofen Kate offered and popped them into his
mouth. Then he took the glass of water from her and drank the

whole thing.

"I'll wait for you in the living room."

Fletcher nodded and waited as she got off the bed and walked out. When the door closed behind her, he slid off the bed and went into the bathroom. He got the shower going then went to the commode to recycle the remainder of the beer he'd drunk last night.

He took a long, hot shower, moving as slowly as possible—both because it hurt to move any faster, and because he wanted to avoid what the day held. When he finally finished and got dressed, he joined Kate in the living room and smelled coffee. He walked straight past her as she waited on the couch and retrieved a mug from the cabinet. He filled it and took a drink. He counted nine bottles on the island. Returning to the living room, he held up the mug and said, "Thanks."

"You're welcome."

Fletcher took another drink and looked at his wife. Even in this moment, she was still beautiful. And not just her appearance. She was caring, compassionate. Why couldn't he have said it more? "You really want to do this?"

Kate stood and said, "Look, Fletch—"

Fletcher held up his free hand to stop her. "Just answer my question. If this is where we're at, it's where we're at."

"It is."

And he was a fool for letting it slip away. "Well then, let's get it over with. I have work to do." He went and topped off his coffee cup, then passed Kate on his way toward the front door. "Where're we doing this?"

"I thought we could do it down at the bank."

"Which bank, Kate? There are dozens of them."

"You don't have to get sarcastic, Fletcher."

"I can be whatever I damn well please. Which bank?" He wasn't an ass by nature, but he wasn't going to pretend that he was okay with this. And besides, she always said he was never emotional enough.

"How about the one across from the courthouse?"

"Meet you there."

Fletcher grabbed his phone and walked into the garage. He eased into his truck, careful not to spill the coffee. The garage door was already open, but he had to wait for Kate to get into her car and pull out since she was parked directly behind him. She had a manila envelope in one hand when she walked past. He checked the messages on his phone while he waited and saw that he had eleven texts from her. It was 9:57.

Fletcher followed Kate out of the driveway, through Prescott Valley, and on into Prescott. There was one parking spot open in front of the bank, which Kate took. He found an open spot in front of Ponderosa's and pulled in. *Rock-star,* he thought. Ponderosa's wasn't open yet, but he knew that by time he finished ending his marriage it would be.

Fletcher walked back up the street toward the bank. He looked across Gurley at the courthouse where he and Kate, eleven years ago, had gone in as a happy couple and applied for their marriage license. And where, mere days ago, Eric had run into Kate returning to the same building picking up the papers so they could end their marriage.

A part of him wanted to tell her he wouldn't sign them—to make her go through the process of having him officially served if she really wanted to do this. But it was only a thought. He wasn't that type of person. If she didn't want to be married to him anymore, he wasn't going to fight it.

Kate was waiting at the front door.

You look beautiful today, he couldn't help but think again. He didn't know why he was so bad at paying her regular compliments. It just wasn't something he thought about. He'd always thought she was beautiful; he was just bad at telling her. Of course, when he was reminded, he did it for a while, but he always slipped back into complacency. Funny that the thought occurred to him now, as he was walking in to have divorce papers notarized.

"Let's get this over with," he said. Kate scowled at him, but he didn't care. In a few minutes, her feelings were not something he would have to worry about anymore.

He let Kate take the lead when they got inside.

"How can I help you?" asked the professionally-dressed woman behind the counter when they approached.

"We'd like to see a notary," Kate said.

The woman gestured behind them and said, "Okay. If you want to have a seat over there. It'll be just a few moments."

They took the available seats. Kate sat opposite him rather than next to him.

A few minutes later, another woman approached them and introduced herself. "Hello. I'm Cynthia Myers. I'm told you need a notary?"

"Yes," Kate said.

"Well, follow me, then." Cynthia led them over to a cubicle where she sat down behind a desk.

Kate looked at him, and he gestured to the seats in front of the desk. Kate sat in one of the plush chairs and Fletcher sat next to her.

Cynthia got a ledger out of her desk and said, "Now, what do we need notarized?"

Kate pulled the papers out of the manila envelope and handed them to Cynthia.

Cynthia did a poor job at hiding her surprise. "Oh… okay," she said. "I'll need both of your IDs."

Fletcher retrieved his wallet from his pocket, pulled his driver's license out, and set it on the desk. Kate's shortly joined his.

Cynthia wrote in her ledger, then said, "Okay, go ahead and sign the document."

Fletcher looked over at Kate. They locked eyes for just a moment before she broke contact and directed her attention to the papers. She flipped to the last page and signed her name, seemingly without hesitation or second thought. She scooted the stapled clump of paper toward him and offered him the pen.

Fletcher took it from her and considered the document before him. He was not unfamiliar with signing documents that would forever change a person's life—he'd just never thought he would be signing one that would change his own. He held the pen, tapping it with his forefinger for a moment, reflecting. Then he scrawled his signature.

Cynthia turned the ledger so it was right-side-up to them. "Now, if I could have each of you sign here."

Fletcher had the pen, so he signed the ledger first, then handed the pen to Kate. The moment she signed her name, Fletcher scooped up his license and walked out. He was halfway to Ponderosa's when he heard Kate yell, "Fletcher!" He kept walking. "Fletcher!" he heard again. A hand grabbed him by the arm.

"What?" he said, spinning around.

"That was rude."

"What exactly? I signed the papers, just like you wanted. As far as I'm—"

"This is *not* what I wanted!"

"Oh? I don't remember being the one who wanted to get a divorce, Kate."

"I didn't *want* to get a divorce, Fletch."

"Then what are we doing?"

"That doesn't mean I wanted it…"

"Well, you got it, whether you wanted it or not. See ya, Kate." Fletcher turned and walked away from her.

"Fletch! Fletch!" Kate grabbed him by the arm again.

"*What* do you want?"

"I don't want to leave things like this."

"Like what, exactly?"

"Like this. You mad. I thought—"

"How did you imagine I'd feel about this? That I'd go in there with a smile on my face and be all, 'Hey! Let's go get divorced today, why don't we'?"

"No. I... I thought maybe we could at least be friends," Kate said. Fletcher noticed for the first time that her eyes were glistening.

"I want to be your husband, Kate. Not your friend."

"So that's it?" The tears welling in her eyes broke free when she blinked and streamed down her cheeks. "You're just going to walk away?"

"Jesus fucking Christ, Kate! I'm not the one who wanted this. Look, I love you. I probably always will. But I'm not interested in being your friend. I'm especially not interested in watching you date other people—which, for all I know, you probably already are."

"No," she answered, a little too quickly.

"At this point it doesn't matter. I can't pretend that I'm just a friend, and watch you go off and find happiness elsewhere. That was supposed to be my job. Now you've got what you wanted, so please—just leave me the fuck alone."

Fletcher turned and walked away.

This time, Kate didn't follow.

With a clenched jaw and fists, Fletcher left her behind. He left the life they had promised they'd share "till death us do part." She had erected a wall between them, but it was no longer his job to try to break it down. It would forever stand between them unless she dismantled it herself.

Fletcher went through the door leading into the atrium mall. Ponderosa's opened at eleven. He pulled his phone out of his pocket and pushed the side button to light up the screen. 11:01.

Perfect.

He pulled Ponderosa's front door open and went in. He walked to the bar section at the back, sat at one of the many vacant stools, and ordered the first of what he knew would be numerous pints of beer.

CHAPTER 21

Fletcher ignored his phone as it buzzed on the bar. After a few more pulls on his beer, he picked it up and saw he had a couple of missed calls as well as a new voicemail. Both Eric and Scott Stephens, the prosecutor, had called. He wouldn't know which one of them had left the voicemail unless he opened the app, but he wasn't the least bit interested in what either of them might have had to say. He also had several texts from Eric.

Eric: *Where are you, man?*

Eric: *Scott's looking for you.*

Eric: *Fletch?*

Eric: *I just tried calling. Where the fuck are you?*

Eric: *Scott's pissed. He got an earful from Tim this morning about your visit with Renee.*

Eric: *Fletch!*

Fletcher picked the phone up and texted Eric: *Tell Scott I won't be in today.*

Eric texted back immediately: *Why not?*

Fletcher: *Because I'm celebrating my divorce.*

Eric: *Fuck, dude, I forgot. Sorry.*

Eric: *What am I supposed to tell Scott? He wants to meet again about the GJ.*

Fletcher: *You handle it.*

Eric: *Shit, Fletch.*

Eric: *Ugh. I'll do my best...*

Fletcher knew Scott would be pissed that he wasn't there to help prepare for the hearing, but he was going to have to make do. Eric was new, but still competent. Somewhat. Besides, he knew that even if he had decided to go in after he'd finished with Kate, he wouldn't have gotten anything done. The motivation he had for working on Renee's case was now completely overshadowed by his own misery.

He still had a headache from the night before, but at this point he didn't care—and after a few pints, it was gone. He ordered food. He wasn't particularly hungry, even though it was almost midday and he hadn't eaten anything, but he knew that if he didn't eat something, his day would be short-lived.

From time to time Mac tried to make small talk. Fletcher would normally have been amenable, but today he politely waved Mac off each time. He didn't want to talk to anyone. All he wanted was to be alone with his thoughts. And those thoughts were dominated by the mystery of how and why his marriage had completely disintegrated in less than a week. But it hadn't been less than a week; he knew that now. It was more like a slow water leak that you didn't find out about—or ignored— until it was too late and the damage was done.

She's found someone else already, he concluded. Why else would she want to get the divorce papers filed so quickly? She'd left him the house, too. Wasn't the woman supposed to get the house? If she had found someone else, how long had it been going on? He tried thinking back on the last several months—it had been at least four since the last time they'd had sex. Even though he was acutely aware of it, it wasn't the first time they'd gone through such a dry spell. But if she was seeing someone else, maybe that was the time frame he had to work with—she wouldn't sleep with him if she had already decided to see someone else, would she?

Did it matter? Even if she was seeing someone else, what difference did it make now? They were divorced. Well, technically, a judge still had to review and sign the papers, but still. Whether she was already seeing someone else or not, Kate had decided long ago that their marriage was over. Nobody came to that sort of life-changing decision in four days. If anything, he was the idiot for not seeing it—or, more likely, ignoring it. He wouldn't place all the blame on her. He'd been a shitty husband.

Fletcher's phone vibrated on the bar. He looked down at the screen and saw that it was a text message from Tina. He swiped the phone open to look at it: *You all right? Eric told me what happened.*

He shook his head, mentally cursing Eric. He knew Eric had his best interests in mind, but he really wished he would just leave him alone. Sure, he felt something toward Tina—he wouldn't consider it feelings; more like a carnal desire. It was hard not to think about her sexually. She was gorgeous. And although he and Kate had still had sex until recently, he could tell her physical interest in him was long dead. But that didn't mean he was interested in sleeping with someone else.

But now he was divorced. Maybe not legally—the judge still had to sign the decree after the requisite waiting period—but for all intents and purposes he was fucking divorced.

Whereas he'd occasionally thought about sleeping with Tina, he had never once thought about *acting* on those thoughts. He would never cheat on Kate. But now he didn't have to worry about that. She was free to sleep with whomever she wanted—and so was he.

But he didn't feel like being with anyone at the moment. He just wanted to be left alone.

He didn't want to be rude, though, so picked up his phone and texted Tina back: *I'm fine.*

Tina: *You sure?*

Fletcher: *Thanks for asking, but yeah. I'm fine.*

Tina: *Well, I've never been married before, but I know you can't possibly be fine.*

Tina: *I just want to let you know I'm here if you need anything.*

Fletcher: *Thanks. I appreciate it.*

He looked at the time on his phone: 2:12. He had no clue how many beers he'd had—and he didn't care—but he knew he couldn't stay here all day. He also knew he couldn't drive. The last thing he needed was a DUI. He really didn't want to see anyone, but he also didn't want to spend the money it would take for a cab to haul his drunk ass all the way out to his home in Prescott Valley. He begrudgingly sent Tina another text: *Actually, I could use a ride to my house.*

Her response was immediate: *Sure. Where are you?*

Fletcher: *Ponderosa's.*

Tina: *All right. I'll be there as soon as I can.*

Fletcher: *No rush.*

Fletcher held up his mostly empty glass and silently toasted his divorce. *Welp, I wish I could say that was fun, but I can't.*

He upended the last of his beer and flagged Mac down. "I'm ready to cash out."

He settled his bill when it came and stood up. He tried his best to walk out of the bar without stumbling, but he was forced to use the bar and the wall to help him keep his balance as he walked. In the atrium, he dropped heavily onto a creaky bench and waited.

Several minutes later his phone buzzed in his pocket. He took it out and saw that Tina was waiting for him outside. He stumbled out and looked for her. A car horn blared, and he saw Tina waving at him through the windshield directly in front of him. *Rock-star parking. How apropos.* Twice in one day. It was the least the parking gods could do. "Take *that*, Kate," he said to himself.

Fletcher staggered across the sidewalk and fumbled with the passenger door. Tina leaned across the center console and opened it from the inside. He plopped down into the seat and said, "Thanks."

"No problem," Tina said as he pulled the door closed.

He had trouble getting his seatbelt buckled, so Tina reached over and helped him push the buckle down into the latch. He looked up at her when her hand touched his. "God, you're beautiful," he said. It felt good to say it. He'd thought it ever since she started working with the department, but had never permitted himself to say it before.

"Thanks," Tina said, looking away and shifting the car into reverse.

"I mean it," he said. He looked down at her hand, which rested on the gear shifter in the center console, and thought about placing his hand on hers. *Too soon,* he thought. Instead, he turned and looked out the passenger-side window. The motion made him feel sick, so he spent the rest of the trip concentrating on not puking in Tina's car.

Wouldn't that be a great way to start a relationship?

Who was he kidding—he didn't want a relationship. His last one wasn't even legally over yet. He wouldn't object to Tina coming in and fucking him, though, and any chance of that happening would evaporate if he puked. But he wasn't going to ask her. And he didn't think she would offer. At least he didn't think she was the type of woman who would, knowing he'd literally signed divorce papers a few hours ago.

"Thanks," he said when Tina pulled into the driveway. She placed the car in park, and he managed to unbuckle his seatbelt on his own. He hesitated for a moment, hoping she would invite herself in, while at the same time forcing himself not to invite her. "I really appreciate it."

"Glad I could help, Fletch." She placed her hand on his shoulder and said, "I'm really sorry."

"It's not your fault." The shoulder was a safe, platonic spot. If she'd been hinting that she wanted to come in with him, she would have put her hand somewhere else—his arm, or maybe his thigh.

She removed her hand. "I know. But it still sucks."

An awkward silence hung between them.

"Thanks again," he said. "I know you gotta get back to the station..."

"Yeah. Look, Fletch, if you need anything, let me know."

"I will." He cracked the door.

"Promise?"

Fletcher nodded. "Thanks again." He pushed the door open and climbed out. When he closed the door, Tina backed out of the driveway and he waved. He watched her pull away, then walked to the front door and leaned his forehead against it while he clumsily fit the key into the keyhole. As if one lock wasn't enough, he had to fit the key into the deadbolt as well.

When Fletcher finally managed to get the door unlocked, he went inside and headed straight for the bedroom. He stopped just outside the room and stared at a photo of him and Kate on their wedding day. It was just the two of them standing next to each other. Their bodies faced the camera, but their heads were turned toward each other. He was looking down at her and she was looking up at him. They were both smiling broadly. And why shouldn't they be? It was their wedding day.

A jolt of sadness shot through him. He went into the bedroom and climbed into bed. He turned his phone off, noting it was barely three in the afternoon, and covered his head with a pillow.

The day had nothing left to offer him.

CHAPTER 22

October 26th

Fletcher sat at his desk staring at nothing in particular. The monitor screen was blank because he hadn't touched the computer in at least ten minutes. He'd thought that after taking Friday off and having the weekend to reflect he would be able to come to work refreshed and focused. Instead, he'd gotten a tongue-lashing from Frey, who felt Fletcher was too distracted by his personal problems to handle such a high-profile case. Eric had managed to help Scott with Nicole's complaint without screwing it up, Frey said, so he was going to let them stay on instead of pulling them from the case. Even after learning that Scott was also annoyed with him—he would be annoyed, too, if he were in Scott's place—he still couldn't concentrate. He also had a nasty voicemail from Renee's lawyer, Tim.

Despite Scott's annoyance with him, Eric reported that Renee's grand jury hearing had gone well. They still lacked a clear motive—or any sort of motive, really—but the evidence was enough for the grand jury to formally indict Renee in the murder of Marlon Williams.

Tim had threatened in his voicemail that if the Scott tried to use anything Fletcher discovered on Renee's dating profile, Tim would move to have it thrown out. He wasn't worried, though—it was just a threat. If he discovered anything useful on the dating site, it would be evidence he had obtained legally. Renee was free to say whatever she wanted, to whomever she wanted. Tim was just mad that Fletcher had gone behind his back.

Frey was annoyed he'd gone behind Tim's back as well, which was largely the reason for his tongue-lashing. Frey hated Tim just as much as he did, so he'd been none too pleased when Tim had called him on Friday and complained. Frey wanted to know if riling up Renee's lawyer had at least been worth it, to which Fletcher had replied that he didn't know yet.

Frey had asked what he'd been looking for, and he'd said he was looking for a motive. They could convict Renee without a motive, but Scott wanted to throw the proverbial book at her. To do that, they would need a motive that proved intent. That left him with the onus of finding a motive in both cases. He also needed to prove that Renee and Nicole knew each other. As wild as their stories were, it was too much of a coincidence to believe that they had both randomly come up with the same thing. The only logical conclusion was that they must know each other and were lying about it. But he needed to prove it. And he thought that proof might be found in the dating site. They were both supposedly on first dates with the same person, so it was possible they were working together, and that Sam Gilkons was nothing more than someone they'd made up to add credence to their story.

He hated dealing with websites; they could be notoriously slow about responding to warrants. So the first thing he did when he got into the office—after his tongue-lashing by Frey, that is—was get a warrant for access to the profiles for Renee Denovan, Nicole Henricks, and Sam Gilkons on Your Ideal Mate.

Fortunately, the manager he spoke to when he called their customer service number ended up being receptive to his request after Fletcher pointed out that he was investigating two separate crimes committed by users of the service, and that it would reflect badly on the website when it inevitably became public. He ended the conversation with the assurance they would comply as quickly as they could.

He had a meeting later in the day with Scott regarding Ms. Henricks. Eric had done a superb job putting together the notes on her investigation, so while he waited to hear back from Your Ideal Mate, he decided to pay a little attention to the missing persons case he'd been working on before Mr. Williams' murder. It was frustrating him that he had run into a dead end.

Fletcher moved the mouse to wake up his monitor. He brought up the file with all his notes and looked over them again.

The afternoon of September 26, Tyrell Gibson's parents had called the police when he didn't come home from school. They hadn't thought much of it when he didn't come home the night before from his evening shift at the Burger Mania on the corner of Willow Creek and Watson Lake; according to them, he sometimes went over to friends' houses to do homework. Their cellphone records indicated they had called his phone numerous times, as well as texting him. His bike was later found in the ditch along the side of Watson Lake Road. The footprints present near his bike didn't indicate any sort of a struggle. As near as Fletcher could tell, Tyrell had ditched his bike, then either walked away on the pavement, avoiding the shoulder, or voluntarily gotten into a car. His cellphone was found a few hundred yards farther down the road.

The gas station/Burger Mania had a surveillance system, but it hadn't worked in years, according to the manager on duty when they went to investigate. None of the interviews with Tyrell's friends had turned up any leads. None of them had seen him the night of his disappearance. He had run into a dead end—just as he had with finding a motive for the two murder suspects he was now investigating.

When he finished looking over Tyrell's case, he went back to his interview with Renee, which he'd been reading when he spaced out. It didn't really matter; he already knew what they said. He'd been over both Renee's and Nicole's interviews time and again, but he forced himself to go through them once more in the hopes of seeing something he might have missed.

Fletcher had to restart frequently because he kept spacing out. When he saw Eric waving both arms in front of him, he realized he had done it again.

"What?" he said.

"I asked if you want to go get something to eat."

"Why, what time is it?"

"Noon-ish. Besides, does it matter? Doesn't look like you're being very productive over there anyways."

"Sure," Fletcher said. He logged off his computer and grabbed his phone. "But I'm not driving."

"What?" Eric said. "I drive. Sometimes."

"When was the last time you drove anywhere?" Fletcher said. He followed Eric through the station, bumping into him when Eric suddenly stopped in the dispatchers' area.

"Hey, Tina!" Eric called out.

Tina looked up from her desk and pulled her headset off. "Yeah?"

Fletcher pushed Eric in the back, trying to get him moving. "Eric…"

"Wanna join Wise Guy and myself in getting some grub?"

Tina looked at Fletcher and he felt a wave of heat rise in his face. Then she said, "Sorry. As much as I'd love to, I've got too much to do."

"Maybe tomor—" Eric started before Fletcher pushed him in the back again. "That was rude," Eric said when they were past the dispatchers.

"I don't need you playing matchmaker, Eric."

"Come on! It's fun."

"Not for me."

"You gotta get back out there."

"I will when I'm ready. Besides, my divorce isn't even

finalized yet."

"You're not gonna let that keep you from asking her out, are you?"

"That doesn't really have anything to do with it."

"But you just said—"

"Don't you think it might be because I'm not ready to date?" Fletcher said.

"Jeez. Sometimes I swear you're such a..."

"Such a what?"

"Nothing." Eric pushed open the door leading outside and said, "How does that Mexican place around the corner from Ponderosa's sound?"

"Sounds good to me."

"Wanna get a beer tonight?" Eric said. Using the remote key, he unlocked the doors of his green Mustang as they approached.

"I probably shouldn't," Fletcher said when they were both sitting inside.

"Why not?"

"Because after this weekend, my liver's going to kill me if I don't give it a rest."

"Dude," Eric said, starting the engine. The exhaust, with its custom pipes, roared. "Why are you being so lame all of a sudden?"

"Now I remember why I like driving," Fletcher said. The noise from the muffler—or lack thereof—reverberated in his body.

Fletcher plopped down at his desk an hour later, his stomach protesting after he'd gorged himself on the fry bread he loved at Antonio's. He wished he could find somewhere dark to take a nap.

"So?" Eric said, sitting opposite him.

"So, what?" Fletcher said, looking across their desks.

"We gonna get beers or what?"

"What's the 'or what'?"

"Beers."

Fletcher didn't want to, but what else was he going to do after work? Go home to an empty house and mope? "Sure, why not," he acquiesced.

Fletcher still had an hour before his meeting with Scott. Unable to think of where to go next with the missing persons case, he turned his attention instead to the Hank Michaels case. He started by reviewing the notes on the crime scene investigation, as well as the interview of Nicole Henricks. Then he looked over the ATF report. She'd bought her gun the same day she shot Hank, just like Renee. *Another thing they have in common.*

Next, he turned his attention to the surveillance video from Connie's. He watched it over and over. It was similar to Renee's video. Nicole came into Connie's, ordered coffee, sat at a table for about half an hour, then got up and left.

What's the connection? Renee's and Nicole's actions the days they had each committed murder were too similar, almost as though they were choreographed. They'd both gone to Connie's to meet someone from Your Ideal Mate. They both seemed to have been stood up. They both left Connie's on their own accord. They'd both bought a gun the same day. But they were both holding to their respective claims that they didn't know each other—and there wasn't any indication that they did. Fletcher couldn't find a connection between the victims, either.

His meeting with Scott came and went. By the time it was over it was close enough to five o'clock that he didn't see any point in returning to the office. He was mentally fried and knew he wouldn't get anything done even if he did go back in. He started walking back to the station from the courthouse.

As he stood at the corner of Cortez and Goodwin waiting for the walking man to light up, he texted Eric: *I'm on my way back to the station. Not planning on coming in. Ready to meet me at Ponderosa's?*

The traffic light changed; the walking man signal came on and Fletcher crossed Goodwin. While he waited to cross Cortez, he got a reply from Eric: *Yeah. Let me wrap up a few things and I'll meet you there.*

Fletcher: *Sounds good.*

Eric: *See you there.*

When the light changed, he crossed the street. He walked past a bronze statue of a bucking bronco with a cowboy on its back and to the employee parking lot. He got into his truck, set his briefcase behind the seat in the extended cab, and drove the short distance down to Ponderosa's. It had been a very long day and he knew a beer from his favorite pub was exactly what he needed. There wasn't any rock-star parking, though, so he drove around the back and found a spot.

The old wooden floors announced his arrival as he entered through the back of the cavernous atrium mall. He looked through the opening leading out to Ponderosa's patio seating and saw that a happy-hour crowd had already gathered, though they hadn't yet spilled out onto the patio.

Fletcher walked through the mall and entered Ponderosa's through its front entrance. He smiled at the hostess, who recognized him, and walked past her to the bar. He found an empty table, dug his phone out of his pocket, and texted Eric to see what he wanted while he waited for a waitress to come take his order. It took a couple of minutes for Jill, one of his favorite waitresses at the pub, to make it over to him.

"Hey, Fletch," Jill said. She held a menu out to him and said, "Something to eat? Or just the usual?"

He hadn't heard back from Eric, so rather than ordering a beer for him and letting it get warm—Eric had a nasty habit of leaving his beer unfinished if he thought it'd gotten too warm—he said, "Just the usual."

"Be right back."

"You snooze, you lose," Fletcher said to himself as Jill walked away.

She returned a couple of minutes later and set his beer down on the table with a coaster. He picked it up and took a long, welcome drink.

"Hey there," a familiar voice said.

Fletcher looked up over his glass and saw Tina standing before him.

"Oh, hi," Fletcher said. He set his glass down.

"I hope I'm not interrupting."

"No, no. I just didn't realize Eric invited you to join us."

"Are you sure it's all right? I don't want to intrude if he didn't run it by you."

He gestured to the seat opposite him and said, "Sit, sit." Tina slung the strap of her purse over the back of the chair and sat. "Did Eric say when he would be here?"

"He said he'd be right behind me."

Fletcher nodded, took a sip of his beer, and mentally cursed Eric. He knew exactly what Eric was doing, but he resisted the urge to pick up his phone and send him a nasty text. Instead, he flagged Jill down so Tina could order a beer. "And I'll take another," he added, after Tina made her order.

"Be right back," Jill said.

"Are you sure it's okay that I'm here?" Tina said. "You look like you'd rather I not be."

"No, really. It's okay," Fletcher said. Whereas it was true that he didn't want her to be there, at the same time he *did* want her to be. He just wished Eric would have let him do it on his own time. He wasn't going to say anything tonight, but he planned on telling Eric later exactly what he thought about this.

Fletcher's phone buzzed. He looked at it. "It's Eric," he said, before picking it up and reading the text.

Eric: *Sorry, forgot to tell you I invited Tina.*

Fletcher: *Yeah… thanks for that.*

Eric: *Crap. I totally forgot I had something planned tonight.*

Eric: *Sorry, dude, won't be able to meet ya after all.*

Fletcher stared at his phone with a clenched jaw. He'd been played. He was supposed to be the Wise Guy, the Wizard, the Sensei, and he got played. By *Eric*, of all people. He resisted the temptation to swear.

"What is it?" Tina said.

Fletcher looked up at her and said, "He says something came up and he won't be able to make it." Before setting his phone back down he sent Eric a quick reply: *I'm going to kill you.*

"Do you want to just go?" Tina said.

"No," Fletcher said. Though, to be honest, that was exactly what he felt like doing. But his alternative for the evening hadn't changed. He took a drink of his beer, then said, "You hungry?"

"I am, actually," Tina said with a smile.

Fletcher got Jill's attention and when she came over, he said, "We decided to eat after all."

"No prob. I'll go grab you a couple menus," Jill said. She returned promptly and set a menu before Tina and another one in front of Fletcher.

Fletcher didn't really need to look at the menu—he pretty much had it memorized—but he picked it up anyway and glanced at it. Knowing what he wanted, he looked over the top of the large, single-page laminated sheet at Tina. She was holding the menu just off the table with one hand, and tucking her brunette hair behind her ear with the other. Her eyes were looking down at the menu so he couldn't see their color, but he didn't need to see them to know they were hazel. She was dressed modestly in a red blouse that suggested curves more than revealing them. However, looking at her, a memory of the department's Fourth of July party came to mind: She'd worn a white tube-top. Admittedly, even as a married man, he ogled her, wondering exactly what the tube-top was hiding. She looked up from the menu and met his eyes, making him look down.

"You know what you want?" Tina said.

"I'm going with the bacon burger." He was afraid to look back up. He set his menu on the table and took a drink of his beer. Still not looking at her, he said, "What about you?"

"I think I'm going with the taco salad."

"Good choice." Man, was he bad at small talk. It had been entirely too long since he'd had to do it. Sure, she occasionally came out with him and Eric, but he'd always felt comfortable talking with her because he was married, and they were just friends. And Eric had always been there. But now... they *were* just friends, and his divorce papers wouldn't be finalized for who knew how long—but it somehow felt different. And he couldn't help thinking about that party.

Kate had been the love of his life and he'd always thought she was gorgeous—although he'd been bad at expressing that to her—but he'd felt something for Tina. A yearning of sorts. She was, in his opinion, drop-dead gorgeous. Brunette hair, hazel eyes. And despite the way he feigned annoyance when Eric talked about her—no, he *had* been annoyed, or maybe jealous of the idea that Eric had a chance with her and he didn't—he couldn't help but agree that she was gorgeous.

And now he couldn't think of anything to talk to her about. *I'm going to kill you, Eric.*

They sat in awkward silence, sipping their respective beers, until Jill came back and took their order. When she left, Fletcher took another sip of his beer and said, "So, how long have you lived in Prescott?"

"I moved up from Phoenix about six years ago."

"Is that where you're from?"

"Born and raised." Tina lifted her glass and took a drink.

"What made you decide to move up here?"

"Pretty much everyone I knew moved away or got married and had kids, so I was getting bored."

"So you decided to move to sleepy ol' Prescott? You know this is where people come to die, right?"

"Yeah, I know it's a 'retirement community'"—she made air quotes as she said it—"but it has its own little life. Besides, I was sick of the heat."

Fletcher started feeling more at ease. After they were finished with their meals, Tina said, "You wanna grab a couple bottles and take 'em back to my place?"

"Your place?" Fletcher said, looking over his glass, surprised.

"Yeah. You know, so we can fuck."

Fletcher coughed on the beer he was in the midst of swallowing and thumped his chest repeatedly. "What?" he eventually managed to croak.

"I said I want to go back to my place so we c—"

"I heard. I just—"

"Yeah, yeah, I know. You just got a divorce. But tell me right now that you haven't thought about it before."

Fletcher stared at Tina, dumbfounded.

"So?"

She was right. He'd thought about it many times. "Let me get this straight. You're inviting me back to your place because you want to..."

"What? Is that so hard to believe?"

"I..."

Tina flagged the waitress down and said, "Will you add a couple bottles of the IPA to our bill?"

"Sure. Be right back."

The next thing he knew, Fletcher was being led out of Ponderosa's by the hand. Tina walked out the front doors of the mall to her car, which was parked directly across the sidewalk. *Rock-star parking.*

As Tina drove, Fletcher looked over at her. She caught him and smiled.

"What?" she said.

"You're beautiful is all."

"You already said that."

"I did?"

"The other night when I took you home."

"Oh."

"You really think so?"

"I do. I could never say it before because it wouldn't have been proper, but I'm saying it now."

Tina looked over at him again, and said, "Good." With one hand on the wheel, she used the other to start unbuttoning her blouse. She stopped after a couple buttons, which was just enough for Fletcher to catch a glimpse of her bra. He put his hand on her leg, and she placed her hand on top of his.

They walked into her house and she gestured toward the kitchen, saying, "Unless you have any objections, why don't you go put the beer in the fridge."

Fletcher had no objections. He knew exactly what that meant. He walked straight over to the kitchen and put the beer in the fridge. When he turned around, Tina was standing by the couch with her hands at the buttons of her blouse. He walked over to her and she gave him a gentle push, sitting him down. She climbed on top of him, straddling his lap, and finished unbuttoning her blouse. She pulled it open, revealing the black silk bra beneath, then slid the shirt off. She leaned forward and cupped Fletcher's face, one hand on each cheek, and kissed him.

He didn't want to get involved with another woman mere days after he'd signed divorce papers, but he was completely unable to convince himself to stop kissing Tina. Her bra came off, revealing what the hungry part of him secretly wanted. His shirt came off a minute later. He twisted on the couch, falling onto his back with her on top of him. He kissed her with a vigor he hadn't felt in a long time. And then all too quickly she climbed off of him and stood.

He was getting ready to object when she held out her hand. Fletcher took it and Tina led him to her bedroom, the two bottles of beer long forgotten.

CHAPTER 23

October 27th

For the first time in a long time, Fletcher woke up with a smile on his face. It was early, still dark outside. Feeling Tina's warm body next to him, he didn't move, not wanting to wake her. He studied her: the shape of her nose, the curve of her lips, her eyebrows, her eyelashes, her hairline. He imagined her hazel eyes, which always seemed to be smiling. Everything about her was beautiful. He resisted the urge to pull the sheets down and kiss her body all over again like he'd done last night. He wanted to taste her skin again but didn't want to disturb her sleep. Instead, he imagined her smooth skin, the shape of her legs, hips, stomach, breasts—all still fresh in his mind.

As much as Fletcher hated the idea of leaving, he needed to make sure he was on time for work today. He was already on Frey's bad side and didn't want to make it worse. He rolled slowly onto his back, then onto his other side. He slid out from under the sheets, trying his best not to disturb Tina. He gathered his clothes from the floor next to the bed and tiptoed into the bathroom, pulling the door closed behind him.

When he was dressed, he slipped back into Tina's bedroom, using the dim light of his phone as a guide so he wouldn't bump into anything on his way to the door. He hesitated and turned back toward the bed: He couldn't be the guy who slips out in the middle of the night after getting laid. He made his way back to the bed and leaned over Tina. He brushed her hair behind her ear with his fingers then kissed her on the ear.

"Huh?" she said in a stupor.

"I've gotta get going," he whispered. "I'll see you later, okay?"

Tina nodded, turning her head toward him. He kissed her lightly on the lips and said, "Bye."

"Bye," Tina murmured. She was asleep again before he stood up.

Fletcher was smiling as he stood in the chilly air waiting for a taxi. But by the time he was back in his truck, driving toward his empty home in Prescott Valley and thinking more about what had happened, he began feeling guilty. His smile was completely gone by the time he pulled into his driveway. *I shouldn't have done it. Should have waited.* He pulled into the empty spot in the garage—no longer Kate's spot—feeling miserable again. He walked into the dark house, straight to the bedroom, and turned on the shower.

Fletcher went through his morning routine without thinking—or at least, trying not to—and was back in his truck with a mug of coffee half an hour later. He had plenty of time to spare before he had to be in the office, but the last place he wanted to be was at home. There was no point in sitting around being leisurely.

He glanced over at the dispatchers' area as he made his way to his desk, thinking about what he was going to say to Tina when he saw her. It wasn't until he sat at his desk that he remembered that today was her Saturday. A sense of relief washed over him when he realized he wouldn't have to worry about running into her today and facing what was inevitably going to be an awkward situation.

What was the 'morning after you sleep with someone'

expectation? Was it like waiting a few days after a date before you call again? He had always been clueless about social protocols. He remembered blowing it with Kate—or at least his friend Trevor said he had, but she didn't seem to have minded. He was glad he didn't have to actually see Tina today; he figured he could ask Eric how to handle it when he got in. Eric hooked up with women all the time. What did he do after? Eric wasn't really a relationship-type person, but did that mean after hooking up with someone he just ignored them? Wham, bam, thank you ma'am? *NO!* He could *not* mention this to Eric. He would never hear the end of it.

Fletcher logged onto his computer and was pleasantly surprised to find an email from Your Ideal Mate granting him the access requested in the warrant. They also provided an IP address for Sam's account, but unfortunately it appeared as though he was using a VPN to mask his location. *That would have been too easy. Ah well.* He wasted no time in bringing the website up on his browser. He started by entering the supplied username and password and logged into Sam's account. He planned on going through everyone's profiles thoroughly, but he wanted to start with Sam's matches.

He had no "New Matches," four "Active Matches," and fourteen "Closed Matches." The oldest of the closed matches was from September 26. *Huh*, he thought. Fletcher clicked on the first name: a woman named Sherry Gonzalez. They had been matched together at 4:59 pm on the 26th, and Sam closed the match without initiating interactions at 7:20 pm that same evening. Fletcher clicked on the next several matches, all beginning and ending the same. Sam had closed all of them shortly after being matched.

Fletcher looked through all the matches Sam had closed so quickly, looking for a reason why, but couldn't find anything. Almost all of them were attractive and sounded like genuinely interesting people from their profile information. Of all the names listed in the Closed Matches section, the only women he'd actually interacted with were Renee Denovan and Nicole Henricks. And each of them had murdered someone after he'd set up a date with them and then didn't show. Coincidence?

Fletcher clicked on Nicole's profile and found that the match had been closed by Sam on the 22nd, the day after she murdered Hank Michaels—just like he'd closed Renee's match the day after she killed Marlon.

Sam closed both matches, Fletcher thought. *Why? He couldn't have already known what happened to them. Unless he was working with them, that is.*

His thoughts immediately shifted to finding out exactly who Sam was since it was looking more and more like he was somehow involved. An email address was the only contact information on the site for him. There was an option for account verification with a cellphone number, but it had been left blank.

Fletcher loaded the National Crime Information System and the Arizona CIS, and ran a few searches. The only returns were a few MVD listings, but there wasn't anyone in the county with the last name of Gilkons. There were half a dozen hits in Phoenix, as well as a couple down in Tucson, but none of them were named Sam, or any of its variations.

He went back to Sam's profile and looked at his current matches. Without clicking on any of the icons, he could see what stage of interaction Sam was in with each of them. The furthest along was a woman named Trudy Norlin. They were actively engaging in direct communication. He clicked on Trudy's profile and read through their communications. The most recent was from Sam, sent yesterday, in which Sam suggested they meet for coffee at Connie's. Trudy had yet to respond.

Fletcher picked up his coffee mug and sat back in his seat. He took a sip, reflecting on the unsettled feeling growing in his gut. Thus far two women had met Sam Gilkons for a date, neither of which he showed up for, and both of those women had subsequently gone out and murdered someone. Was Sam somehow targeting women? If so, why? What for? Was Trudy next? Or did it make more sense that he was somehow working with the women he interacted with? He looked back through the closed matches. With the exception of Renee and Nicole, Sam had almost immediately closed the matches. Why? Did he not like what they looked like? That didn't make sense; many of them seemed to be just as attractive as Renee and Nicole. He also didn't see any obvious red flags in the information they provided in their profiles. It was almost as if Sam knew in advance who he was going to interact with and who he wasn't.

Did he already know the women he was currently interacting with? And if he did know them, did that mean that they knew each other? Not necessarily, he determined. It was possible he knew them individually, without the women knowing or even being aware of each other. But why would he only match with women he already knew? Wouldn't that defeat the purpose of internet dating? That didn't make sense either.

Other detectives began filtering into the back corner room. Fletcher saw shapes move past him in his peripheral vision—his desk was close to the front—but, completely absorbed in his coffee and train of thought, he didn't acknowledge them. A snapping in front of his face, however, brought him to attention.

"Drifting off already, are you?" Eric said. He was leaning over their desks from his own side, his arm extended out as far as he could reach.

"No. I was just thinking."

"I'm sure you were," Eric said with a wink.

"I'm going to kill you, you know."

Eric sat in his chair and leaned back, then put his feet up on the desk. "So...?"

"So, what?"

"What happened?"

"What happened is I think I'm onto something." He turned his screen so Eric could see it. "Look at this."

Eric whispered, "I meant with Tina."

"We ate dinner and had a few beers. Now, look at this,"

Fletcher said, pointing to the screen.

"That's it?"

Fletcher tapped the monitor. "Look."

"What?" Eric said, leaning forward to get a better look at the monitor.

"Your Ideal Mate complied with the warrant. This is Sam Gilkons' profile—the guy who Renee and Nicole were supposed to meet. He's trying to set up another meeting."

"What time did you get in this morning?"

"Early-ish."

"Did you come straight from her house? You dog."

"Would you pay attention?" Fletcher said. "And no. We don't have much on this guy. The only contact information on his profile is an email address. But so far he's the only connection linking the murders."

"You think Renee and Nicole worked together?"

"Why else would they have identical stories? There's no way two separate murder suspects would randomly come up with the exact same weird stories."

"True. So what're you thinking?" Eric looked intently at the monitor. "You think this... Trudy... might be involved?"

"I don't know. What I *do* know is that so far, both women Sam scheduled a date with have ended up murdering someone." Fletcher sat back in his seat again. He took a sip of coffee and said, "Here's something interesting I noticed about the women he matched with. Look at these closed matches..." Fletcher clicked each name individually. "Notice anything?"

"Give me a hint of what I'm supposed to be looking for, Holmes."

"The dates they were matched, and the dates Sam closed the matches."

"They're all the same date."

"Exactly. And *he* closed every single match."

"So..."

"So? I've never done internet dating before, but don't you

think it's odd that *he* closed every match? Wouldn't the women have closed some of them?"

"Maybe he didn't like them for one reason or another," Eric said.

"Okay, but don't you think it's a bit odd that every match he closed, he closed almost instantly? Without initiating interactions with any of them? I mean, he's either all in, or all out."

Eric bobbed his head. "All right, Sherlock, I guess I see what you're getting at."

"I can understand if he looks at a few of them and closes them, uninterested. But all of them? Shouldn't he have initiated interaction with at least a few of them?"

"Makes sense. But the women didn't initiate any interaction with him either."

"That's because he didn't give them a chance. I mean"— Fletcher clicked through the closed matches again—"in every case he closed the matches within a couple hours or so of being notified of the match. It could be that the women didn't even have a chance to log on and see that they'd been matched with him. I mean, unless they just happened to log in right away."

"So what are you suggesting we do, Merlin?"

"*Merlin?*" Fletcher said with a look over at Eric.

"Yeah. You know, the wizard?"

Fletcher shook his head. "Not sure yet."

"Wanna run it by Sarge?"

"Why not?" Fletcher set his mug on his desk and pushed his chair back. He walked to the office in the corner, Eric following close behind, and knocked on the door. "Hey Sarge," he said, leaning against the jamb. When Frey looked up he said, "May we come in?"

"By all means." Frey waited for Fletcher and Eric to sit then continued, "What's on your mind?"

"The dating site Renee and Nicole used complied with the warrant," Fletcher started, "and I think I might have a lead."

"Go on…"

Fletcher filled Frey in on what he had discovered and what he was thinking.

Frey pursed his lips. "So you think… What's her name again?"

"Trudy Norlin," Fletcher said.

"You think Ms. Norlin might be working with the other two suspects?"

"It's possible. I'd like to find out. Seems like it would make the most sense of their stories."

"If they were working together," Eric interjected, "wouldn't they at least have different stories? They can't be that stupid."

"Unless it was intentional," Fletcher said.

"Well," Frey said, "let's bring her in for questioning."

"Actually," Fletcher said, "what I was thinking is that, if Trudy agrees to meet this Sam guy, we should let the date happen and see if we can't catch them in the act."

CHAPTER 24

October 29th

I still can't believe you fucked her," Eric said. "I didn't know the great Sherlock Holmes was a ladies' man!"

"Would you stop already? It's been three days," Fletcher said. "You'd have already slept with two other women by now."

"I know. But it's *Tina*. And besides, you still haven't said shit about what happened."

"What happened," Fletcher said, taking a sip of his lukewarm coffee and looking out the window of the car, "is that you lied to me. So what makes you think I'm going to tell you anything?"

"Are we still on this? I did it for you."

"Yeah, right."

"You got laid, didn't you?"

Ignoring Eric, Fletcher scanned Connie's parking lot from their spot in the corner. They were backed into their spot and had an unobstructed view of the entrance to the coffee shop.

Eric was right, though, Fletcher knew. Eric's plan *had* resulted in him spending the night with Tina—but it had also created an awkward work situation for him. And he'd completely screwed it up. He'd managed to text Tina minimally during her two days off, but this morning when he ran into her at the office it was nothing but awkwardness. When she saw him walk by, she came over and made like she wanted to hug him, but for some stupid reason he stepped back. They engaged in some idle chitchat, then she returned to her desk. He could tell her feelings were hurt, but he didn't really know how else to handle it. He wasn't ready for another relationship.

"I don't know why you gotta complicate things, Doc," Eric added a few moments later.

"Because I'm not you." Fletcher looked at the time on the dashboard—3:45. It was almost time for Trudy Norlin's date with Sam Gilkons.

When Fletcher and Eric had gone in to talk with Frey, Trudy had yet to respond to Sam's request, but when Fletcher came in to work the next morning her reply was in. She agreed, at his suggestion, to meet for coffee at Connie's at four o'clock on Thursday. The pattern was becoming obvious. A date at Connie's was their alibi. But if they were working together, why would they plan the murders so they all had the same alibi? It didn't make sense. Well, it did actually—not all criminals are smart. If they were indeed working together the smart thing would be to have a unique alibi for each murder. But he still didn't know who Sam Gilkons was, or if he was even real. Fletcher had thus far been unable to turn anything up on him.

After seeing the date confirmation, Fletcher spent some time looking into Trudy before he had to meet with Scott Stephens to prepare for Nicole Henricks' upcoming grand jury. The case itself would be pretty much a slam dunk since they'd already convinced the grand jury to indict Renee Denovan under practically the exact same circumstances. What wasn't a slam dunk was what he discovered about Trudy: not much.

Trudy Norlin was a twenty-five-year-old receptionist at Blake's Dentistry. Her name didn't appear in either Renee or Nicole's phones. They didn't appear to be connected on social media either. He had found nothing that suggested Trudy knew either Renee or Nicole. He hadn't even found anything that connected Renee and Nicole. There was nothing connecting *any* of them—except Sam Gilkons, a person who, as far as he could determine, didn't even live in the Prescott area.

"There she is," Eric said. "One o'clock moving toward Connie's."

Fletcher looked over to where Eric indicated. The tall red-headed woman walking across the parking lot matched Trudy's profile picture on YIM to a tee. He looked down at the clock on the dash—3:56—then watched her enter Connie's.

About an hour prior to the scheduled meeting, Eric and Fletcher had both gone into Connie's and ordered coffee before settling into their unmarked car. While they waited, they looked around to see if anyone resembling Sam was already in the shop, but didn't see anyone matching his description. Patrons entered and left the shop while they waited in their car, but none of them were Sam.

"If she's in on this," Fletcher said, thinking aloud, "she should come back out in half an hour or so."

"Should I go in and have a look around?" Eric said.

"Nah. We already have eyes inside with the surveillance system Connie has. If we need it, we can get it."

"Ugh. With you unwilling to kiss and tell, all this sitting around is boring."

"What did you think being a detective would be like?" Fletcher said.

"I don't know. I mean, I knew it was boring most of the time… I guess I just secretly hoped it wouldn't be."

"Sorry to disappoint."

"It wouldn't be if you'd be a little less of a prude."

"It's called respect."

"*Respect?* What respect?"

"Do I really have to explain it to you?"

"Yes."

"Sorry to disappoint."

They passed the time largely in silence after that. Eric didn't know what to do with his hands, since Fletcher wouldn't let him text while they waited. It seemed the only thing Eric thought interesting enough to talk about was his night with Tina. He'd certainly enjoyed himself and was still in complete shock that it had happened—Tina, in his opinion, could do much better than him. He just wished it had been under different circumstances. The whole thing left him feeling conflicted—guilty, even. He still loved Kate. And he couldn't believe that they were divorced. Even the *word* "divorced" made him feel wrong. And although he knew Tina understood where he was coming from, he couldn't help but feel he had messed things up even more by sleeping with her.

The sight of Trudy exiting Connie's was a welcome relief for Fletcher. The idleness had been sending his mind in circles. "Here we go," he said.

Fletcher waited until Trudy was in her car, a red SUV, then started the engine. When she pulled out of her parking spot, he pulled out as well and followed behind her. She turned onto Sheldon Street toward Pawn Paradise, where Renee had bought her gun. He reported their position over the radio, so the strategically placed patrol cars could move to follow. He kept a comfortable distance behind Trudy, but when she drove past the pawnshop, he closed the distance a little so he wouldn't lose her at a light.

At the junction of Sheldon and Gurley, Trudy turned left onto Gurley, then followed it to the right when it turned into Highway 69. As they continued, he kept their position updated with the participating officers. When they reached the Prescott city limits Fletcher knew their plan had just become a little more complicated, but fortunately they'd planned for this possibility. They had already coordinated with the Prescott Valley PD, and they, too, had officers standing by in case they were needed.

They drove past the mall, following the winding highway through the hills to Prescott Valley. Trudy made a left turn at the second light upon entering Prescott Valley then an immediate right onto the frontage road.

Instead of following her, Fletcher drove through the light then pulled off on the side of the road. They watched Trudy's car pull into the parking lot of Prescott Valley Pawn.

"Looks like it's happening," Fletcher said. He picked up the hand mic and said, "We're on scene at Prescott Valley Pawn. All units on frequency, prepare for an armed red-headed woman, five-foot-four, and possible shooting at unknown location."

"Adam Ten is available at 69 and Glassford," a voice said over the radio.

That's just ahead, Fletcher thought.

"Adam Fifteen is available at Glassford and 89," another voice said.

"Adam Five is available at 69 and Robert."

Good. No matter which way Trudy went when she left the pawnshop, they should be covered.

Half an hour later Trudy emerged and got into her car. She pulled out of the parking lot, turned left, and drove down the frontage road.

"Suspect driving east on frontage in a red SUV," Fletcher said over the radio. He shifted the car back into drive and started driving down the shoulder. He pulled out into the traffic, and lost sight of Trudy as the road curved and she drove behind a building. "I've lost sight of her," he said.

"Suspect in sight," Adam Ten said. "Turning left onto Glassford."

"Ten-four," Fletcher said. He accelerated, flipping on the car's lights. He signaled for a left turn as he approached the intersection of Glassford and 69, pulling into the turn lane. The light was red, but he inched into the intersection as the cross traffic saw him and stopped.

Turning onto Glassford, Fletcher turned the lights off and punched the accelerator. The road curved right, then left, then Trudy's car came back into view. "I've got visual," he said over the radio.

Fletcher followed Trudy as she drove down the four-lane divided thoroughfare. A police car was visible in his rearview mirror, tailing him from a distance.

After a few miles, Glassford ended at Highway 89A. "Suspect approaching 89," he said over the radio when the crossing highway came into view. They passed a subdivision on the right, and Fletcher saw a police car sitting on the side of the road fifty yards into the subdivision.

Trudy turned right onto the onramp.

"Suspect entering highway eastbound."

"Adam Five en route to Robert and 89," Adam Five said over the radio.

Fletcher slowed to allow a little space to build between his car and Trudy's before he turned onto the highway to follow. He pulled onto 89 and accelerated. Trudy was visible a few hundred yards ahead. After a little over a mile, she signaled and exited the highway. "Suspect turning left onto Viewpoint," Fletcher said.

He turned left at the light and followed a little closer as the road wound into a subdivision. A couple of miles in, she turned right onto a side street. Her car was still in view as Fletcher neared the intersection, so he slowed down and pulled off on the shoulder. The red SUV stopped. A moment later, Trudy emerged with a purse slung over her body.

"We're on scene at North Viewpoint and"—Fletcher looked at the street sign—"Courage Butte. Suspect exited car and is proceeding on foot." He turned to Eric and said, "Let's go."

Fletcher climbed out of his vehicle and saw two police cars approaching from behind. He started jogging down Courage Butte, drawing his gun as he ran. There were several houses in various stages of construction on the street, and the street was littered with construction debris and large waste bins.

Trudy stopped in front of one of the houses in the framing process. She reached into her purse.

Fletcher broke into a sprint. When he drew near, he slowed to a walk, raised his gun, and shouted, "Trudy!"

Eric stopped next to him, his gun up as well.

The red-headed woman turned around. Her eyes went wide, and she pulled her hand slowly from her purse, showing it was empty, before raising them above her head.

"Drop the purse!" Fletcher shouted.

Officers appeared in Fletcher's peripheral vision, guns drawn.

Trudy lowered one arm, lifted the purse strap over her head, and dropped it to the ground.

"On your knees!" Fletcher shouted.

Trudy put her arm back above her head then lowered herself to her knees.

Fletcher and the other officers approached. He put a hand out to his side and said, "Stop. Put your guns away." He waited for the others to holster their weapons, but kept his own aimed. "Trudy?" Trudy looked up at him. "My name is Detective Wise. What are you—"

Trudy let out a piercing scream. Her arms lowered to her stomach. She pushed herself into a crouch, then, extending her hand toward Fletcher and the officers, she started moving backward. She took a few hunched steps, then fell onto her bottom.

"Wait right here," Fletcher said to the officers. He holstered his gun and motioned for Eric to follow. Construction workers had stopped working and were watching them.

Fletcher picked up the purse and knelt next to Trudy. She looked at him, tears streaming down her face and fear in her eyes. "Trudy, what are you doing here?"

"I don't know. I…"

Fletcher looked inside the purse and found a gun. "You what?" he said, looking back at her.

"I don't know!" She looked around and started sobbing. "I… what happened?"

"What do you mean?"

"How did I…?" She looked around again. "Where am I?"

"You don't know where you are?" Fletcher said.

"No, I..."

"Here," Fletcher said, holding out his hand. "Let me help you up."

Trudy took Fletcher's hand and he pulled her to her feet. "Are you all right?"

"Yeah. I think so. I just..."

Fletcher reached into Trudy's purse and pulled out a .45-caliber handgun. "I don't suppose this is yours?"

Trudy's eyes went wide, and she immediately started shaking her head back and forth. "I've never seen... I don't own a..."

"You didn't just buy this?"

Trudy shook her head again. "No."

Fletcher looked at Eric, who shrugged his shoulders. He felt as confused as Trudy seemed to be. Was she acting? She had to be. The alternative was impossible. "What were you doing at the pawnshop then?"

"What pawnshop?" She looked from him to Eric, then past them at the officers standing behind him. "Who are you? What's going on?"

"Detective Wise," Fletcher repeated. "And this is Detective Harris."

"What happened to me?"

"What do you mean?"

"I... I went to Connie's Coffee Shop, then..."

Fletcher wanted to finish for her when she stopped, but he also wanted to hear what she had to say. "Then what?" he finally prodded.

"Then I... I was..." She stopped and started crying.

"Trudy? Are you all right?"

"I... I'm so scared."

Fletcher looked at her, confused. "Scared of what?"

"I don't know..." Trudy looked around her again. "I just want to go home." She looked over at her car then started walking toward it.

Fletcher stopped her. "Trudy..." She hadn't actually done anything illegal, but only, as far as he was concerned, because they had intervened. She was connected to Renee and Nicole somehow, and since her arrival at Connie's, she had followed in their exact footsteps. He couldn't simply let her go without questioning her. She looked at him expectantly. "Do you mind if I take you back to the station and ask you a few questions?" It wasn't really a request. He needed to question her.

"About what?" She looked around nervously.

"About what happened today."

"I don't understand. What about my car?"

"You don't have to worry about it. We'll take care of it."

Trudy looked around nervously for a bit, then nodded.

Fletcher led her down the road to his car, then helped her into the back seat. He closed the door, then turned to Eric, who had followed him back to the car, and said, "You mind staying and interviewing these workers? See if we can figure out who the target was?"

Eric nodded. "Sure thing, Seer."

"Seer?" Fletcher said. "That's a bit of a stretch, don't you think?"

Eric shrugged his shoulders and walked away.

"And stop by the pawnshop too, would ya?" Fletcher said.

Eric held both arms straight out to his sides with his thumbs up as he walked away.

Fletcher was certainly no seer. If he had the ability to see into the future, he would already know what was going on with these women—the evidence of their collusion would already be revealed. *And* he would have known what was happening between him and Kate.

No. Whatever he was, he was definitely not a seer.

CHAPTER 25

Trudy!" a voice shouted.

Gabe turned around and saw two men dressed in business casual approaching with guns drawn.

Shit.

The urge to flee overwhelmed him, but he resisted.

Who are they?

What are they doing here?

Realizing the men didn't know who Gabe was, he pulled his hand from Trudy's purse. He was safe—he could linger a moment longer to find out what was happening. He showed his hand to the two men so they could see it was empty, then raised both hands above his head.

"Drop the purse!" the man on the right shouted.

He saw the badges hooked to their belts.

Cops. Are they undercover? But how could they…?

Three police officers approached from behind the two men. They had their guns drawn as well.

Gabe lowered one arm, lifted the purse strap over his head, and dropped it to the ground.

The man who had spoken previously shouted, "On your knees!"

He lifted Trudy's arms back above her head then sank awkwardly toward the ground, the miniskirt making it difficult. *How do women wear these things?* He had to find out who they were or he was screwed.

The undercover cops and uniformed officers approached. The first man put his hands out to his sides and said, "Stop. Put your guns away."

Gabe watched them, thinking, forcing himself to resist the urge to flee. Everyone holstered their guns, except the undercover cop who had been giving orders.

"Trudy?" the man said. "My name is Detective Wise."

That's all I needed to know.

"What are you—"

Gabe shifted back to his own body. Darkness enveloped him.

"Shit. Shit. Shit. Shit."

He felt around in the dark until he found the corner. He stood up on the tips of his toes and found the key taped to the wall. He pulled it free, then, with a hand against the wall, found the doorknob.

Gabe walked up the stairs and into the kitchen. Somehow a detective had caught on to what he was doing.

He paced back and forth between the table at one end of the room and the wall at the other, trying to figure out how the cops could possibly have known where he would be. Who was Detective Wise? They weren't following him; they'd been following Trudy. Why?

They must have figured out the connection between the three broads. It was the only link between them.

Gabe went into his bedroom and sat at his computer. When the monitor woke up, he opened the internet browser and logged into his Your Ideal Mate account. He navigated to the account settings screen and found the link to close his account. He hesitated, tapping the mouse with his forefinger. If he closed it, he wouldn't be able to accomplish everything he had planned.

But this Detective Wise must have figured out the link connecting Renee, Nicole, and Trudy. Why else would he have been there? He knew who Trudy was. And they had acted like they knew what he was about to do. If they already knew enough to find him, they knew too much. He had to consider Sam Gilkons compromised. As much as he hated to do it, Gabe clicked the "Close Account" button.

"Are you sure you want to close your account with Your Ideal Mate?" a popup message said.

Gabe hovered the mouse over the "yes" button and clicked.

"Would you mind sharing why you are leaving YIM?" another popup message said.

Gabe read through the list of answers and thought, *Because you only matched me with superficial bitches, that's why.* He selected the "other" option and was greeted with a final message, "Your account is now closed."

Angry that his high had been interrupted, Gabe pushed his chair back and laid in his bed. He'd been denied the satisfaction of killing Tanner, but at least he'd gotten to experience being a woman again. He closed his eyes and replayed his visit to the bathroom at Connie's.

It was dark outside when he woke. His high was completely gone. He had nothing now. He was back to square one. After Nicole, he had managed to limp to his next high by attending Marls' funeral on Saturday, and attending the store meeting at Book World when the management team brought in grief counselors. Consoling Jenny at the funeral had brought him great pleasure, as had watching his stupid coworkers sob throughout the meeting. But now he was back to where he'd been before this all started. With his Your Ideal Mate account closed, and Jenny deciding to go to a motel instead of "imposing" on him anymore, what was he supposed to do? How was he supposed to get his next high?

Gabe rolled out of bed and went into his living room. He needed to think. He grabbed a bag of chips from the kitchen counter, plopped into his chair, and turned on the TV. He needed a new plan. But he also had a new threat: Detective Wise. He couldn't accomplish what he wanted with a cop snooping in his business. If he was going to continue, to do what he wanted to do, to become who he wanted to be, the threat needed to be neutralized.

CHAPTER 26

Fletcher stood outside the interrogation room and looked through the one-way glass at Trudy Norlin. The ride back to the station had passed in silence, but he'd watched her through the rear-view mirror. Her body visibly trembled. She kept her arms tight against her body—one wrapped across her stomach, her hand gripping the elbow of the other arm, which she held against her chest with that hand pressed against her neck. Her demeanor had not improved after he'd put her in the room. She was obviously frightened. The question, though, was why? Was it because she had been caught?

"So?" Sergeant Frey said, walking up to him. He looked through the glass and said, "How'd it go?"

"Exactly as I thought it would. After arriving at Connie's, she left by herself, went to Prescott Valley Pawn, then drove to a construction site in the Viewpoint subdivision on the north side of PV. We found a gun in her purse, which she claims isn't hers."

"What about that other nonsense? The 'dark room' thing?"

"She hasn't mentioned it yet," Fletcher said.

"You interrogate her yet?"

"No. I brought her in but haven't decided how to proceed.

Eric stayed back at the site to see if he could figure out who the intended target was."

"Good," Frey said. "If you ask me, there's evidence enough to show that she's working with those other two gals, so whatever you decide, I want it to end with her being booked."

"On what charges?"

"You're the wise guy so figure it out."

Fletcher nodded.

Frey walked away, leaving Fletcher standing alone, looking in at Trudy. She was now chewing on one of her nails. The only angle he could really settle on was just to be straight with her. Let her know she was going to be charged and hope that she talked.

He opened the door and went in. Trudy looked up at him as he entered, the fear in her eyes evident. He placed her purse on the table and said, "Could you please, for the record, state your name?"

"T-Trudy Norlin."

"And how old are you, Trudy?"

"Twenty-five."

"What's your home address?"

"701 Sanctuary Road. What exactly am I doing here, Detective?"

"Ten days ago, a woman by the name of Renee Denovan walked into a house off Watson Lake and shot a man in his home. Eight days ago, another woman, Nicole Henricks, walked into Book World and shot one of their employees. Both victims died."

"I-I read about that on the news," Trudy said. "Why are you telling me?"

"What were you doing at Connie's Coffee Shop?"

"I… I went there for a date."

"Did you know that, before murdering their victims, both of the women I mentioned *also* went to Connie's for a date?"

Trudy shook her head.

"Could you please state your answer?"

"No."

"They were meeting someone they met on Your Ideal Mate." Fletcher stopped, waiting for a reaction from Trudy. She simply stared at him, blank-faced. "Only their date didn't show. Did your date show?"

Trudy shook her head again and said, "No."

"Both of them left Connie's and proceeded to a pawnshop where they purchased a handgun," Fletcher continued. "Renee murdered a man in his home and Nicole murdered someone in the bookstore.

"The reason I'm telling you this is because we watched you go into Connie's a few minutes before four. You emerged about half an hour later and drove straight to Prescott Valley Pawn where you likely purchased the gun we found in your purse—I'll know that for certain in the very near future. You left the pawnshop and drove to a construction site in the Viewpoint subdivision. I watched you get out of your car, with your purse in hand and approach one of the houses being built." Fletcher paused and watched Trudy as she shook her head in small rapid shakes. "Were you planning on murdering someone at that site, Trudy?"

"No!" Trudy said, looking up at Fletcher. "I'm telling you the truth, Detective. I... I didn't buy that gun. I don't even know how I got out there. I don't even know where *there* is! I hardly ever go out to PV. Last I remember I was..."

"You were what?" Fletcher said, when Trudy stopped talking.

"I was at Connie's Coffee Shop. You say I left, but I didn't. I never got up out of my seat."

"I watched you walk out and get into your SUV."

Trudy shook her head. "One minute I was there, the next I was..."

"You were what?"

"Somehow... somehow I was in a... a dark room."

"A dark room?" He knew what she was going to say, but he played dumb just so he could get her to actually say it.

"I don't know. I was sitting at the table, then I wasn't. I was in a dark room. I couldn't see anything."

"Just like that?"

"Yes. Just like that."

"So you just teleported there?"

"I... I don't know. All I know is that one minute I was sitting at a table in Connie's waiting for my date to arrive then... then I was in a dark room. And Detective..."

"Yeah?"

"There's something else."

"What?" *Let me guess; you were a man.*

"I... I wasn't myself."

Yep. "What do you mean?"

"I know this sounds crazy, but I swear I'm telling the truth: While I was in that room, I was... I wasn't myself. I was"— Trudy shivered visibly—"a man."

Fletcher sat back in his chair. *Yep, they're colluding.* "The problem, Trudy, is that your story... it's the *exact* story both Renee and Nicole told. And we have video footage of them walking out of Connie's and *not* somehow being magically transported to a 'dark room.' We have proof that they both purchased handguns the very day they used them to murder someone. We have proof that they were both the ones who pulled the trigger. And I watched you walk into Connie's, walk *out* of Connie's, drive to a pawnshop where you likely purchased a gun, then drive to a location where you were probably going to murder someone."

"But I didn't murder anyone—"

"Because we stopped you." Fletcher sat back up in his chair.

"I would *never* murder anyone!"

"Based on the evidence, we have every reason to believe you were about to."

"What are you saying, Detective?"

"I'm saying that, once we get the video footage from Connie's and the bill of sale from Prescott Valley Pawn, we'll have evidence that rather closely resembles evidence we have against Renee and Nicole."

Tina's eyes went wide. "You have to believe me! I would never murder someone! I don't even know who Renee and Nicole are!"

"Does the name Sam Gilkons sound familiar?" Fletcher said.

"How do you...?"

"So it does?"

"Yes. How do you know that name?"

"Because both Renee and Nicole were supposedly meeting Sam Gilkons for coffee right before they committed their murders. Just like you."

"I... I want to speak to a lawyer," Trudy said.

"All right," Fletcher said. He was surprised that one of them had finally lawyered up. "But we'll soon be able to prove that you bought that gun today. It won't be hard for our prosecutor to connect the dots of similarity between the other murders. They're facing trial for murder, but you... you have the opportunity to plead a lower charge. Attempted murder isn't as bad as what they're facing, but you'll still see some time behind bars. If you cooperate, it might not have to be that way."

"Attempted murder?" Trudy said, looking up. "But I didn't attempt to murder anyone. I'm telling you detective, that gun isn't mine. Something happened today—I can't explain it—but something happened!"

Fletcher pushed his seat back and rose to his feet. "If you cooperate and tell us what's going on—why you, Renee, and Nicole are doing what you're doing—you might not have to go to prison like them. It's up to you."

He hated playing bad cop but sometimes it was necessary. Trudy was rattled. Enough pressure and she would spill the beans. He waited a moment to see if she had anything else to say. But she just sat there, staring at the table. All he needed to do now was wait, to give her time to think about what she was facing.

Fletcher walked out of the room.

CHAPTER 27

October 30th

Fletcher sat at his desk staring blankly at the screen. His mind kept replaying the awkward exchange he'd had with Tina yesterday instead of focusing on the video footage of Trudy's visit to Connie's.

Tina normally worked four ten-hour shifts—Friday through Monday—and got in at 7:00 am, a few hours before he was required to be at his desk. But she'd picked up a shift on Thursday, and it had surprised him when he'd shown up at work and passed her as she was returning to her desk from the break room. The coolness of his responses to her texts over the last three days had had their effect. His pulse increased when he saw her, but he quickly averted his eyes, wanting to avoid a conversation with her. It worked. She walked by him without stopping, but he could sense that she wanted to talk.

He picked up his phone and looked at the text she'd sent about ten minutes after he sat at his desk: *I'm sorry, Fletch. I shouldn't have been so forward. Can we please go back to the way it was before?*

He hadn't responded yet.

You're such an idiot, he thought, setting his phone down and looking back at the monitor. *Why can't you be more like Eric?* "Because I'm not," he said.

"Huh?" Eric said.

"What?" His eyes focused on the screen for a second before he looked over at Eric.

"You said something."

"I don't know." He looked back at the screen, dragging the progress bar of the video back. Checking the time in the corner of the monitor, he saw that he still had a few minutes before he had to leave for Nicole Henricks' grand jury session at the courthouse. Everything was in order there so, wanting to clear his head of Tina so he wouldn't be distracted in court, he refocused his attention as best he could on Trudy's case. Fortunately they basically had Connie's Coffee on speed dial by now, and were able to get the footage they needed of Trudy's visit quickly.

It wasn't a slam dunk like Renee's and Nicole's cases were, but they had video footage of Trudy's visit to Connie's, and a copy of the bill of sale from Prescott Valley Pawn for the gun she'd bought—two eerily similar coincidences to both Renee's and Nicole's actions. They also had a list of every construction worker present at the site Trudy had approached yesterday with her newly purchased gun. "So no one at the site recognized Trudy?" he said.

"Nope."

"Then who was she going to murder?" Along with motive, that was another answer they needed to find.

"Your guess is as good as mine. Better, probably."

"You come up with any other connections between the three of them yet?"

"Have you?"

"No."

"So we're stuck at Sam fucking Gilkons and their lame ass stories."

"Which is enough, I think, to prevent the judge from

dismissing Trudy's charges." Fletcher logged off his computer and gathered his material for Nicole's hearing. "Her lawyer's demanding we let her go so if we want to keep her through the weekend we need to get the judge's orders."

"Yes, Boss," Eric said.

Fletcher looked up at Eric. "What? You've exchanged witty nicknames for sarcasm?"

"I wasn't being sarcastic."

"Boss?"

"You don't like Boss? What about Go-to Guy?"

Fletcher shook his head and snapped his briefcase closed. He snatched it off his desk and left the detectives' room, glancing over at the dispatchers as he passed. He didn't see Tina.

He hated the position they were in. He shouldn't have slept with her. She had insisted back at Ponderosa's that they were just friends but no matter what people say, things are never the same after you sleep together. And the awkward exchange they'd had when they ran into each other this morning proved it.

He tried to put it out of his mind—he needed to focus on Nicole's grand jury hearing.

* * *

"How'd it go?" Eric said when Fletcher returned and set his briefcase on his desk.

"We got the indictment," Fletcher said.

"That's good. Hey, it's Friday. You wanna bug out early and get a beer?"

"You get that complaint to the judge?"

"I did."

"And?"

"He agreed to hold her on five hundred K."

"Then, yes. A beer sounds like an excellent idea."

Fletcher put his briefcase away, then followed Eric out of the station.

"Why didn't you invite Tina?" Eric said as they crossed the parking lot.

"For one, she wasn't even there, and two, do I need a reason?"

"I thought you guys hooked up."

"We did."

"And?"

"And nothing. I'll see you over there, all right?" Fletcher said. "And Eric..."

"Yeah?"

"If you're not there when I get there—"

"Yeah, yeah, yeah."

Normally he would only have a couple of beers, then head home to eat dinner with his wife, but since he didn't have a wife to go home to anymore, he ate at Ponderosa's. He liked their food, so he couldn't think of a reason not to.

"You wanna go down to CJ's with me tonight?" Eric said through a mouthful of burger.

"Really?"

Eric swallowed and said, "Yeah."

"You know that place is for college kids, right?"

"Yeah. And?"

"We're not... never mind."

"So? Do you?"

"I don't think so. It's been a long week, so I think I'll just call it a night." Fletcher finished his beer then signaled to Jill that he was ready for his bill.

"So, what's the deal with Tina?"

"There is no 'deal.' I just don't want to date anyone right now."

"Who said anything about dating?"

"I... look, I don't have to explain myself to you, all right? Besides, I'm still annoyed at you for what you did."

"What I did was get you laid."

"I'm perfectly capable of looking after myself."

When Jill delivered the check, Fletcher dug some cash out of his pocket and laid it on the plastic tray. "See ya Monday," he said as he stood to leave.

"You know where to find me if you change your mind," Eric said.

Truth was, he didn't want to go home. He used to look forward to his weekends with Kate. It had been one of the many reasons he'd decided to become a detective—it afforded him the opportunity to have more regular hours. True, there were nights he was on call and times he had to work odd hours—such as the night Marlon Williams was murdered—but the hours were much better than being on a beat. But now there was nothing for him at home but an empty house.

Kate had been extremely quick about moving her stuff out. The house was virtually empty. She'd left him the bed, the couch, the TV, and a few other pieces of furniture. She must have had a mover come while he was away; he'd left for work one morning, and when he got home that evening everything was gone. He hadn't even bothered to text Kate about it.

He pulled out of the rear parking lot, turning left onto Montezuma. He turned left onto Gurley at the light and at Cortez he turned right, deciding that he did not, in fact, want to go home. He also wasn't interested in hitting on college girls with Eric, so he decided to go back to the station and see if he could make some sense of the Denovan, Henricks, and Norlin cases.

The second floor was dark, with everyone except the dispatchers gone for the night. He glanced over at the dispatchers' area as he passed and saw Tina sitting at her desk. *Did she switch to swings?* She was talking into the headset and typing on the keyboard. He stopped at the doorway separating the dispatchers from the detectives and looked back at her. God, she was beautiful. And he really liked her company. Why did he have to be such an idiot? Maybe Eric was right. Maybe they could see each other casually without officially "dating."

Tina didn't notice him in the darkened room, so he watched her for a bit, then went to his desk. Leaving the lights off, he sat down and logged onto the computer. The only link he had so far between the three women—two accused of murder, and the third probably interrupted on her way to commit murder—was Sam Gilkons. He opened the Your Ideal Mate website and entered the credentials for Sam Gilkons' account.

A message in red letters popped up: "Invalid username or password."

Fletch furrowed his brow and re-entered Sam's credentials, which he had already memorized.

"Invalid username or password."

He tried it a third time.

Same message.

"Huh," he said. He typed the username and password slowly to make sure he was getting it right, but got the same message. Had the password been changed? He logged into Renee's profile instead. When it loaded, he clicked the Closed Matches link, then clicked on Sam Gilkons' profile. Even after someone closed a match, the person's basic profile information was still viewable—but when Sam's page loaded, he received the message, "This account has been closed."

"Dammit," he said to himself.

He stared at the screen for a moment then realized something: Renee, Nicole, and Trudy were all in custody. None of them could have closed the account.

This whole time he'd been trying to figure out if they were working together, but hadn't found a link between them—except Sam Gilkons. They had all been matched to Sam. And now his account was closed, which meant there *was* someone behind it. Sam Gilkons actually existed.

Even if Renee, Nicole, or Trudy had been using Sam as an alias, they couldn't have possibly closed the account. There had to be someone else. But who? And how was he going to find them now that Sam's account was closed?

Facing a dead end, Fletcher sent an email to the site administrators requesting a list of the remaining women Sam had been matched with, as well as the date and time the account had been closed. Then he directed his attention to the list of construction workers.

He cross-referenced the names to the men Renee and Nicole had been matched with on YIM, but none of the names stood out. He would have to wait until the website responded to his request for access to Trudy's account to see if any of the names matched the people she had matched with. He also called the construction company's office and left them a voicemail. Hopefully he could coordinate interviews for all the men on the list early Monday. Until then, they were just a list of names.

Fletcher thought about going home but couldn't shake the desire to make some sort of a breakthrough. His stupid idiosyncrasy of needing immediate resolution, which had always driven Kate crazy, kicked in. Now that he knew there was another party involved, he wanted to know who it was.

With nowhere else to turn, he loaded the surveillance video of Trudy from Connie's. He watched the video at 5X speed, then loaded the other two videos and watched them all simultaneously. Trudy's visit to the coffee shop didn't differ much from Renee's or Nicole's except that she spent about ten minutes in the bathroom before she left. After watching them through a few times he started them all over. They all started at different times in the day, but they all began an hour before each of their respective dates was scheduled to begin.

He watched each video in 2X time; it was fast enough to save time but not so fast that he missed what was happening. He'd watched them all before, but he knew there had to be something he was missing—some sort of clue to link the three women together. He sat back in his chair, put his feet up on the corner of his desk, and watched as patrons came and left Connie's at twice the speed.

All three videos played simultaneously in their own windows. He made it through them once, but partway through the second time his eyelids suddenly got heavy. He nodded a couple of times, then startled awake when someone shook his shoulder and said his name.

"Sorry," Tina said. "I didn't mean to startle you."

Fletcher yawned and shook his head.

"What are you still doing here?"

"I didn't really want to go home so I came back after dinner. Must have fallen asleep."

"Considering I heard you snoring from my desk, I'd say so."

Fletcher fumbled for his phone and asked, "What time is it?"

"Eleven-thirty."

"Oy," he said. He slid his feet off the desk and sat up. He looked up at Tina's silhouette and said, "Why're you still here?"

"I switched with Terrance to help him out." Tina sat on the edge of the desk where his feet had just been and said, "Fletch?"

"Yeah?"

"Can we please stop being awkward with each other?"

"Tina, I'm sorry. I just don't—"

"Want to date anyone right now, I know. Neither do I."

"So what happened..."

"Was just sex. We've already been over this. So we fucked—who cares? I know you're in the middle of a divorce and obviously aren't looking to date anyone. I still made the decision I did."

"I—"

"Wait here just a second," Tina said. She pushed herself off the desk, darting agilely through the door dividing the dispatchers from the detectives. Fletcher watched, wondering where she was going. She returned a minute later and held out her hand. "Here."

He opened his hand, and she dropped a key into it. "What's this?"

"The key to my place. And no, I'm not asking you to move in with me. But you did say you didn't want to go home—so I'm offering you somewhere else to go."

"You want me to go to your place?"

"My bed's comfortable, isn't it? I don't get off until six, so it's not being used right now. And... if you can get over your weirdness about sex, maybe I'll wake you up when I get off."

"You're serious?"

"I wouldn't be offering if I wasn't."

Fletcher looked up at Tina in disbelief.

"Take it," she said.

Fletcher nodded.

"Now, go get some sleep. I'll see you in the morning."

CHAPTER 28

November 2nd

As much as Fletcher hated to admit it, Eric was right. The thought of dating someone was the furthest thing from his mind, but that didn't mean he had to wallow in self-pity either. So long as Tina kept to her end of the agreement, there was no reason they shouldn't be able to be friends—or "friends." It had been months since he and Kate had slept together, but at the same time he wasn't Eric—he wasn't interested in hooking up with someone he'd just met at CJ's. But Tina wasn't just someone. The only regret he felt about spending the weekend with her was that Eric would never let him hear the end of it if he found out. He could never know.

He arrived at work Monday morning early, refreshed. It was a new month. The hell that had been October was behind him. He didn't normally make New Year's resolutions, but in this case, he felt as though he'd broken free from the old and started new. He loved Kate, and probably always would, but she'd decided it was over between them. And now that it *was* over, he planned to only look forward.

He had a lot of interviews to conduct prior to Trudy's upcoming grand jury, but he couldn't actually get started on them until the construction company office opened. He fired up the videos again instead. It didn't take long before his mind started to wander, though. He couldn't help but think about his weekend.

He'd fallen asleep almost instantly when he'd crawled into Tina's bed late Friday night. Or had it been early Saturday morning? The smell of her on the pillows had lulled him into a sense of calm that washed over his tired body and sent him straight to the land of slumber. He woke some time later to kisses on his chest. It had taken him a moment to gather his senses, but when he'd opened his eyes and saw Tina lying next to him, he said, "What time is it?"

"Kissing time," Tina said.

"Kissing time?"

"What?"

"Nothing. I've just never heard that phrase before." He slid his arm under Tina and pulled her closer to him.

Tina nuzzled in close. "I know you're probably going to laugh, but I read it in a book."

"Oh yeah? What book?"

"Just this fantasy novel I read."

"Fantasy? You mean like orcs and elves and such?"

"Yeah, but there were no elves or orcs in this particular book."

Fletcher smiled.

"What?" Tina said.

"It's just... I haven't done this in a really long time."

"What? Kiss?"

"Get to know someone. I didn't know you liked fantasy books."

"Yeah. I'm looking forward to it... I mean, if you are."

"If we take it slow. I mean, I just—"

Tina put her hand over Fletcher's mouth. "We'll take it as slow as you like."

Fletcher pulled her hand down and kissed her.

"And what kind of books do you like?" Tina said after the kiss ended.

"Actually, I'm not much of a reader," Fletcher admitted.

"Okay, then if you did read, what would it be?"

"I mean, if I was forced to read, I guess I'd pick a crime novel or something."

"Seriously? A crime novel?"

"What?"

"Nothing."

"Oh, I get it. I'm a detective, so it'd be 'cliché' or something for me to read crime novels?" Fletcher said. "Who knows, maybe I'd learn something."

"I thought you were the Wizard?"

"That's just a stupid game the other detectives play because of my name. I'm not any better than anyone else. Which reminds me—if we're going to do this, no stupid nicknames. I get enough of that at work."

"Whatever you say, Smart-ass," Tina said. She threw the sheets back and climbed on top of Fletcher.

They slept in until almost noon. It was Saturday, but Tina had errands to run before she had to be at work that evening. As she was about to leave, she asked Fletcher, "What are you planning on doing this afternoon?"

"The weather's almost as gorgeous as you, so I thought I'd ride my bike."

"Will you be wearing those stretchy shorts?"

"Biker shorts, you mean? I will."

"You mind riding by the station so I can see?"

"Don't make fun," Fletcher said, "or I'll be sure to make fun of you when you're wearing them."

"I don't ride bikes."

"Maybe you will one day."

"Oh?"

"I'm reminded of an old adage," Fletcher said. "The best thing about cycling, besides its obvious health benefits, is the hours of opportunity to get to know someone better."

"Old adage? Isn't that kind of redundant?"

"As redundant as a French baguette. Will I see you tonight?"

"I don't know. Will you?"

"I thought maybe I'd come by again tonight."

"I don't get off until—"

"Six am, I know."

"I thought we were going to take it slow?"

Fletcher still had reservations about getting involved with Tina, but he was perfectly fine being nonchalant with her.

"We are," he said. "Doesn't mean we can't hang out. But if you don't want to, I'll see you Monday."

That afternoon Fletcher enjoyed the best bike ride he'd had in a long time. The weather was almost too perfect for the last day of October—sunny in the low seventies. He spent the majority of the ride thinking about Tina. He hoped she would agree to try riding with him. It was Halloween, so he stopped at the store on his way home and bought some candy, then spent the evening handing it out to the steady stream of trick-or-treaters. When they tapered off to almost nothing, he packed a bag and returned to Tina's.

She woke him with kisses again when she got home from work. "I hope you don't mind," she said, "but I took tomorrow off."

"Oh?" he said, pulling back a little, not sure what to think.

"I was thinking about what you said all night, and I was sort of hoping you'd take me riding."

The idea of her taking off work to be with him had initially disconcerted him a bit, but when she said she wanted to go riding, his moment of wariness vanished. "That'd be awesome," he said.

Sunday had to have been the best day he'd experienced in years. He took Tina to his favorite bike shop and got her fitted with some biking shorts—which she looked phenomenal in. He rented a bike, helmet, and shoes for her, and they went for a gentle ride down Highway 89 south of town—his favorite ride—turning back at the ten-mile mark. She proved to be quite the rider and he could tell she enjoyed herself quite a bit. When they returned, she even asked the kid at the shop a bunch of questions about the different bikes they had for sale.

The ride itself didn't take very long, so after going back to her place for a shower they went out to eat and watched a movie on Netflix.

"I haven't done this in a really long time," she said as he drove her back to her place.

"What? Watch a movie?"

"Dinner and a movie with a guy."

"Neither have I," Fletcher said.

"It was really fun."

Before he knew it, it was the wee hours of the morning and he was crawling out of her bed so he could get home and back to work on time.

"*Hello?*"

"Huh?" Fletcher said, looking up.

"What in the hell are you thinking about, Butch?" Eric said.

"What?" He paused the video. "Nothing."

"Nothing, my ass. You look like a hormone-crazed boy who just accidently saw his best friend's older sister naked." Eric plopped down in his seat.

"And 'Butch'? Really?"

"Yeah, what's wrong with that?"

"They were train robbers."

"So? Why're you changing the subject?"

"I'm not—"

"Wait a minute," Eric said, leaning forward. "What *exactly* did you do this weekend?"

"I told you, I handed out candy to trick-or-treaters and rode my bike a little." It wasn't technically a lie, Fletcher thought. He *did* do those things. But he had definitely omitted other parts of his weekend. Eric could never know about those.

"I call BS."

"What? The weather was beautiful."

"Beautiful weather? Is that why you, Mr. Sherlock Holmes himself, were so zoned out you didn't notice me trying to get your attention for over a minute?"

Fletcher shifted his gaze from Eric to his monitor. "We're trying to solve a couple of murders if you hadn't noticed."

"Weather my ass. I've never heard you talk about the weather before. No. I think—" Fletcher glanced over at Eric but quickly averted his eyes. "...you bastard. You were with Tina, weren't you?"

Fletcher stared at the frozen video feed showing Trudy waiting for her supposed date. "How did I miss..."

"Weren't you?" Eric repeated.

Fletcher loaded the video of Renee.

"I can't believe it. After all that talk of not wanting to date someone."

He slid the progress bar forward until he saw Renee sitting at a table. "You gotta be kidding me."

"No, *you've* gotta be kidding *me*," Eric said.

"Would you focus for a moment?" Fletcher turned the monitor so Eric could see it. "Look at this."

"Quit trying to change the subject. Admit it."

"Eric..." Fletcher said, tapping on the screen.

"What?" Eric glanced at the monitor.

Fletcher loaded the video of Nicole at Connie's and forwarded it until she too was sitting at a table. "There," he said.

"I'm not seeing it. What am I supposedly looking at?"

"All three of them told the exact same story, right?"

"Yeah."

"Which was what?"

"That they were at Connie's for a date."

"Right—with Sam Gilkons. But he never showed. Why would a guy stand up three separate women?"

"Because he doesn't exist," Eric said.

"That's what I thought, too," Fletcher said. "But what if he really *does* exist? Someone closed Sam's account after we apprehended Trudy. Look." Fletcher pointed at a man in the paused video, just past Renee, frozen mid-stride. He then pointed to the exact same man in the other two videos.

"Holy fuck," Eric said. "But that's not Sam Gilkons..."

"No. And obviously coffee shops have routine customers, but what are the odds that the exact same guy would be at Connie's Coffee Shop at three very different times of day that just so happen to be the exact moment our murder suspects were there?"

"Unlikely, to say the least. Who do you think this guy is?"

"I don't know. He's definitely not Sam Gilkons, but then I never thought there *was* a Sam Gilkons."

He had been racking his brain to find some connection between Renee, Nicole, and Trudy, but the only thing he'd found was the man they'd were all matched with on Your Ideal Mate. But that man didn't exist—or at least there was nobody by that name living anywhere near Prescott—which explained why no one showed up for any of the three supposed dates. But someone had closed the account.

"Wait a second..." Fletcher said. "I recognize this guy!"

"You do?" Eric said.

Fletcher opened the web browser and typed in the URL for Your Ideal Mate. "What if Sam Gilkons really *was* made up, but not by these women?" He logged into Renee's profile and navigated to her closed matches. "Aha!" he exclaimed. "Look. This guy—Gabe. What if he's the one who made up Sam Gilkons?"

"That's definitely the guy in the videos," Eric said. "But why would he make a fake profile just to stand her up?"

"But not just Renee," Fletcher said. He opened another window on the browser and brought up Your Ideal Mate again, but this time he logged into Nicole's profile. "Nicole, too," he said, seeing Gabe's profile listed in Nicole's closed matches as well. "And I'm willing to bet that when YIM gives us access to Trudy's profile we'll find him there as well."

"Why would he do that? And how does this relate to them going out and shooting people?"

"I don't know. Maybe they're telling the truth and don't know each other, but they all independently know this Gabe guy." Fletcher clicked through the interactions Gabe had had with Renee and Nicole. "And look, in both cases, it was Renee and Nicole who closed the match with him."

"So... what, you think he somehow made them kill people?"

"Coercion? Maybe? Or maybe he hypnotized them. I don't know. Right now, it doesn't make sense, but it's a lead. Let's find out who this guy is and go pay him a visit."

CHAPTER 29

Gabe sat in his car munching on some fries while he watched the front door of the Prescott Police Department. His weekend had been a shitstorm of paranoia that the police were going to come bust down his door at any moment. He'd spent Friday night and the better part of Saturday—Halloween—sitting by the front window, peering through the curtain with his gun gripped in his meaty hand. But when kids started showing up at his door trick-or-treating, his paranoia abated. *As long as kids keep coming by,* he reasoned, *the cops won't be stupid enough to try anything.*

He went back to gaming on Sunday until his evening shift at Book World. By the end of his shift, he concluded that even if the cops didn't come for him right away, they needed to be dealt with—at least the ones investigating the murders. If he left the detective to his own devices, he would eventually catch up to Gabe. *That's their job. It's what they do.*

Gabe thought about simply walking into the police station and shifting into the detective's body—but if he went in there, he likely wouldn't leave. The best plan he had come up with so far was to stake out the station and hope the detective went somewhere Gabe could follow. That way he could try to get close without being seen. At this point, if he got the opportunity, he planned to shift into the detective's body, with his own locked in the secret room, then taking him out to the woods like he'd done with the cashier.

While he waited, he thought about what his new plan would be once he'd dealt with the detective. The dating site made it so easy for him to interact with girls who had treated him unfairly, without them ever knowing it was him. It had worked so well—they were clueless and fell for his plan without even a hint of suspicion. But that option was no longer available. Even if he succeeded in disposing of the detective, he had to consider the dating site compromised.

"Shit," Gabe said when he realized he had another problem. His plan had worked perfectly—he wasn't sure about Trudy, but he was certain he had successfully ruined Renee's and Nicole's lives. But if he didn't stop the detective, they were going to get off scot free.

Gabe really wished he could have been in the room when Renee and Nicole were being interrogated by the cops. He imagined the looks on their faces when they told their stories. Just as he was fully aware while in their bodies, they would have been fully aware while in his. But who would ever believe a story like that? Even if several people told the same story, no one would believe them—shifting into someone else's body was impossible. If the cops didn't think they were just batshit crazy, at most they'd decide the women were colluding. At least, that's what he hoped.

But if he didn't stop the detective—if the detective somehow proved it wasn't them—his efforts would be for naught. And he couldn't let that happen.

Slowly a plan coalesced in his mind.

That's it!

Gabe couldn't go into the station and ask to see the detective because the detective would know it was him, but someone else could.

CHAPTER 30

A re you sure Sam and Gabe are the same guy?" Eric said as they pulled into the driveway of the house Gabe rented.

"He was in all three videos at the coffee shop," Fletcher said. "What are the odds?" He stared at the house as he put the car into park.

"About the same as three women coming up with the same outlandish story, I suppose."

"So don't you think it's at least worth looking into?"

"All right, say he's somehow been coordinating this. Why would women who rejected him on a dating site later work *with* him to murder people?"

"Maybe it was all some kind of elaborate ruse." Despite the click-clacking of Eric's phone, Fletcher didn't take his eyes off the house. "How long do you reckon it would take to drive from Connie's to here? About five minutes?"

"Give or take," Eric said. The clacking stopped. "Why?"

"Because in the videos, all three women get up and leave Connie's about five minutes after he walks by them."

"And...?"

"Nothing. It's crazy."

"The great Sherlock Holmes isn't suggesting that he's

beginning to believe them, is he?" Eric was looking over at him with a look suggesting he thought Fletcher was just as crazy as the women were.

"They all reported that they were locked in a dark room in a man's body. A fat man's body."

"Yeah, but you and I both know that can't happen!"

"And the only lead we have in these murders is a fat guy. A fat guy who happens to walk past all three of them five minutes before they get up and leave—the exact amount of time it takes him to drive home. There are too many coincidences here."

"Please don't tell me that you're starting to think that this guy somehow changes bodies with these women, then goes and kills people?" Eric said. "Forget *why* he would do that—*how?* How on God's green *earth* would he do that?"

"I don't know," Fletcher admitted, shaking his head. "But you know what I think?"

"Go ahead, Einstein. I know you're going to tell me no matter what I say."

"I ain't no Einstein."

"You were going to tell me…?"

"Both Renee and Nicole closed their match with Gabe. And as near as I can tell, they did so without ever meeting him. What if Gabe intentionally created a fake profile in order to trick these girls into going out with him?"

"But he *didn't* go out with them. He left shortly after they showed up." Eric resumed typing furiously on his phone.

"Right. So he must have had other plans. He didn't want to meet with them, he wanted to *use* them."

"To murder people?"

Fletcher put the car into reverse. He looked over his shoulder and backed out of the driveway.

Looking up from his phone, Eric said, "Where are we going?"

"Sorry. It's crazy, I know. I don't know why I even considered it."

"Considered what?"

Fletcher looked over at Eric. "You know, sometimes I wonder about you."

"What do you mean?"

"Half the time I wonder whether or not you're paying attention."

"So where are we going?"

"I thought of something else I want to look into." Fletcher shifted into drive and pulled away from the house. "Besides the part about being in a man's body trapped in a dark room, what else hasn't made sense?" Eric didn't answer, and after a moment, he answered his own question. "The lack of motive. Why would Renee kill Marlon? She claims she didn't know him. And Nicole didn't know Hank. But what if Gabe did?"

"We'd have a motive?"

"Exactly."

"So where are we going?"

"First, Book World," Fletcher said.

"Why?"

"Do I really need to spell it out for you?" Fletcher looked over at Eric, who was just staring at him, phone in his hand. "To see if he knows Hank."

"But he wasn't on the list of witnesses."

"What's his alibi?" Fletcher said.

"I don't know. He's not a suspect."

"Not yet. But if he *had* been there, we could immediately rule him out."

"So we see if he knows Hank, then bring him in for questioning?" Eric said.

"Maybe."

"Sounds like a bit of a stretch to me. Just because you know someone doesn't mean you have a reason to murder them."

"True. But if he knows either of them, it'd be more of a connection than either Renee or Nicole has. Even more so if he knows them both. Besides, we don't have any other leads right now."

CHAPTER 31

If Gabe showed up at the police station and the detective recognized him, it would all be over. Not only would his life be over, but his work to ruin Renee and Nicole's lives would be undone as well. But if he showed up as someone else, someone the detective wouldn't expect, he could eliminate his new threat without anyone being the wiser.

Gabe tapped the steering wheel, thinking. His previous murders had been done with two goals in mind: to get vengeance on the superficial women Your Ideal Mate had matched him with, and to get revenge on other people who had wronged him. But what he needed right now was to eliminate a threat, and he didn't have immediate access to any of the women on his list. Once the detective was out of the way, he could develop a new plan, but until then, he would have to use whatever resources he had available. And if it meant ruining an innocent person's life, well... nobody was truly innocent.

He drove toward his house and when he was a few blocks away, he looked at the driver of the car next to him—a middle-aged man with a beard. He concentrated on the man, willing himself to be him. He had the process down; the feeling came on demand.

Gabe turned onto the side street leading to his house and pulled into his driveway a couple of minutes later. He hurried inside as quickly as he could, the urge to shift into the random stranger's body right on the edge, beckoning to him.

He locked the door behind him, dropped his keys on the table next to the door, and went straight to the kitchen. He descended the stairs, taking them two at a time. He stopped at the washer and dryer in the basement, grabbed a fresh piece of scotch tape, and stuck it to the key sitting on the dryer. He emptied his pockets onto the dryer, leaving behind his phone, a pocketknife, and Chapstick, then went into his dungeon. After locking the door, he felt his way to the corner and reached up as high as he could on the tips of his toes and stuck the key to the wall. Then, his hand on the wall, he felt his way around the room and sat down opposite the door.

Gabe relaxed his resistance to the shift, and waited for the feeling to overwhelm him. But nothing happened. Instead of the yearning growing stronger until he shifted, it was growing weaker. "No, no, no!" he shouted. When the feeling was completely gone, he screamed, "Dammit!" and pushed himself to his feet.

This had never happened before. Had the man moved out of range? It was the only thing he could think of.

Gabe felt his way around the room again and pulled the key from the wall. He found the door and unlocked it, then grabbed his phone and other belongings from the dryer. *I'll just go to Connie's, where my victims aren't moving.*

He went back upstairs and headed for the front door. He picked up his keys—and froze. Through a gap in the blinds covering the window next to the door, something had caught his eye. There was a car parked in his driveway.

"What the…"

Gabe went quickly to his bedroom and got his gun down from the closet. Returning to the living room, he sat in the chair he'd placed next to the window back on Halloween. The blinds were closed, but he could see out between them and the edge of the window.

The car wasn't marked, but it was a Crown Vic—the standard model of a police car.

"Shit, shit, shit," he said. What was he going to do? There wasn't anything he *could* do. He couldn't kill them—if he did, his life would be over. *Maybe it's not the cops.* He couldn't tell. He could see two men inside, but they weren't wearing uniforms, so he couldn't know for sure. Then he recognized the man driving. "That *fucking* detective."

He watched for a few minutes, scrambling to think of something, then the car backed out of his driveway. Then it hit him. He knew exactly what he was going to do.

CHAPTER 32

Fifteen minutes later Fletcher pulled into a parking spot at the mall. He looked for a spot right outside the store, but the parking lot gods weren't with him. Instead, he parked in the larger general parking area, farther from the store entrance.

As they walked inside, Fletcher took out his phone and brought up the screen shot of Gabe he had copied from Renee's profile. They found the nearest employee, who promptly asked them if she could help them find anything. Fletcher looked at her name tag and said, "Actually, Liz, I need to speak to a manager."

"Sure thing," Liz said.

Fletcher watched her as she walked away, then looked around the store. He couldn't see the registers from his vantage point, and didn't see anyone resembling Gabe, so he turned his attention to a display of books on a nearby table.

"Can I help you?" a voice said a moment later.

Fletcher looked up at the smiling middle-aged woman who greeted him. "Are you the manager on duty?"

"I am."

Glancing at her name tag, he said, "Hi, Sally. I'm Detective Wise and this is Detective Harris." Eric was staring off into the distance. Fletcher followed the direction of his gaze and saw an attractive woman perusing a shelf. He swatted Eric on the arm, then unlocked his phone. He held the screen toward Sally and said, "Do you recognize this man?"

Sally leaned in, squinted her eyes, and said, "Gabe? Yes, sir. He's an employee here."

Fletcher hadn't expected that. After a brief pause, he said, "Is there somewhere we can talk?"

"Sure," Sally said. "What's this about?"

"I'd rather not say until we're somewhere more private."

"Of course." Sally led Fletcher and Eric through the store to a hallway by the bathrooms. They passed a break room, then Sally ushered them into an office. "How can I help you?" she said once they were seated.

"We're investigating Hank Michaels' murder," Fletcher said.

"Hank? I thought you already had the murderer."

"We have a suspect, ma'am, but we're still trying to connect all the dots."

"Okay... so how can I help?"

"You said Gabe works here?"

"Yeah. He has for a few years."

"Can you tell me anything about the nature of Gabe's relationship with Hank?"

"Hank?" She looked surprised at the question.

"Yes. What was their relationship like?"

"I don't know. Okay, I guess."

"Do you have any reason to believe Gabe would want to hurt Hank?"

"*What?* No! I mean, Hank had a reputation for being stern, but hurt him? Heavens, no. Gabe is harmless and sweet."

Fletcher ran his finger back and forth across the crease in his chin, just below his mouth. He flipped through his little notebook and said, "And what about the customers? How did Hank treat them?"

"So far as I know, he was always very cordial with the

customers."

"What about the other employees?"

"He... well, Hank was ex-military or something, and he ran a tight ship. Most of the employees, including myself, didn't care for his techniques."

"Anyone ever complain? To the store manager or anything, I mean?"

"Not that I'm aware of," Sally said.

Fletcher nodded. He read through his notes once more and said, "I have you down as being one of the witnesses who saw Miss Henricks shoot Hank. Is that right?"

Sally nodded.

He pulled a business card out of his coat pocket and set it on the desk. "If you can think of anything else, please call me."

Eric scooped the card up before Sally could pick it up. *What the hell*, Fletcher thought as Eric flipped the card over, looking at both sides.

When Eric handed the card to Sally, Fletcher stood. "Thank you for your time," he said.

"Detective?"

"Yes?"

"You think Gabe had something to do with Hank's murder?"

"I'm not sure. I'm just trying to ensure Hank and his family get the justice they deserve. When does Gabe work next?"

"He usually works evening shifts."

"Does he work tonight?"

"Yeah, I think so."

"Do me a favor—please don't say anything to anyone, especially not to Gabe. I'm just trying to make sense of what's happened by exploring every possible option. So until we know more, there's no reason to worry, okay?"

"All right," Sally said.

On their way back out to their car Eric said, "Harmless..."

"Huh?" Fletcher said.

"Nothing," Eric said, waving him off. "I was just thinking."

So you do know how to think... Fletcher thought. "You can print yourself your own cards, you know."

"What?"

On second thought...

When they were back in his car, he said. "So we have an ex-military manager with an iron fist in charge of a guy who's not up to his militaristic expectations. You think Hank harassed Gabe to the point where Gabe snapped?"

"Possibly," Eric said, "but where's the proof?"

"Sally said he was stern, so it might give him motive—something Renee and Nicole don't have."

"You can be strict without harassing someone. I think it's a bit of a stretch to assume someone would kill a boss just because they were a hardass."

"You're right." Fletcher started the engine. "But I'm thinking that, at the very least, we should get a warrant to check the employee records. If Hank has a documented record of treating employees poorly, then we might have something."

"Ah. Right. So where to next?"

"I'd like to talk to Jennifer Williams."

"Marls' wife?" Eric said, his voice rising slightly. "Why?"

"Marls?" Fletcher said with a look over at Eric.

"What? It was in the report. That's what his wife called him."

"Anyways. Remember that both Renee *and* Nicole claimed not to know the people they shot, but if Jennifer knows Gabe—or at least if she can attest that her husband knew Gabe..."

"You're not suggesting—"

"...then he would be connected to both murders."

Fletcher left the mall, taking the Prescott Lakes Parkway that cut through the hills from Highway 69 to Highway 89. Eric seemed to be taking a break from his incessant texting, so Fletcher enjoyed the rare silence. He cut across Highway 89 at the bottom of the hill and into the Watson Lake residential area.

After a few more minutes and a couple more turns, Fletcher

pulled the car to a stop in front of 1542 Lakeview Drive. A carpet cleaning van was parked in the driveway and two hoses ran from the loudly humming van in through the front door. Eric followed Fletcher as he made his way to the open door.

Poking his head in, Fletcher saw a man cleaning the carpet in the area where Marlon had died. He approached the man slowly, trying not to startle him, but the man jumped anyway when he saw them. "Hi," Fletcher said, holding his hands up. "Sorry if I scared you." The man waved him off. "Is Mrs. Williams h—" he began, but stopped when Jennifer Williams walked out of the kitchen cradling a mug with both hands.

"Can I help you?" she said.

"Detective Wise," Fletcher said, offering his hand. "I don't believe we've met." Jennifer shook his hand and he added, "This is Detective Harris."

"It's a pleasure," Eric said. He took Jennifer's hand, shook it, then covered it with his other hand. "A real pleasure."

Fletcher swatted Eric on the arm again, and he let go of Jennifer's hand.

"What can I do for you?" Jennifer said.

Fletcher glanced at the cleaning man and said, "Is there somewhere we can talk? We're trying to get to the bottom of what happened to your husband, so we'd like to ask you a few questions."

Jennifer gestured toward the bedroom, and Fletcher and Eric followed her in as the carpet cleaner resumed his work. The hum was still audible through the thin walls after she shut the door.

Eric stepped over to an antique-looking dresser and picked through the jewelry littering the top.

"Eric," Fletcher said.

"Huh?" Eric said.

"What are you doing?"

"Just… looking."

"Would you knock it off?"

"Sorry."

"I have to admit, I'm a little confused, Detective," Jennifer said when Eric had stepped away from the dresser. "Don't we already know who murdered Marls? There were witnesses—"

"She's right," Eric interjected.

"Yes," Fletcher said. "But the problem we're having, Mrs. Williams, is that we can't find a motive."

"What does motive have to do with anything?" Jennifer said. "Several witnesses saw her come out of our house. She *was* in our house."

"True, but so far as we can tell, Renee didn't know your husband and had absolutely no reason to murder him."

"So! You know she was here!" Jennifer exclaimed in clear agitation. "Why is there even a question about her guilt?"

"Because, Mrs. Williams, in order to see that your husband receives all the justice he deserves, we have to convince a jury beyond a reasonable doubt that Renee not only shot your husband, but had a *reason* to."

Jennifer strode over to the door. "The fact that she *did* shoot my husband"—she aggressively opened the door and pointed out in the living room—"right there isn't enough?"

Fletcher held up his hands in an effort to calm her. "Please, Mrs. Williams, try to understand what I'm trying to say. There may be no doubt that Renee is guilty of murdering your husband, but if we want to get the maximum conviction—which we do—we have to also prove that she came here with the intention of doing so. And so far, we have no evidence that Renee even knew your husband."

Jennifer dabbed at her eyes with a tissue she pulled from her pocket. "I'm sorry."

"No need to apologize, Mrs. Williams. We completely understand."

"Um… can I have a minute."

"Sure," Fletcher said. "Take your time."

"You need anything to drink?"

"No, thanks," Fletcher said, at the exact same time Eric said, "Sure."

Fletcher shot Eric a look, but Jennifer said, "Just a sec."

She made her way out of the room, and Eric followed close on her heels.

I swear to God, if he hits on her I'm sending him back to the beat.

They both returned shortly, Eric with a glass of water in his hand. Fletcher glared at him, but Eric just happily sipped his water.

Jennifer sat heavily on the bed. "So you think she might get off?"

"Not entirely, but proving Renee had a reason to kill your husband will help us get the maximum sentence from a jury. And as I said, we're having trouble proving that. And not only are we having trouble finding intent, but we're having a hard time finding any connection between your husband and Renee whatsoever." Fletcher paused for a moment and looked over at Eric, who was just standing there staring at Jennifer. He really hoped he didn't try to start flirting with her. He mentally rolled his eyes and turned back to Jennifer. "Mrs. Williams, are you aware that there was another murder as well?"

Jennifer looked up and shook her head. "I haven't paid much attention to the news lately, with the funeral and... I haven't been back here since..." She pointed toward the door and said, "And today I forced myself to deal with this."

"I'm so sorry," Fletcher said. "Truly, we both are." Eric still hadn't moved. *Please don't hit on her, you idiot.* "But two days after your husband was murdered another woman walked into a bookstore at the mall and killed one of their employees, Hank Michaels. Do you happen to know him?"

Jennifer shook her head. "No, don't recognize the name."

"Well, apparently neither did the woman who killed him. There were witnesses there as well who saw her walk into the store and shoot him."

"Okay? I don't understand what you're trying to tell me."

"In the span of three days, we've had two murders—more than we had in Prescott all last year—where two women, unrelated to each other, kill strangers, seemingly without a motive. So far as we know, Renee didn't know Marlon, and according to your statement you don't know her either."

"Yeah. I'd never seen her before."

"And you also said that your husband didn't know her."

"No."

"So far we have no reason to believe that that isn't true."

"So, she's lying," Jennifer said.

"That's the most logical explanation. But parts of her story have checked out. Until the second murder, we were busy trying to fill in the parts of the story that don't add up."

"Like what?"

"Sorry…"

"You can't talk about it."

"No. But there's something else we came here to ask you."

"Sure. Anything you think might help."

Fletcher held his phone up. "Do you know this man?"

Jennifer's eyes widened. "*Gabe?*"

"You do know him, then."

"I… yes, I do. Why do you ask?"

"How do you know him?" Fletcher said.

"He was a friend of ours—me and Marls."

"*Was?*"

Jennifer looked down at her hands, which she held clasped in her lap. "We had a sort of falling out."

"What kind?"

"He didn't handle me and Marls being engaged very well."

"Why not?"

"Gabe and I were friends for a long time. We met in college and we were both gamers, so we started playing together. It wasn't until after Marls and I started dating that I realized Gabe liked me. What is this about, anyway?"

"I know this might not make any sense—it doesn't even

make sense to us yet, which is why we're here—but I'm starting to think he might have somehow been involved in what happened to your husband."

Jennifer looked up. "What? How?"

"Have you spoken with him recently?"

Jennifer nodded. "I hated that we'd fallen away from each other, so after Marls was... I reached out to him."

"Okay," Fletcher said. "What about before? How long had it been since you'd heard from him?"

"About a year and a half or so. What does Gabe have to do with this, Detective?"

"Well, as I've said," Fletcher said, "the problem we're having is that we haven't found a connection between Renee and your husband, but now we know that Gabe knew your husband."

"So?"

"He also knew the other victim, Mr. Henricks. And, he knew Renee."

"He did?"

"He did. They met on a dating site."

Eric coughed suddenly. "Sorry, wrong tube," he said, pointing at the glass of water. He thumped himself on the chest a few times.

"The other suspect as well," Fletcher added.

Jennifer stared at Fletcher seemingly in disbelief. "You think he's working with them somehow?"

"Possibly. We don't know how yet. Maybe Renee didn't know your husband and didn't have a reason to kill him, but Gabe knew them all."

"So, what you really want to know is whether *Gabe* had a reason to kill Marlon," Jennifer said.

Fletcher nodded.

Jennifer sat silently. Eventually, she said, "I don't know. He's not a violent person."

"Can you be sure?"

"No. But I've never seen him behave in a way that would suggest otherwise."

Fletcher rubbed his chin. Jennifer didn't seem to know anything that might prove useful, other than that Gabe knew her husband and that they'd had a falling out. But he was convinced now that Gabe was involved. He was in all three videos, knew both the victims closely, and had been matched with at least two of the three suspects. "Thanks for talking with us," he said. "I know how hard this must be, but I want to assure you that the only reason we're here is because we want justice for your husband."

"No, no worries," Jennifer said, rising from the bed.

"I know it's probably easier to think that Renee acted alone, but if at any point you can think of anything that might help us—with Gabe, I mean—please call me," Fletcher said. He handed her a business card.

"I will."

Fletcher thanked her, and he and Eric followed Jennifer as she ushered them to the front door.

"What the hell was that?" Fletcher said when they were back in his car.

"What?" Eric said.

"You were distracted as hell back there."

"I don't know."

"You have to pay attention, Eric, or you're never gonna make it as a detective."

"Sorry." After a moment of awkward silence, Eric said, "So, what are you thinking?"

"I'm not sure. But Gabe is the only person we've found thus far who knew both Williams *and* Henricks. Renee and Nicole as well."

"So you think he matched with these women, met them for a date, and somehow convinced them to commit murder? How?"

"Maybe he hypnotized them somehow. I don't know," Fletcher said with frustration. "But his connection to all of them can't be coincidental. At the very least we need to bring him in for questioning."

CHAPTER 33

Should we call for backup?" Eric said as Fletcher pulled back into Gabe's driveway.

Fletcher put the car in park. "Why?"

"In case he goes all crazy on us."

"We don't even know for sure if he's involved."

"Right."

Fletcher stared ahead at the house, thinking through what he knew.

"So, what?" Eric said. "We gonna haul this guy into the station and ask him if he's been hypnotizing people?"

Fletcher ignored Eric's obvious sarcasm. "No."

"Cause if you do that, Fletcher, everyone's gonna think you're crazy. Especially since we can't prove it."

"I know."

"What, then?"

"I'm thinking," Fletcher said, then looked over at Eric. "Wait, what?"

"If you go hauling this guy—"

"I heard what you said, Eric. What did you call me?"

"What?"

"You called me Fletcher."

"So? That's your name."

Fletcher's eyes narrowed.

"You never—"

Eric reached for his gun.

Fuck!

Fletcher swung his arm, hitting Eric in the nose with the back of his fist. When Eric's hands went up to his face, Fletcher leaned over and pulled Eric's gun from its holster, then reached for the door handle with his other hand. He rolled out of the car and drew his own gun as well, then pointed both of them at Eric.

"Holy shit!" Eric said.

Fletcher didn't move. "Gabe?"

"They're telling the truth!"

"Who's telling the truth?" Fletcher said. He wasn't sure who he was talking to—Eric or Gabe—so he kept the guns trained on Eric.

"All three of them. What are you doing?" Eric felt his nose. "And why is my nose bleeding?"

"Who am I?" Fletcher said.

"Huh?"

"What do they call me at work?"

"Dickhead?"

"Eric..."

"Wise Guy, Smarts, Wizard, Sherlock—"

"Okay, okay," Fletcher said. He lowered the guns. "What happened?"

"I don't know. We were sitting outside the house a while back, then I was in a dark room."

"A while back?"

"Yeah—an hour or so, if I had to guess. It was dark. I swear," Eric said, touching his nose delicately, "if this bruises, I'm gonna be pissed."

"Wait—you were in a dark room?"

"That's what I'm trying to tell you. They're telling the truth. All of them!"

"Holy shit," Fletcher said, echoing Eric's earlier sentiment. He looked over at the house. "Then he knows that we know."

"Shit." Eric said. "What now?"

"I don't know."

"How the fuck does he do that? We should probably get out of here."

"Yeah," Fletcher said. But before he could move, his heart suddenly started racing. His vision blurred, then his skin started tingling. *What the hell?*

When his vision cleared, he was peering through window blinds, looking at himself standing next to his unmarked squad car. He watched himself lift one of the guns he held toward the car and, muted by the window and wall, heard himself say, "Get out!"

He looked at Eric, in the passenger's seat of the car.

"Get out!" he heard himself shout again.

The car door opened, and Eric stepped out and put his hands in the air.

Fletcher watched himself gesture with a gun toward the house. Eric said something he couldn't hear, then started walking toward the door.

Inside the house, Fletcher held up his hands—they were meaty, the wrists thick. He looked down at the stomach protruding out in front of him, covered by a plain gray t-shirt with a stain on it. He looked around at the room he was in, which was littered with pizza boxes, empty chip bags, and other food waste.

The door opened and Eric stepped into the living room, Fletcher himself—his body—right behind him. He saw himself hit Eric in the back of the head with the butt of a gun. The other one was pointed at him. Fletcher—Gabe, in Fletcher's body—said, "Don't move."

"I was right," he said, his voice unfamiliar, sort of weak and squeaky. "Even though I dismissed it because it was crazy, I was right."

"About what?" Fletcher—Gabe—said.

Hearing his own voice was strange—just like when he played back the interrogations he taped and listened to himself talking.

"That it was you who killed Marlon somehow. Hank too."

How had he done it?

Fletcher—Gabe—gestured toward Eric with the gun. "Does he know?"

"What, that you killed two people?" Gabe—Fletcher—said. *I feel tired.*

"Two that you know of," Fletcher—Gabe—said.

"There's more?"

I gotta get back to my own body. But how?

"Does. He. Know?" Fletcher—Gabe—snarled.

"Until now, even I wasn't sure."

"Meaning he has an idea."

"I—"

Fletcher—Gabe—pointed the other gun down at Eric.

"Don't!" Gabe—Fletcher—shouted, holding out a fat hand. Fletcher—Gabe—looked up. In Gabe's body, Fletcher took a step toward himself, holding the meaty hands up as if showing that he wasn't armed. "You don't have to do this."

"Stay right there!" Fletcher—Gabe—yelled.

"You don't have to do this," Gabe—Fletcher—repeated.

"You think I can just let you two *live*? You know! And I can't allow you to ruin everything I've done."

"Everything you've done…? Two innocent people are dead, Gabe."

"They weren't innocent!"

"Maybe not, but killing us won't solve your problems. There are others who know, too."

It was a lie. But if something happened to them, others would certainly figure it out.

Fletcher stared at himself. It was incredibly surreal to be standing apart from himself, seeing himself moving and talking. He was having a hard time processing it. His brain almost wanted to collapse in on itself, completely disassociate from what was happening. It was impossible! Nonetheless, he watched as his own fingers flexed and loosened on the grips of both guns.

He wondered if his skills transferred to Gabe now that Gabe was in his body. Could Gabe shoot? Was he as accurate a shot? He was holding the guns single-handed. It was harder to control than a two-handed grip, which meant his accuracy would automatically suffer. And depending on whether he was left- or right-handed, the non-dominant hand would be almost useless. But at this range, would it matter that much?

Maybe if he lunged at Gabe—at himself—he could get the guns away. But as he moved in Gabe's body, he didn't think he could lunge anywhere—not quickly enough, anyway. And if he got shot in Gabe's body and died, would it be *him* who died, or Gabe? His brain was really freaking out right now.

Eric moaned, and Fletcher took his eyes off his own body to look down at his partner. Eric touched the back of his head where he'd been hit, then tried pushing himself to his knees. Fletcher watched as his body moved toward Eric and kicked him in the side. Eric curled up into a ball again with a groan.

Then Fletcher's body turned toward him and, with a flick of one of the guns, said, "Move."

He hesitated.

"I said, move!" Fletcher heard himself shout.

"Where?" he said, in Gabe's squeaky voice.

"Outside."

Fletcher's mind was whirling. He had a gun pointed at his head, but the person holding the gun was… himself. Too dazed to disobey, he walked out the front door.

He had been right. Somehow the outlandish stories Renee, Nicole, and Trudy had told weren't stories at all—they were the truth! Gabe could change bodies with people. This whole time he'd thought that the only reason he was even entertaining the possibility that Renee might be telling the truth was that his mental clarity had been clouded by his marriage problems. But this whole time he'd been right.

"Get in the car," Fletcher heard himself say in his strange-sounding own voice. Fletcher opened the driver's door, then heard himself say, "No. In the back."

He didn't want to get in the back. He was still trying to think of a way out of this situation, and once the back door closed, he'd be trapped. But he was already trapped. He had no idea how Gabe was switching bodies with people, and he had no way of switching back. All he could do at this point was comply and hope he could talk some sense into Gabe. He opened the back door and climbed in, sitting with a grunt. The rear shocks groaned. His movements felt awkward, less agile. And he felt drained of energy.

He watched himself put the key in the ignition and start the car. The car lurched into reverse, wheels screaming, and stopped abruptly on the road. Fletcher—Gabe—shifted the car into drive and they lunged forward, the wheels screaming a second time as they accelerated. Fletcher—Gabe—took the turns in the road without slowing, blowing through the stop signs.

"Where are we going?" he said.

Fletcher—Gabe—didn't reply.

They flew down Willow Creek Road, the speedometer reading sixty-five miles per hour—thirty miles over the speed limit.

"Look," he said, leaning as far forward as his new stomach would allow, "there's no sense in getting us killed."

Still no reply from Gabe.

"Can we just please talk?"

Fletcher—Gabe—looked over his shoulder. His brain was still doing mental gymnastics at seeing his own face. He looked into his own eyes briefly before Gabe turned back. Fletcher felt nauseated. He felt disconnected. Off.

"Renee and Nicole were telling the truth. This whole time, it was you..."

"Shut up!" Fletcher—Gabe—shouted.

"Renee didn't kill Marlon. She didn't know him. No wonder I couldn't find a motive. It was you. *You* killed Marlon."

"I said shut the *fuck* up!"

"I think I understand about Marlon—you loved Jennifer—but why Hank?"

Fletcher—Gabe—looked over his shoulder again and held a gun up next to the plexiglass separating the front and back seats. "If you don't shut the fuck up, I'm going to pull over and put a bullet in your fucking head."

Fletcher sat back in his seat. He wouldn't get anywhere by agitating Gabe. Each time they approached a traffic light, he put his hand on the ceiling to brace for a possible collision. Horns blared as they sped through intersections. After a few miles, they approached Highway 89, going way too fast. "Slow down, slow down slow down!" he yelled.

Gabe slammed on the brakes so hard the automatic braking system engaged, making the car vibrate as they slowed quickly. Gabe yanked on the steering wheel, making the car careen sharply to the left. He somehow maintained control as they turned onto 89, then floored the accelerator again.

They sped down the highway, accelerating to ninety miles per hour. Gabe weaved through traffic, sometimes veering into the southbound lane when both northbound lanes were blocked.

"Please, Gabe! Talk to me! What are we doing?"

They entered the next town and the speed limit dropped to thirty-five. Gabe, however, didn't slow down. The town was a long, sprawling community, and the highway widened into four lanes with a turning lane in the center. For people going the speed limit, the road was wide and comfortable, but at their speed it was precarious and deadly. If they hit another car—or, god forbid, a pedestrian—people were going to die.

They flew through a red light and swerved around a truck pulling into the intersection. "Slow down!" he screamed. "You're going to get us killed!" He was truly starting to be afraid they were going to crash and die. He saw a police car sitting at the light on the opposite side of the road and turned as best he could to look over his shoulder; Gabe's body wasn't particularly flexible. The lights of the police car turned on and it turned around to follow them.

A voice sounded over the radio: "This is Adam Twelve. I've got a reckless driver, possible stolen police car. Heading north on 89. Silver Crown Vic with government plates. Request urgent assist."

"Roger," a voice answered. "All available units please resp—"

With an audible click, Gabe turned off the radio.

"You're attracting attention, Gabe," Fletcher said. "They know this is a stolen police car; they've called for help. You need to stop before you lose control." But Gabe had already lost control. Whatever Gabe was thinking, he wasn't thinking logically. "They know where you are. You're not getting away. The best thing to do is to just stop so we can talk."

"You don't want to talk," Gabe said. "You just want to put me in prison. To pay for my crimes."

"Did you commit any crimes?" Fletcher said, fishing even though he already knew the answer. "I mean besides assaulting a police officer?"

They left the sprawling town behind and entered the open highway again. They were still going precariously fast, but Fletcher breathed a sigh of relief—though still dangerous, their speed was closer to that of the traffic they were passing. He looked over his shoulder and saw that there were at least three police cars following.

Gabe drove a few more miles, then slammed on the brakes. The tires squealed and smoke billowed, and Fletcher flew into the plexiglass divider before he could brace himself. The car lurched sharply to the right and bounced as it drove off the pavement. Fletcher hit his head on the roof, then hit the hard plastic seat roughly on his side. He groaned as he tried pushing himself back into a sitting position. The jostling of the car as it bounced down a dirt road made it difficult, but he finally managed. Looking out the back window, he couldn't see any other cars through the billowing dust.

"Where... are you... going?" Between jolts, Fletcher stared at the back of his own head. He braced one hand on the roof and the other against the door, but he didn't have the strength to keep himself from bouncing around on the plastic seat.

After several more minutes Gabe slammed on the brakes and the car skidded to a stop. A cloud of dust drifted past them.

In Fletcher's body, Gabe looked into the back seat—the sight of himself was still disconcerting—and said, "Get out!"

"It's a police car." When Gabe—himself—stared back with a blank stare, he added, "I can't. The doors don't open from inside."

Gabe furrowed his brow—Fletcher's brow—then climbed out of the car. Fletcher watched himself open the back door. "There."

Fletcher scooted closer to the door and placed his hand on the frame to give himself the leverage he needed to climb out. He heard sirens in the distance. "I don't know what you have planned, Gabe, but the police are going to be here any minute. You weren't exactly being covert back there."

The cloud of dust around the car was still thick, but it was starting to settle. Gabe grabbed Fletcher by the arm and yanked him away from the car. He was fit, he knew, but the tug did little to budge the bulk of the body in which Fletcher found himself. He gave in to the pull as Gabe led him by the arm away from the car. They walked out of the settling dust into a landscape of juniper trees.

The sound of the sirens grew louder.

"Gabe," he said. "What are you hoping to accomplish here?"

Gabe let go of Fletcher's arm and stepped away. Fletcher turned toward him, and Gabe pointed the gun at Fletcher. He froze.

"You don't know how it feels," Fletcher—Gabe—said.

"How what feels?"

"To be made fun of your whole life!"

"I..."

"To have people incessantly call you names and pick on you just because you're different."

"You're right, Gabe. I don't. But how's this going to help?"

"It's going to solve everything!" Fletcher—Gabe—shouted.

"Look, Gabe. I don't know how you're doing this, but—"

"Shut up!"

"We can come to some sort of an—"

Gabe raised the gun, aiming at Fletcher's head. Fletcher instinctively put his hands up. "What? You think killing me's the answer?"

"Why not? Then I'd be rid of that *fucking* body."

Fletcher's heart broke for Gabe. He had obviously lived a tormented life. He didn't know what Gabe had been through, but he could empathize to an extent. He hadn't had an ideal life himself. But who did? "But you wouldn't be you, Gabe." He looked in the direction of the approaching sirens. He hoped he could resolve this before they arrived—things would only get worse when they did. He had no idea how Gabe would react once he got cornered. And if the approaching officers mistook him for Gabe then Fletcher might be the one who wound up dead, not Gabe. Looking back at himself, he said, "You can't be me, either. Do you think *my* life is perfect? It's not." He laughed. Gabe looked at him curiously. "Have you ever been divorced, Gabe? Well, I have. Do you have any idea how that feels?" A look of surprise crossed his face—Gabe's face. "It fucking sucks. You think that just because I'm not... because our bodies are different... that my life is any better? It's not. A person is more than what they look like. I was married for ten years. And I thought my life was pretty good—I have a job I enjoy and a wife that I loved. But it's not. My wife wanted a divorce. So I know what it feels like to be rejected. I never thought I'd be someone who got divorced. But here I am." He held both arms out at his sides. "She didn't love me anymore. And I hated it. I hated how it made me feel." Fletcher—Gabe—shifted his feet and glanced toward the sound of sirens. Their arrival was imminent. He was running out of time. "Look, Gabe…" For some reason, in that moment, he thought of Tina. "Just because you get dealt a bad hand doesn't mean there isn't hope for the future. I know this is all because you were in love with Jennifer and she chose—"

"No!" Fletcher—Gabe—yelled. He stepped forward and placed the gun against Fletcher's forehead. "You think this is about Jenny?"

Fletcher held his hands up in submission. "I… I talked to her. She said—"

"She's just one of countless superficial bitches who will feel what I've felt my entire life!"

"Just because she didn't choose you doesn't mean she's superficial, Gabe. It means she—"

"No? Why do you think all those girls refused to go out with me?"

"I… I don't know."

"Because all they're into is looks. Every time I showed them my picture, they closed our match."

"You can't possibly know that."

"But I do. I always showed my picture in step five—"

"Step five?"

"And *that* is exactly when every single one of them closed our match. Then I shifted into that Burger Mania kid's body, and I got to thinking…"

The missing boy… so that's what happened to him.

"I didn't know they were superficial at the time—I mean, that's what I figured, it's been that way my whole life, but I needed to prove it—so I created another profile."

"Sam Gilkons," he said. Gabe's eyes widened when he said the name.

"The thing about dating sites," Gabe said, "is that they're all algorithms. The way you answer questions determines who the computer matches you with. So I created another profile identical to mine. And sure enough, I got matched with the same people. And you know what happened?"

Fletcher shook his head.

"When they saw my picture—a fake picture, of some random dude—not a single one of them closed the match."

That's why they didn't recognize him at Connie's.

"In fact, every single one of them agreed to meet me."

"That doesn't prove anything, Gabe." Though he knew it sort of did. "It just means—"

"It proves exactly what I thought. That they're all superficial bitches. That they only go skin deep. None of them were actually interested in who I was, only what I looked like."

Several police cars came into view and pulled up next to Fletcher's car. Their doors opened and officers got out, drawing guns.

"It's all right, guys," Fletcher's body said, looking over his shoulder.

"No!" Gabe's body shouted in his squeaky voice. He stepped back from Fletcher.

Fletcher felt like he was losing control of his bike at thirty miles an hour and was about to fly over the handlebars. He wryly remembered the adage: 'Only ride as fast as you are willing to crash.' It applied here too, apparently. He'd chosen a career that put him in danger of crashing. "No no no no! H-he switched bodies with me!" he shouted when the officers trained their guns on him.

"You're crazy, Gabe," said Gabe, from Fletcher's body. "You think anyone will believe you're some sort of X-Man?"

The officers walked around the doors of their cars, guns up, in defensive stances.

"I'm Fletcher Wise," Fletcher said, patting himself on Gabe's meaty chest. "That's Gabe Snyder," he said, pointing at his own body. He had to disarm this situation fast. If they shot him, he didn't know whether it'd be him who died or Gabe. And if they shot Gabe, would he forever be stuck in Gabe's body? Shit. What would Tina think? Why was he even thinking of her now, of all times? Would it matter to her how he looked?

Fletcher recognized a couple of the approaching officers. "Mike? Pete? It's me, Fletcher." Though he really hated how everyone made fun of his last name, he used it now to his advantage. He knew they'd know about it. "Wise Guy, Smarts, Wizard, Sherlock."

The two officers he'd named stopped and lowered their guns a little.

It worked. "I-I can't explain it but... somehow he—" He looked over at Gabe, at himself, still holding a gun and aiming at him, and froze. *The look in his eyes...* "Gabe..." he said, holding his hands up. He took a step back. He recognized the look—he'd seen it too many times when he'd been a patrol officer. It was a look of finality.

Gabe turned the gun on himself, pointing it at the side of his head.

"Gabe! No!" he shouted. He was flying over his handlebars now, staring straight down at the approaching pavement—he'd always had the habit of going too fast, he knew. This crash was going to hurt.

Gabe, in Fletcher's body, turned the gun back on Fletcher, in Gabe's body.

Gunfire reverberated.

Pain consumed Fletcher and he fell to the ground.

"Drop the gun!" several officers yelled.

Out of the corner of his eye, Fletcher saw the gun fall to the ground. He tried to clutch at the pain in his chest, but he couldn't get his arms to move.

His heart raced and his vision blurred.

A tingling sensation replaced the pain, and simultaneously, his vision cleared. Fletcher found himself looking down at Gabe, who was lying on the ground, a gunshot wound in his chest.

An officer crashed into Fletcher's side, tackling him. He felt himself being rolled onto his stomach and his arms pulled behind his back. As the cuffs clicked into place he said, "Guys! Guys, guys, it's me, Fletcher!" The officer got off him, and he rolled onto his side. Mike stood over him.

"Prove it," Mike said.

He'd known Mike since the academy. "Okay, but the only thing I can think of is the night they surprised us with Indian food back at the academy," Fletcher said. "I'd never seen someone run to the bath—"

"All right, that'll be enough," Mike said. "You want the cuffs off or not?"

Fletcher rolled back onto his stomach and lifted his arms up off his back. When Mike had the cuffs off, Fletcher pushed himself into a sitting position. "Well, that was by far the weirdest thing that's ever happened to me."

"What the hell *was* that?" Mike said.

"You wouldn't believe me if I told you," Fletcher said.

Mike held a hand out to Fletcher and helped him to his feet.

Pete approached Gabe's body, checked his pulse, then called into his radio, "Subject down! Ambulance needed at..." Pete turned toward them and said, "Either of you know what road this is?"

Fletcher shook his head and Mike said, "Hell if I know. Some Forest Service road."

Mike turned to Fletcher and said, "You all right?"

You mean other than my mind going a million miles an hour? "Yeah, I think so."

"Then, I'll go back and flag the ambulance down."

"We're off 89 north of Chino," Pete barked into his radio. He dropped to his knees and started performing CPR.

Feeling completely vulnerable and helpless, all Fletcher could do was stand by and watch.

CHAPTER 34

Fletcher walked through the front door of Ponderosa's and headed back toward the bar. Tina jumped out of her seat and ran toward him the moment she saw him. She embraced him in a hug, wrapping her arms tightly around his neck.

"I don't care if you want to go slow," she said into his ear. "When I heard what happened it scared the shit out of me."

Fletcher hugged her just as tightly. "It scared me too." He breathed in the scent of her hair.

Tina let him go and took him by the hand. She led him back to the table where Eric, Sergeant Frey, and several officers awaited him. They clapped as he approached. All the occupants of the pub clapped. Attention... the exact opposite of what he would have wanted.

Sergeant Frey clapped him on the shoulder. "Well done, Wise."

"What? No smart-ass nickname? No synonym befitting my unfortunate last name?"

Eric, who was bruised across the bridge of his nose, visibly shuddered. "Ugh. That was the single worst experience of my life." He handed Fletcher a beer and said, "What took you so long to figure out that it wasn't me sitting next to you in the car?"

"I should have figured something was wrong when you didn't spend the entire drive clacking away on your phone. Can't you at least turn off the godforsaken sound?" He took a healthy, and much-needed, swig of his beer. "And I'd decided that if you hit on Jennifer—"

"You have to admit, she's hot."

"—I was going to recommend sending you back to the beat."

"Hey! That wasn't me. Unlike you, I'm able to separate work from pleasure." Fletcher punched Eric in the arm at the obvious insult. "What happened to my nose, anyways?" Eric reached up and gently pinched the bridge of his bruised nose. "You know how much this is going to slow me down?"

Tina laughed.

"What?" Eric said. "You think this is funny?"

"Seems like you need a challenge to me," Tina said. She slipped her arm back around Fletcher.

Having Tina's arm around him felt good, Fletcher decided, and he pulled her closer. "Sorry about that," he said. "When I realized what was happening, Gabe reached for your gun, so I hit you in the nose to stop him."

"Well, thanks," Eric said.

"Why don't you just tell them you got into a fight protecting a young damsel in distress from an old man who wouldn't stop hitting on her?"

"Har, har."

Fletcher looked at Frey and said, "What about Renee, Nicole, and Trudy?"

"Neither Scott or Judge Sinclair had any qualms about releasing them, so they're being processed as we speak," Frey said.

"That's good. I can't imagine what they've been through." Fletcher shuddered. "Well... I guess I sort of can."

Eric shuddered as well, but in an exaggerated fashion.

Even though he had completely stumbled into solving the

crime—well, really, Gabe had solved it for them—Fletcher was pleased with the outcome. Renee, Nicole, and Trudy wouldn't have to spend their lives in prison for crimes they didn't commit.

"It's too bad the bastard didn't make it," Frey said. "Would have loved to have seen *that* trial. Would've been a real circus!"

"And I'd liked to have seen ol' Matlock in action," Eric said.

"See," Fletcher said, "now that one just plain doesn't work."

"Why not, *Ben?*"

"Because Matlock was a lawyer."

"He investigated crimes though."

Fletcher gestured around with his beer. "Are you *trying* to ruin this whole gathering thing for me?"

"Geez, lighten up will ya."

"Yeah, Fletch," Tina said with a squeeze. "He's just messin'."

Fletcher rolled his eyes and took a swig of beer.

"So…?" Eric said.

"What?" Fletcher said. He wiped his upper lip with the back of his hand, careful not to spill.

"How'd you figure out it wasn't me sitting in the car with you? It couldn't have been the texting thing. There's been plenty of times I didn't have anyone to text."

"Really? Remind me when, exactly."

"Come on. Seriously. How'd you figure it out?"

"You know what it was?"

"I wouldn't be asking if I did."

"It was your stupid nicknames."

"How'd that give it away?"

"Because you called me by my name," Fletcher said. "Something you haven't done since, well, I can't remember the last time you called me Fletcher."

"Huh," Eric said. "They're not so stupid now after all, are they?" Eric raised his glass and said, "To Fletcher!"

"To Fletcher!" everyone shouted. Glasses clinked and everyone drank. Then someone shouted, "Speech!" which was quickly followed by a chant of "Speech, speech, speech!"

Fletcher felt himself flush. He absolutely hated being the center of attention. The room quieted down, and all eyes were on him. He really had no idea what to say, or why he had to say anything at all. He'd just been doing his job. There was no reason to single him out from any of the other detectives who worked on the cases. If it hadn't been him, it would have been someone else. But his colleagues expected him to say something. He lifted his half-empty glass, gestured around the room with it, and said, "Well, first of all, I wish I could say this was fun, but I can't..."

THE END

ABOUT THE AUTHOR

Patrik grew up in the southwest and presently lives in Idaho. Earlier in life he almost exclusively read fantasy novels but has since broadened his horizon and enjoys many genres, both fiction and nonfiction. He has wanted to write a book for a long time but never really had any ideas. Then, one random day, when he least expected it, he had an inkling and started writing. In his spare time, he enjoys hanging out with his family and entertaining his exuberant dog Pearl (or the Black Pearl when she is naughty, and yes, she is black).

Thank you for reading *Shift*! Please consider leaving a review on Amazon as well as on Goodreads. If you enjoyed *Shift*, consider Patrik's *Blessed of the Dragon* series. You can also follow Patrik on his website as well as on Facebook.

CPSIA information can be obtained
at www.ICGtesting.com
Printed in the USA
FSHW010008220721
83348FS